TRAP, NEUTER, DIE

TRAP, NEUTER, DIE

A DEELO MYER CAT RESCUE MYSTERY

SHARON MARCHISELLO

LEVEL
BEST BOOKS

First published by Level Best Books 2024

This novel is entirely a work of fiction. The names, characters and incidents portrayed in it are the work of the author's imagination. Any resemblance to actual persons, living or dead, events or localities is entirely coincidental.

Sharon Marchisello asserts the moral right to be identified as the author of this work.

Author Photo Credit: Linda Edmonds <edmonds@numail.org>

First edition

ISBN: 978-1-68512-798-5

Cover art by Level Best Designs

This book was professionally typeset on Reedsy.
Find out more at reedsy.com

To all the animal rescue volunteers who speak for those without a voice.

Praise for Trap, Neuter, Die

"Discover the purr-fect recipe for murder in *Trap, Neuter, Die*, a witty, fast-paced addition to the genre of cozy animal mysteries that will keep you guessing to the last page. DeeLo, recently single and fiercely independent, stumbles into a mystery with an ever-growing list of suspects as danger prowls around every corner"—DL Mitchell, author of *Trust the Terrier: A Coral Shores Veterinary Mystery*

"Animal rescue fans and cozy mystery fans will fall in love with DeeLo Myer and the quirky characters at the Pecan Point Human Society. In *Trap, Neuter, Die*, Sharon Marchisello has penned a purr-fectly claw-ver mystery that I enjoyed from tip to tail!"—Larissa Reinhart, *Wall Street Journal* bestselling author of the Cherry Tucker Mystery and Maizie Albright Star Detective series

"Sharon Marchisello's *Trap, Neuter, Die*, is a delightful entry into the world of cozy mysteries. It features thirty-year-old divorcee, DeeLo, who balances solving a murder against successfully completing her hours of ordered community service under the watch of a prickly woman who runs an organization that traps, neuters, and releases feral cats. With well-drawn characters and quick paced action, *Trap, Neuter, Die* offers twists and turns that will keep readers engaged from the first to the last page."—Debra H. Goldstein, author of the Sarah Blair mystery series

"A new cozy queen is on the scene! *Trap, Neuter, Die* is everything a cozy should be: a satisfying whodunit with a smattering of romance and bursting with cattitude. Cozy readers are in for a delicious treat.—Cathy Tully, *USA*

Today bestselling author of the ChiroCozy Mystery Series

"*Trap, Neuter, Die* is, let's say, feral, and you'll love it. This is not a cat cozy. There are cats, but the book has a seductive edge. Sharon Marchisello's engaging protagonist, Delores Diane Myer-Johansson, who goes by DeeLo, knows she was wrong when she drove her car after imbibing too much wine. I was invested in her story from the first chapter. The writing purrs and if you're familiar with Sharon's previous work, she's planted a little surprise for you."—Lane Stone, author of the Big Picture art thriller trilogy

"Meet kindly DeeLo, a new volunteer at the local animal rescue. While learning how to trap stray cats on her very first night, she stumbles across the body of a local bookstore owner. She begins asking questions and quickly learns that feral cats are not the only ones with enemies in the community. And, most importantly, that one should never underestimate the loyalty and craftiness of a cat."—Rebecca Saltzer, author of *Murder Over Broken Bonds* and *Not Accounting For Murder*

Chapter One

Catherine Foster preferred cats to people. I made that assessment shortly after I reported for my first assignment with the Pecan Point Humane Society: helping Catherine with the Trap-Neuter-Return program for feral felines.

When I arrived at her house at eight p.m. as scheduled, Catherine met me in the driveway in front of a rusted, dingy-white cargo van—the vehicle of choice for serial killers. Examining my neatly typed timesheet, she scrunched her flat face that reminded me of a Persian cat. "Delores Diane Myer-Johansson sounds like too many names." She ignored my extended hand.

"I go by DeeLo." I smiled like a salesperson trying to close a deal but got nothing in return.

Her flinty blue eyes swept my small frame from head to toe, judging whether I had dressed appropriately for traipsing around in the woods at night. She'd told me to wear comfortable shoes and warm clothes but to put on layers. Nothing too new or fancy. I had complied, from my oldest cashmere sweater down to last season's suede boots.

"Why do they always send me the criminals?" Catherine pushed a strand of stringy, shoulder-length blond hair behind her protruding ear.

I winced. *Criminal* sounded harsh.

"What?" She raised her never-been-plucked eyebrows. "You're not here of your own volition."

That wasn't fair. I'd always loved animals and had owned cats until my marriage. When the county clerk gave me a list of approved charities where

1

I could perform my community service, I was happy to find the Pecan Point Humane Society as one of my choices. Working with furry pets beat picking up trash along the highway in an orange jumpsuit. "I... I wanted to be here."

Catherine took a pack of gum out of her jacket pocket and removed one stick. "Yeah, right. You'll finish your forty hours or however much the judge sentenced you to, and then I'll never see you again." She peeled off the wrapper and popped the gum into her mouth.

I didn't have a comeback. I'd always meant to do volunteer work, give back to the community. But between a full-time job, loose ends from my divorce, and the move to Georgia from California, a mother in memory care—and, of course, Barry—there was never time. Until now, when I had no choice.

"What did you do anyway?" Catherine heaved a small-animal wire trap into her van. The long, rectangular contraption looked almost as big as she was. "Speeding? Shoplifting?"

"D.U.I." It came out a whisper.

"Drunk driving?" She almost dropped the trap as she whirled to face me. "How many people did you kill?"

"None! It was my first offense."

"Once is too many. Guess the cops did something right for a change. Got you off the road." She straightened the trap on the van's floor and headed toward the open garage for another. "Well, don't just stand there gawking. Earn your hours or I won't sign your timesheet. Bring me another one of these traps, D.D."

"D.D. isn't—"

"I like it. Stands for Drunk Driver, doesn't it?"

One of the volunteers had warned me not to let Catherine's caustic personality rattle me. *D.D. is short for Delores Diane. I'll pretend that's what she meant. My new nickname.*

The nightmare of my arrest replayed like a video loop for the hundredth time. Flashing blue lights in the rearview mirror. The dreaded order, "Step out of the car, ma'am." Barry staring at me through the bars of a jail cell before he bailed me out, disappointment clouding his face.

Because of Catherine's disheveled appearance, I expected her garage to be cluttered to match. But the concrete floor was spotless, and although the two-car space brimmed to capacity, every item was neatly labeled and stored on industrial-strength metal shelves or in white laminate cabinets. I lifted a trap from the stack she'd set out and carried it to her van.

"Are you an alcoholic?" Catherine smacked her gum as she took the trap I was carrying and stacked it on top of the others. "Guess you know there's no drinking on this job."

"I'm not an alcoholic. And I don't make a habit of drinking and driving." I hated that she judged me because of one infraction. "I made a mistake."

"Ya think?" Catherine let out an exaggerated sigh.

If only…. If only I hadn't stayed for a second glass of wine. If I'd worn flats instead of my new stilettos. If I'd come to a full stop at that intersection. Barry always warned me about my rolling "California stops."

Maybe if I'd acted more businesslike with the cop who stopped me. Flirting had spared me a speeding ticket several years ago, but it was the wrong move this time.

"You could have killed someone."

"I know, but it's a good thing I didn't." I met Catherine's gaze. If our partnership was going to work, she'd have to cut me some slack. "Look, I can't change what happened. But I'm trying to make amends."

"And they sent you to me."

I smiled. "And I'm happy to help. Just tell me what you need."

With a grunt, she slammed the cargo door and headed toward the driver's seat. "Get in."

I'd hoped to follow her to the site in my own car and drive straight home after we finished trapping, but she hadn't given me that option. I rounded the vehicle and climbed in on the passenger side. Although the inside of Catherine's van looked tidy, it reeked of cat urine and dead fish.

Hands on the steering wheel, she turned to me. "What do you know about TNR?"

"Trap-Neuter-Release?" My friend Jill Hernandez made donations every year to Alley Cat Allies, a national nonprofit promoting TNR, but that was

3

all I knew.

"Trap-Neuter-*Return*. More accurately, Trap-Neuter-*Vaccinate*-Return. After we've spayed or neutered the free-roaming, community cats and vaccinated them, we return them to the same location—their outdoor home."

I nodded, wondering why she had not started the engine. Not that it mattered; I was on the clock. "Sounds like TNVR is your passion."

"Been doing it for years."

"Tell me more about it." The longer I sat here listening to her lecture, the less time I'd have to spend getting dirty, and the sooner I'd finish my community service hours.

"The Pecan Point Humane Society is a nonprofit animal rescue group focused on adoption." Catherine's voice softened; I could tell she'd made this speech many times before. "But the most important part of our mission is spay and neuter. They told you that in orientation, right?"

I nodded again. The trainer who'd conducted the orientation meeting had graciously not revealed my status as a "community service volunteer" to the other attendees—eager teenagers, restless empty-nesters, and new retirees—all donating their time to the animal charity for purely altruistic reasons. But we both knew. Maybe her disdain was in my imagination because I felt mortified for what I'd done.

"Fact is," Catherine said, "overpopulation of companion animals, especially cats, is a serious problem." She still had not started the van; I'd already racked up almost an hour of community service. "Did you know approximately four million healthy cats and dogs are put to death in animal shelters in America every year because they don't have homes?"

Four million a year? I'd never realized the figure was so high.

Her face grew flushed. "It's murder, and no one wants to talk about it. They whitewash what they're doing by calling it 'euthanasia.' Ha! Euthanasia is putting a terminally ill or injured pet out of its misery. Killing a healthy animal is murder."

I'd never thought about what happened to all those pets abandoned in shelters. Like the time my stepfather took the energetic puppy I'd found off to find its forever home...

4

"We can't adopt our way out of the problem." Catherine clenched her jaw. "Spay and neuter is the only solution."

"I've always had my pets fixed," I assured her.

"Well, that's good." The sarcasm in her voice told me she didn't believe anything from a drunk driver.

She turned the key in the ignition. The engine started to turn over, then sputtered and died. She tried again. Same result.

With a sigh, she squinted at the dashboard as if confronting a misbehaving child and then turned to me again. "Not everyone is a responsible pet owner. Especially here in the South where they don't value companion animals." Her accent was not Southern; like me, she probably hadn't grown up in Georgia.

I started to chuckle but stopped myself when she gave me a look that reminded me of my arresting officer. Memories of that horrible night, the reason I was here, resurfaced.

"People move and leave the cat behind." Catherine seethed. "Think it can fend for itself. All these free-roaming cats reproduce. Exponentially. Most of the ones who grow up outside never become socialized, so if they end up in an animal shelter, they don't make it out alive. That's why we do TNVR. Return them to their colonies where they can live out their natural lives."

"Colonies?"

"Groups of cats who don't have owners. Some are stray, some are feral, some are lost or abandoned pets. Community cats, we call them. It's like a big family, or a village." She tried starting the van again, but the engine refused to cooperate. She pounded the steering wheel. "Piece of—"

"Does this happen often? Maybe it needs gas?"

With a curse, she flung open the door, walked around to the front of the vehicle, and lifted the hood.

"Need some help?" I stuck my head out the window and craned my neck to see her. Not that I knew anything about auto mechanics, but maybe I could call Triple-A.

Ignoring me, she jiggled a few wires.

I picked up my phone to compose a text to Barry, describing my first night of community service. And this piece of work, Catherine Foster.

The van shook as Catherine slammed the hood. She eyed my phone when she got back inside. "You'll have to put that on silent while we're out in the field. We don't want to scare the cats, or they'll never go into the traps." She turned the key in the ignition, and this time, the engine roared to life. Over the sound of the motor, she added, "I hope you're not one of those volunteers who's on her phone all the time."

I pressed Send and put my phone away.

* * *

Catherine pulled the van into a run-down strip mall comprising an independent bookstore, a Mexican restaurant, an insurance office, a dry cleaner, a Dollar Tree, and some vacant storefronts. I couldn't help noticing the giant Whitehead Realtors poster pasted in one of the windows. Dominated by fake-smiling, top realtor Victoria Barton, Barry's ex-wife.

After dodging a few potholes, we parked next to a dumpster by the back door of José's, the Mexican restaurant. The greenbelt behind the buildings looked like a good place for feral felines to hide.

"I told the caretaker not to feed the cats today," Catherine said as we climbed out of the van. "They should be good and hungry."

I stood next to the vehicle and waited for instructions.

"Sometimes she forgets to tell the neighbors not to feed them, and the cats won't go in the traps." Catherine opened the van's doors and reached for a trap. "People aren't too bright."

"Who's the caretaker?"

"Azmina Patel from Black Cat Books," Catherine replied. I'd shopped at that bookstore several times and could picture the proprietor: a middle-aged Indian woman with delicate features, usually draped in an elegant silk sari. Knowledgeable about obscure books and like me, a fan of murder mysteries. Her shop also sold a wide selection of teas and coffees, the perfect accompaniment for a good book on a chilly night.

Catherine pulled out the first trap and motioned for me to pick up another.

"Azmina loves those feral cats like they're her pets. José complains they raid his garbage, and he threatens to poison them." She shook her head. "Personally, I think raccoons are raiding his garbage, not Azmina's well-fed cats. But I don't have time to mediate stupid disputes between business owners. I told Azmina to move the cats' feeding station farther away from the dumpster, and I warned José that if he tries to poison a single cat, I'll have him arrested for animal cruelty."

I helped Catherine unload two more traps, and we carried them to a wooded area off the pavement, where we set up one, partially camouflaged behind bushes. She opened a package of pungent mackerel then showed me how to bait the trap and set the gravity door.

"It doesn't hurt the cat when the trap door is sprung?"

Catherine shook her head. "They make these traps long and narrow, and you put the food way in back, so the cat won't get hit when the door goes down. I hang around and watch, and then I cover the trap as soon as I catch a cat. The towel makes it nice and dark like a little cave; the cats calm down and feel less vulnerable." She pointed to another trap. "Your turn. Prove you paid attention."

I located a hiding place where the ground was level and carried the trap over, the bulky metal banging against my leg. I cleared the entrance, then grabbed a slimy piece of mackerel. As I set it in position, a fishy odor invaded my nose. I understood now why Catherine wore gloves. Note to self: bring a pair next time.

Trying to remember how she'd done it, I set the trap, propped up the wire door, and waited for her to criticize me.

But she didn't. "Okay then," was all she said. "Let's set the other two."

"Now, what do we do?" I asked when we'd finished, and she'd inspected my work.

"We wait." She handed me a paper towel and some hand sanitizer so I could neutralize the mackerel slime on my fingers.

We walked toward the van, where we'd have a view of the area. Catherine had tied a fluorescent pink ribbon on each entrance door so we could tell from a distance whether a cat had stepped on the trip plate; if the ribbon remained aloft, the trap was still empty.

As we crossed the pavement, a shadow streaked in front of us. A moment later, a large black tom rubbed against Catherine's legs. He sniffed the overpowering mackerel odor that clung to our clothes.

I stiffened. A feral cat? Would he bite?

Catherine reached down and stroked the cat's head. "Manny! What are you doing here? Azmina never lets you outside."

I'd seen the bookstore's mascot sleeping behind the counter but never noticed the left corner of his ear was missing. I gave his head a pat, careful to avoid the cut. "What happened here?"

Catherine eyed me like I'd asked the stupidest question she'd ever heard. "You don't know anything about TNVR, do you?"

Thanks to her lectures, I knew more now than I'd ever wanted to.

"When we TNVR a cat, the veterinarian clips the tip of its left ear." She gave Manny another pat. "Most cats who've been trapped won't make that mistake again, but some juveniles will take the risk for a taste of mackerel. Their ear tip saves them another trip to the clinic."

"I never knew that, but it makes sense."

Catherine looked down at Manny. "And what are you doing out here, Mister? What are you trying to tell me?"

Manny refused to say.

Catherine shook her head. "Manny was born in the greenbelt, and Azmina brought him inside last year when he was still a kitten. Some predator had taken a bite out of his leg, so we couldn't release him after he was neutered. Azmina nursed him back to health, and he became a cuddle bug."

My eyes shifted toward the bookstore. "Is the back door open?"

Catherine followed my gaze. "They close at seven. Azmina should have gone home long ago."

We walked to the bookstore; Manny crept alongside us. Sure enough, the back door stood open. The inside was dark.

Catherine stuck her head into the black hole and fumbled for a light switch. "Azmina?" A musty smell camouflaged the store's usual scent of print books and exotic teas.

As light flooded the bookstore's back room, we gasped.

Azmina's body lay sprawled on the linoleum floor, her head twisted in an unnatural position. The color had faded from her brown face, and her unseeing eyes stared straight ahead. Purple bruises covered her neck.

I froze as the horror of what we'd encountered seeped into me like a dementor.

Clutched in Azmina's fist was a partially crumpled piece of paper imprinted with the logo of my workplace: Barton, Barton & Barton. Barry's law firm.

"Azmina! Oh, my God," cried Catherine. Her eyes widened as she turned to me. "What's going to happen to the cats?"

Chapter Two

I stood paralyzed at the sight of the body on the floor. Those bruises on Azmina's neck meant she had not died of natural causes. Or by accident. My stomach heaved.

I fumbled in my pocket for my phone. Hands trembling, I tapped nine-one-one. This couldn't be happening. Who would do this to such a sweet person? Was her killer still in the building?

Catherine grabbed the phone from my hand before my call connected. "Don't! We can't get involved."

She started toward the door and motioned for me to follow.

"But…" *Is she as crazy as everyone says?* "A woman is dead. We're already involved!"

Still holding my phone, Catherine pulled the door closed behind us. "You call, and I'll be blamed."

"Blamed? How?"

Clink! We both turned toward the bushes where I'd set my trap.

Catherine muttered something under her breath, then rushed back to her van for a towel and ran to the trap. I could tell the gate was down because the pink ribbon was no longer waving in the air.

I raced after her. "Hey, my phone!"

A large brown tabby with an enormous head thrashed at the sides of the trap and howled.

Catherine grinned. It was the first time I'd seen her smile, and at such an inappropriate time for any emotion besides shock and horror. "You caught Big Mack!" She slipped the towel over the trap, and the tom immediately quieted down. "This cat is the daddy of ninety percent of the colony. I'll wager he's Manny's father." She looked at the trap and crowed, "End of the road for you, Big Mack. Balls are coming off tomorrow."

I helped her carry the trap, weighted down with the huge cat inside. "We have to tell the police about Azmina."

A light went out at José's Mexican restaurant next door. A moment later, a door slammed, and a car engine revved.

As we loaded the trap into the van, the towel slipped slightly, and I adjusted it. Through the bars of his cage, Big Mack's wild, golden eyes stared at me, a look of betrayal on his dark face as he licked mackerel from his furry chops.

Catherine cast a wistful glance at the other traps. "We need to get out of here."

I jogged after her as she gathered up the rest of the traps. "We'll be in more trouble if we leave the scene of a crime and don't report what we saw. Give me back my phone so I can call the police."

As we loaded the traps into the van, Azmina's cat rubbed his body against Catherine's legs.

"You better come home with me." She lifted Manny, planted a kiss on his head, and placed him inside her vehicle. In a tone much softer than she'd used with me, she murmured to the cat, "I'm sorry you lost your mommy."

Catherine still had my phone, so I had no choice but to climb into the van with her. A feeling of impending doom enveloped me as the engine rumbled to life.

Just as Catherine shifted into reverse, flashing blue lights bounced off the rearview mirror. I twisted in my seat to see a police car blocking us. My heart pounded. All I needed was to get arrested again. While performing my court-ordered community service, no less. *I'm making the wrong kind of splash in this town.*

A stocky figure exited the patrol car, and boots crunched on gravel.

So much for no one knowing we were here.

The uniformed officer swaggered to the driver's window. "Well, well, if it ain't Cat Foster." I recognized the ruddy complexion and pursed lips of the middle-aged cop, Officer Stan Friendly, the same officer who'd arrested me for driving under the influence. I slumped into the seat, turned my head, and let a lock of hair hang over my face.

"Officer *Fiendly*." Catherine turned off the engine. "Sorry... Friendly."

Why was she antagonizing him? A chorus of feline yowls emanated from the back of the van as the cats joined me in protest.

"Breaking the law again, Cat?" The officer shifted a wad of chewing tobacco against his cheek.

Catherine snorted. "I don't know what you mean."

"Trespassing. Releasing nuisance animals onto public property." His tongue caressed his thin lips like a snake slithering from a burrow. "I can charge you with at least three violations of the county ordinance."

"You're harassing a law-abiding citizen," Catherine hissed, arching over the steering wheel. "I have permission to be here."

"Permission? From who?"

"Azmina Patel asked me to trap cats on her property. She owns this whole shopping center if you want to check the public records."

I flinched at the mention of the dead woman. "Officer, we—"

Ignoring me, he addressed Catherine. "She may own the shopping center, but the greenbelt is public property."

"Do you see me in the greenbelt?"

He tamped the tobacco in his cheek. "Prove you have permission." Only when he placed his hand on his hip did I notice his holstered gun.

"Unfortunately, I can't." Catherine's voice grew husky. "The back door to the bookstore was open. We found Azmina lying on the floor. Looks like she's been strangled. Tried to call nine-one-one but couldn't get a signal, so we were heading to the police station to report the crime. We didn't want to tamper with the scene, and besides, we were afraid the killer might still be inside."

I had to commend Catherine for thinking so fast on her feet and for coming up with such a plausible lie.

"Dead?" The officer's eyes narrowed. "You're making that up."

My mouth flew open. Why did he think she was lying about a death?

"Check it out. Save us a trip to the police station."

He spit tobacco juice onto the gravel. "Making a false police report is a misdemeanor."

"I'm not making a false police report."

He kicked the van's front tire. "Get out of here, Cat Lady. Stop causing trouble."

"Gladly, if you'll get out of my way." Catherine started the engine again. "I take it we don't need to stop by the precinct to report what we saw?"

The cop glowered. "Quit wasting my time, Cat Foster."

I expelled the breath I was holding as Officer Friendly strolled toward the bookstore. "I can't believe he let us leave without checking it out first. Shouldn't he take our statements?"

"He hates me. Doesn't believe a word I say." With a glance in her rearview mirror, Catherine backed out of the parking space and then accelerated. "Besides, he knows how to find me."

We hit a pothole. Catherine gritted her teeth. "Azmina said she was going to repave this lot once she got her insurance check."

"Insurance check?"

"Yeah, her husband passed away last spring. Had quite a bit of life insurance, and she was going to use the money to make some necessary repairs. Guess that's not going to happen."

I couldn't dismiss the image of Azmina sprawled on the floor in such a bizarre pose. "Why would someone kill her?"

Catherine's eyes watered. She sniffled and focused on the road. "I have no idea." Her voice cracked.

"Do you think she surprised a burglar? Like you said, the store was supposed to be closed."

Catherine wiped her cheek with her sleeve.

"I'm sorry, Catherine. I forgot you two were friends."

"Ha!" With another sniff, Catherine straightened. "I have no friends."

No friends? Not that surprising. I changed the subject to ease her discomfort. "What did Officer Un-Friendly mean about you breaking the law? At least three violations of the county ordinance?"

Catherine harrumphed. "Our county's animal ordinance was written in the dark ages."

"I don't understand."

"First of all, the ordinance defines 'owner' as anyone who feeds or houses an animal for forty-eight hours or more." Talking about cats again seemed to mask her feelings about finding Azmina dead. "Because I trap cats at night, take them to the clinic the next day, and then house them overnight while they recuperate from their surgery, the ordinance considers me their owner."

"But that's crazy. The authorities should know you're not—"

"And this idiot county has a leash law. For cats as well as dogs. Owners are supposed to keep their cats inside or on a leash."

"A leash law for cats? Who keeps a cat on a leash?" Why were we talking about leash laws when we just found a dead person?

Catherine rolled her eyes. "I'm in violation of the county's leash law. And I own too many cats. There's a maximum of three pets per household."

"But you don't own them."

We stopped at a red light. Catherine continued, "Officer Fiendly likes to threaten me with the 'abandonment' clause. The way the ordinance is written, when I release a community cat I've had fixed back where I found it—to its outdoor home—the county defines it as animal abandonment."

"That's stupid." I shook my head. "If community cats don't have owners, they're different from house pets. Why don't they update the ordinance to make exceptions for TNVR?"

"Ha!" Catherine snickered. "Our county commissioners are good ol' boys who've never heard of TNVR and wouldn't support it if they had."

We rode the rest of the way back to Catherine's house in silence. I couldn't stop thinking about those purple bruises on Azmina's neck. And what about that paper she was holding, with our logo on it?

As we unloaded her van, Catherine eyed my new Lexus SUV parked on the street. "You drove here?"

I nodded.

"They let you keep your driver's license?"

"With some limitations." It helped to know a good lawyer.

14

"Then you can take Big Mack to the clinic tomorrow morning. I have an early appointment."

Through my fatigue, it took a moment to grasp what Catherine was asking. "The spay/neuter clinic? Where is it?" This task sounded like more than I'd signed up for. And what should I do with a feral cat between now and then?

"College Park. It's called the LifeSaver. Gray building just off the freeway. Take the exit for the Connector. You know, the one by that big billboard about the new movie studio coming to town."

I groaned. "College Park is forty-five minutes away. I start work at eight."

"No problem. The LifeSaver opens at seven." Catherine picked up the trap containing Big Mack and lugged it toward my car. "And don't be late, or they'll turn you away. The cats must be there no later than eight to be prepped for surgery."

With apprehension, I opened my hatchback for her. "What do I do?"

"Big Mack should be fine in the trap overnight. You have a garage, don't you?"

I nodded.

"Park in the garage. Don't feed him; the cats aren't supposed to eat after midnight because of the anesthesia they get with their surgery."

"What should I do when I get to the clinic?"

"Tell them you're with the Pecan Point Humane Society, and they'll give you the right paperwork to fill out."

"Speaking of paperwork—" Would I get credit for the time it took to drive the cat to the clinic?

"I'll sign your timesheet tomorrow." Catherine fished my phone out of her pocket and handed it to me.

I climbed into the driver's seat as she headed toward her house. Squeezing my eyes shut, I tried to dispel the image of Azmina sprawled on the floor of her store.

And what would happen when Officer Friendly found her body?

Chapter Three

I phoned Barry as soon as I pulled into my garage and closed the door behind me. My boyfriend and boss wasn't a criminal attorney, but he had a law degree and should be able to tell me how much trouble I was in.

The call went straight to voicemail, and his soothing greeting instructed me to leave a message. I noticed the time—almost midnight—and remembered he had an early breakfast meeting. Of course, he'd be sound asleep. At the beep, I whispered, "Babe, there's so much to tell you about tonight, but we'll talk in the morning. See you at the office."

Catherine had assured me Big Mack would be fine in the car overnight, but I rolled down the windows to provide ventilation. And maybe dissipate some of his wild animal odor.

Heading inside, I kept thinking about the murder and felt vulnerable for the first time since I'd moved to safe, sleepy Pecan Point. Had Azmina's killer been a random robber who surprised her? Or had someone she knew attacked her?

Armed with an umbrella—the closest object within reach that might be used as a weapon—I made a thorough search of my small house. Behind the drapes, under beds, inside closets and shower stalls. Only after I'd verified that no one lay in wait for me, and all the doors and windows were locked, was I able to relax.

I plugged in my phone to recharge and imagined Barry's reassuring voice counseling me. He could organize details and lay out options so life's roadblocks didn't seem so daunting. Like the logical way he'd handled my mother's transition into memory care. After I'd spent months wrangling with my sister and niece without reaching a solution, Barry's assistance had been a godsend.

There was so much about tonight's events to process, I doubted I could relate a coherent story right now anyway. I'd stumbled across a dead body—of someone I'd known and liked. A death that was most likely murder. Catherine and I might even be considered suspects.

I kept picturing the crumpled paper in Azmina's hand, with the coral and cobalt Barton, Barton & Barton logo on it. What connection did she have with our firm?

As I reached to extinguish the lamp on my nightstand, my eyes strayed to the whodunnit I'd bought last week at Black Cat Books. *Going Home*, by a little-known Georgia author, involved a murder suspect who had Alzheimer's; Azmina had recommended the novel after I told her my mother was suffering from the disease. A tear crept down my cheek as I felt the impact of losing someone in my life, even though her role had been small.

I'd set my alarm for five, but when it sounded, a drugged sensation swathed me, pressing me into my pillow. All night, visions of Azmina's lifeless face, reflected in the fiendish, reproachful eyes of Officer Friendly—Officer Fiendly, as Catherine called him—wouldn't allow me any peace. I hit the snooze button and slipped back into the fog of sleep.

After delaying the inevitable a few more times, I forced myself out of my warm cocoon and headed to the kitchen to make coffee.

Big Mack.

Catherine had not given me the clinic's address. Though not genuinely Southern, she had adopted the habit of giving directions by landmarks rather than actual street names and compass headings. I googled it. What was the name of the place again? Life something. I should have written it down. After some searching, I found the address of an animal clinic called LifeSaver, located in the general vicinity Catherine had described, and typed the address into the GPS on my phone.

I checked on Big Mack before getting into my car. An ammonia-laden stink of tomcat spray had replaced the delightful new-car smell I'd been inhaling until yesterday. Dousing the interior with air freshener did little good.

"Are you trying to ruin my new car?" I chided the feral cat. Oblivious to my discomfort, the cat's fully dilated eyes stalked my movements.

At least he was quiet during the drive, although his pungent odor didn't fade, despite my leaving the windows rolled down.

Atlanta traffic was worse than the L.A. freeways, and drivers zoomed aggressively between vehicles, avoiding collision by only inches. Hunting for the movie studio billboard Catherine had described, I ended up in the wrong lane. I signaled to move over, but the jerk in my desired lane sped up to cut me off. I flipped him my middle finger, and Big Mack chose that moment to howl in solidarity. The driver didn't notice, but my gesture made me feel vindicated.

A story on the radio caught my attention, and I turned up the volume. "...sought in the death last night of Pecan Point bookstore owner Azmina Patel. In other news..." I'd missed it. Had they identified the killer? Was I a suspect?

Too late to heed my GPS instructions to move into the right-hand lane, I passed my exit. I had to drive several miles out of my way, got turned around again, and took an exit that didn't allow easy access back onto the freeway. The robotic voice of my GPS sounded increasingly impatient as it made constant recalculations. "Make a U-turn," she instructed crossly.

"I can't!" I screamed back.

And then I hit more traffic. Some careless driver had caused a fender-bender, and we'd come to a stand-still.

Incensed, I glanced at the clock on my dashboard.

Big Mack let out another yowl. I felt sorry for him, but there was nothing I could do.

I passed the tiny plywood building twice. It looked like an abandoned residence, not a place of business. On the second pass, Siri's declaration, "You have arrived," sounded even testier. I shut off the GPS to silence her and then pulled into a parking lot the size of a postcard. Maybe someone inside could give me directions. Did this clinic even exist? Had Catherine played a cruel trick on me? *Just you wait, Cat Foster.*

A twenty-something woman with an amber-tinted Afro and four silver rings in her ear looked up from the counter as I walked in. "May I help you?"

"I'm trying to find the LifeSaver Spay and Neuter Clinic." Could this be it? The lobby smelled of wet dog, and barks echoed from the back room. A promising sign was the logo pasted on the counter: a circular red lifesaver, like a blown-up piece of candy with the faces of a puppy and a kitten inside.

"You got it."

"Great." I sighed, trying to smooth tangled, windswept hair out of my face. "I have a feral cat from the Pecan Point Humane Society."

The woman looked at the clock on the wall. It showed five minutes past eight. She shook her head. "You have to get them here before eight o'clock."

The big analog wall clock taunted me as its minute hand inched another notch forward. Not only would I be late to work, I wouldn't accomplish my errand. Catherine might not even count the hours I'd spent on my trip to the clinic in vain. And what would I do with an angry, unaltered feral tomcat, who was now starving, stuck inside a cage? Tears flooded my eyes. "Please, miss. It's not even five after."

"Our policy is eight at the latest, so we can administer the anesthesia before surgery. All the trappers know that."

I took a breath so deep I was afraid my lungs would explode. "Look, this is my first time here, and I got lost. And I hit traffic. You don't have any signs out front. I drove by the place twice." I eyed the clock, willing the hands to move backward. "Your clock is fast."

The woman gazed at me with more curiosity than sympathy, unused to having customers challenge her.

"I can't take this cat to work with me. You want me to release him so he can continue to procreate? And never go into a trap again? I can't believe you're not going to take him because I'm five minutes late." I pulled my phone out of my purse to call Catherine. *Unbelievable.*

The woman sighed. "Let me check with the vet. How many cats did you say you have?"

"Just one." I pressed my hands together as if in prayer. "Big Mack. If you

19

could please take him today..."

Holding up an artfully manicured finger with turquoise nail extensions, the woman turned and disappeared through a door behind her.

My eyes roved the room while I waited for her to return with a verdict. The threadbare brown carpet had dark stains in several spots. The dingy yellow walls needed a fresh coat of paint. Two framed veterinary licenses hanging behind the counter gave the establishment its only glimmer of legitimacy.

Pinned notices about lost and found animals, humane traps for sale, and services available for hire covered a cork bulletin board. One handwritten flyer warned, "Stop Oakwood Studios from destroying Pecan Point." I was reading the LifeSaver's "Instructions for Trappers" and pricelist when the receptionist returned.

"He'll make an exception," she said, with a hint of a smile that exposed straight, white teeth. "Just this once." She produced a stack of forms. "Fill these out and bring in the cat. Need some help?"

"Please."

"Jason," she called over her shoulder.

A clean-cut, blond teen materialized from the back room. The badge on his scrubs read, "Intern." He accompanied me to my car to retrieve Big Mack, effortlessly lifted the trap I'd found so cumbersome, and carried it inside.

By the time we returned to the front desk, the receptionist had filled out most of the paperwork for me. I just had to verify the information and add my signature.

"Will you be the one picking up the cat this afternoon?" she asked.

The pen froze in my hand. "Pick him up?" Catherine had only asked me to drop him off. I better be racking up some hours. "Uh..."

"We close at four. Be sure you're here by then."

Great. Not only would I be late to work, I'd have to leave early. To perform my community service.

* * *

It was nine o'clock by the time I arrived at the office. Barry was meeting with a client in the conference room.

Jane Guidry, the receptionist, whose tight bun, long skirts, and plain, high-collared blouses made me think of the Amish, consulted her Timex and smirked. "Good afternoon, Delores." She hated me.

"I had an errand to run this morning. Barry knows about it." Or he would have, if I'd been able to reach him last night. But he'd understand.

No need to admit the errand was related to my court-ordered community service. I whisked past Jane and parked myself in my cubicle.

A stack of papers awaited my attention, but I couldn't concentrate on work. When I shut my eyes, I saw Azmina's tortured face. I shivered. Who would want to kill her? And did the police think Catherine and I had something to do with her death?

I stared at my computer. The events of last night replayed like streaming video across my screen.

The Barton, Barton & Barton logo had been visible on the paper in the bookstore owner's hand. It was our old logo; the current one said Barton & Barton. I typed "Azmina Patel" into our database. No match. Either she was not our client, or Jane had yet to pass her file to me to archive. Maybe the document in her hand had nothing to do with the reason she was killed.

Someone had been at the Mexican restaurant when we arrived at the site, but they'd left about the time Catherine and I found Azmina's body. It had been hours since closing, but perhaps this person was staying late doing paperwork or cleaning up. I remembered Catherine mentioning animosity between José and Azmina. Could the person leaving have been Azmina's killer? José, the owner?

Maybe they'd had another disagreement about the cats, and it got out of hand.

And what was Officer Friendly doing there? What made him show up when he did? And then not ask us to stick around after what we'd told him. Did he just want to harass Catherine? Maybe he had something to do with Azmina's death. What would be his motive?

I shook my head. Who was I kidding? I could be in so much trouble. I'd thought about calling nine-one-one after I left Catherine's, but would that have helped? The cop knew Cat and I had been inside the bookstore. What if he thought we killed Azmina?

Even worse, the real killer was still out there. I needed to find out who committed this grisly crime before the finger pointed at me.

Chapter Four

Without turning around, I sensed Jane Guidry's presence, the shadow from a cloud passing in front of the sun. She set another stack of papers in my inbox.

"How's that database coming?" Her tone implied she knew I was not as far along with my project as Barry expected me to be. Part of the problem was her glacially slow method of granting me access to the files.

"Great." I flashed my best public relations smile.

Jane grunted something unintelligible and headed back toward her desk.

I couldn't blame her for disliking me. When I first moved to Pecan Point from Beverly Hills, devastated by my nasty divorce, overburdened with my mother's entry into the memory care facility—on top of my turning thirty—Barry had given me a job. Even though I had no legal training. I could argue that recent personal experience taught me more about the legal system than I'd ever cared to learn.

The job Barry created for me kept Jane from getting the raise she'd been angling for; it wasn't in the budget anymore.

And in two weeks, he was taking me with him to an estate lawyers' conference in Savannah while Jane would be stuck in the office. He was also paying for me to take an online paralegal certification course, which he'd never done for Jane.

Another concern Jane had—legitimate, admittedly—was that Barry had hired someone with whom he had a personal relationship. As a lawyer amid the #MeToo movement, Barry should have known better. Not that I'd ever make trouble for him if our romance went south, but Jane didn't know that.

Initially, Barry had hired me as his public relations manager; I'd held a similar job with my ex-husband's company, Johansson Productions. Shocked that Barton & Barton didn't have a website, I'd promised to build one and create an advertising campaign so Barry could grow his business, which was a hodge-podge of elder law, estate planning, contracts, and wealth management. But when I arrived on the job, I realized his firm was in the technological dark ages. They couldn't handle any more business until they brought their systems into the twenty-first century. I couldn't market new services to our customers if I didn't know what services they'd already used, and what they might need.

Switching gears, I'd embarked on a project to set up an electronic database so we could quickly locate essential documents without digging through boxes of disorganized papers, and so we could create a mailing list for future marketing efforts. Jane did not embrace change, and she fought me every step of the way.

Out of her loyalty to Barry's ex-wife, Jane also resented his feelings for me. Even though his divorce from Victoria was final before we met, Jane glared every time she saw us together. Never mind that Victoria's flagrant affair with Roy Don Whitehead, one of the county commissioners, had caused the demise of the Barton marriage. I was merely the one to pick up the pieces. But, like a child of divorced parents, Jane still held out hope that Barry and Victoria would get back together, and I was preventing their reunion.

When I was entrenched in asset negotiations with my cheating, Hollywood-mogul husband, Barry had visited Los Angeles. He'd gone to college with Tony, my divorce lawyer, and they'd remained close friends over the years. Tony introduced me to his friend Barry at a chance meeting in his office. Our mutual attraction was instant. *Un coup de foudre*, as we would have said in my college French class—love at first sight.

While my lawyer was busy in court, Barry and I spent a long afternoon commiserating over margaritas on the patio of a Mexican restaurant on Sunset Boulevard, and our cuckold status bonded us. Both of us had married with the promise of "till death do us part," only to discover we were not enough to hold the interest of our respective partners.

By that evening, Barry and I had become kindred spirits, ignoring the customary caution against a rebound relationship.

My eyes flitted around my cubicle and landed on our photo, face-down on the desk again. The frame's stand was sturdy enough that I doubted it had fallen on its own. *Jane.*

I righted the photo, smiled at our laughing faces—Barry and I, arms draped around each other, with the Pacific Ocean as a backdrop—and then pushed it back to its spot next to my computer.

Coincidentally, I'd learned that Barry practiced law in Pecan Point, Georgia, a small town near Atlanta. After my stepfather passed away, my older sister, Desiree, and her daughter, Demi, persuaded Mom to move to Atlanta with them for a fresh start. Both worked as flight attendants and were based there.

When Mom transitioned from senior independent living in midtown Atlanta to a memory care facility in Pecan Point, Barry's help had been invaluable. As usual, Desiree and Demi were useless throughout the process.

While I reminisced about how we met, Barry appeared at the entrance to my cubicle. "DeeLo, there you are." No chastisement about my being late, which I'm sure vexed Jane.

I swiveled my chair around to give him my full attention. The studious, black-framed glasses and button-down blue Oxford shirt made Barry look like a typical young lawyer, in a Clark Kent/Superman sort of way. With slightly thinner hair than Clark.

"What are your plans for lunch? I have a client here, and we're on a tight deadline, but perhaps you'd like to join us."

I needed to review last night's events with him, get his opinion on possible suspects, ask his advice on how to proceed, but I couldn't do it in front of his client. "Sounds like you need a working lunch, and I don't want to interfere. Why don't I go pick up something and bring it back to the conference room?"

"Sure." He seemed relieved. We were still in the honeymoon phase of my employment, and he often tried to include me in his lunch arrangements even if it wasn't always appropriate.

"How does Mexican food sound? Do you like José's?" I opened my bottom desk drawer to retrieve my purse. "You know that's my favorite."

Barry rubbed his clean-shaven chin. "José's sounds fine. Do you have their menu?"

I set my purse on the desk and shut the drawer. "I'll print it out for you." I googled José's Mexican restaurant and brought up their menu, pleased to have created an opportunity to snoop around the scene of last night's crime.

* * *

The strip mall where Catherine and I had trapped cats last night looked worse in daylight. Poorly patched potholes riddled the uneven asphalt parking lot, and most of the decorative shrubbery had withered to a parched brown.

Two blue-and-white police cars and yellow crime scene tape blocked the entrance to Black Cat Books. A crowd of curious onlookers gathered on the sidewalk. I parked and strolled over. "What happened?" I asked the woman standing nearest to me.

"The owner was found dead last night," said the man on her other side. "The police suspect foul play."

I pressed a hand to my chest. "How awful! Do they have any idea who did it?"

A plain-clothes detective, notepad in hand, emerged from the building. He was fortyish, fit, and the competent way he carried himself made me believe he had to be smarter than Officer Friendly. "Folks, I need you to clear out. There's nothing to see here."

As the murmuring crowd dispersed, I hung back.

The officer turned to me, and before he could open his mouth to repeat his command, I spoke, "Sir, I was here last night. I found the body. Before Officer Friendly did."

His face froze. "What did you say?"

I launched into a rapid retelling of my first cat-trapping experience, how we'd found Azmina's cat, Manny, outside, and how we'd come across her body on the floor of the bookstore. I stuck to Catherine's version about

Officer Friendly driving up just as we were leaving for the police station to report our discovery. Even with that distortion, my guilt about leaving without making a statement lifted.

The detective held up his hand. "Slow down, ma'am."

I took a breath.

He extended the hand he'd just raised. His eyes were a brilliant shade of emerald, impossible to ignore. "I'm Detective Paul Ross. And you are…?"

"Delores Myer." I shook his hand. Catherine was right. Myer-Johansson was too many names, and I should sever the symbolic tie to my ex-husband.

The detective waved his notepad; he hadn't written more than my name while I talked. "I need you to come down to the station to make an official statement."

I glanced at my watch. "Can I do it later? I have to pick up lunch for my boss and get back to work."

"Later today is fine. Give me your contact information."

I rattled off my cell phone number, and he handed me his business card. "See you this afternoon, Delores Myer."

I headed into the Mexican restaurant. The smell of frying tortillas and chili grease permeated the air.

Piped-in mariachi music competed with clattering dishes and the din of the lunch crowd. I blinked, letting my eyes adjust from the bright autumn sunshine to the dark interior. Business was hopping, and there was a long line at the cash register.

José Garcia appeared from the kitchen with a salsa-smudged apron tied around his waist. The short, silver-haired man walked like a penguin and was about the size of the actor Danny DeVito—who'd played the penguin in *Batman*—only slightly rounder. In Spanish, he barked orders at one of the waiters. On his way to the cash register, he brushed by me, and his eyes flashed recognition. In the short time I'd lived in Pecan Point, I'd become a regular customer; the food José served rivaled that of the best Mexican restaurants in Los Angeles.

Touching his arm as he shuffled by, I remarked, "José, isn't it terrible about Azmina Patel?"

Color drained from his leathery face. His brown eyes widened, and he shook his head, backing away. "I know nothing." Changing direction, he hurried into the kitchen.

The woman in front of me in line turned around and gave me a quizzical look. "What did you say? What happened?"

"The owner of Black Cat Books was murdered last night," I explained. "José says he doesn't know anything about it."

"What? Murdered?" The man behind me leaned forward. "Who?"

"The bookstore lady next door," someone else offered. "It happened last night. Didn't you see the cop cars over there?"

The woman in front of me covered her mouth. "Oh, my goodness! Is José a suspect?"

I shook my head. "I didn't say he did anything wrong."

"They never got along," another customer added. "They were fighting the other day about those cats she feeds."

"But José!" exclaimed the woman in front of me. "I can't imagine him hurting someone."

I gazed at the kitchen door, willing José to come out again. I'd asked him the wrong question. I should have asked who I'd seen leaving last night, right after we found Azmina's strangled body.

Most likely, he'd tell me it was none of my business.

It was my turn at the register. I picked up my food order and paid the tab with Barry's credit card. When I turned to leave, I almost bumped into one of the servers who'd been standing too close behind me, arms crossed. "Excuse me," I said.

Face dark with anger, she tugged at my sleeve. "My father didn't kill anyone." Before letting go, she muttered, "Mind your own business."

Too shaken to argue or even apologize, I hurried out of the restaurant.

* * *

The conference room door was closed when I returned to the office. Low voices inside confirmed Barry was still meeting with his client.

28

Jane had left for lunch. I'd offered to include her in our order, but she declined. I knew she would; she was not a fan of Mexican food.

I tapped lightly on the mahogany door.

A chair slid across the carpet, and Barry's footsteps approached. The door opened.

"Ready for lunch?" Smiling, I held out the bags of warm burritos and crisp tortilla chips.

Bent over the granite conference table, the client pored through stacks of papers and file folders. She looked up, and our eyes met. Barry's client was Catherine Foster.

Chapter Five

Our hands grazed as Barry relieved me of the bags of food and ushered me into the conference room. "DeeLo, this is our client, Catherine Foster."

Catherine wore a smug expression and did not rise to shake my hand. "Hello, D.D."

"Please join us, DeeLo." Barry motioned toward an empty chair at the conference table.

I continued to stand. "Small world, Cat. By the way, I got Big Mack safely to the clinic this morning, once I found it."

Barry's brow furrowed in confusion. Then a light came on. "Of course, the Pecan Point Humane Society."

Some of the smugness retreated from Catherine's flat face.

I turned to Barry. "I'm going to eat lunch at my desk so I can catch up. Unless you need something from me, I'll let you two continue your work." I plucked my burrito from the bag. "Oh, Catherine, the LifeSaver wants us to pick up Big Mack at four, and I don't think I can get away that early to do it. Will you be free by then?"

Catherine looked down at the papers in front of her. "No problem."

I headed back to my desk to tackle the stack of filing in my in-basket. Seeing Catherine made me think about Azmina's murder again, but I willed myself to focus on work.

As I munched my burrito, I read through the documents, organized them into stacks by client, and then into sub-stacks by type of legal work, which I would later cross-reference in the electronic database. Pecan Point was a small town with few attorneys, and Barry's firm served most of the town's prominent citizens. A newcomer to the area, I didn't know many of them, but I was starting to recognize a few names. Working with Barry's files gave me access to lots of confidential information. Wills and trusts. Investment plans, powers of attorney, and other business dealings.

After I finished eating and washed up, I went back to my computer, created more electronic folders, and scanned the documents I'd sorted into the database.

Caught up with my morning's stack, I browsed our server, searching for a record of Catherine Foster. Until yesterday, her name had meant nothing. No folder had been created yet; her file must be in the conference room with her and Barry. It amazed me how the firm had been able to function with paper file folders and so few documents stored electronically. I'd have to wait until Catherine had gone before I could satisfy my curiosity about her business. She'd been with Barry all day; most of his appointments didn't last that long. How complicated could her affairs be?

I glanced at the time. Was she still in there? Had she mentioned Azmina's murder?

Jane's heavy footsteps clomped across the tile floor as she returned from lunch. She took an unnecessary detour past my cubicle and gave my inbox a surreptitious glance. I was facing the computer and thus had my back to her; she must not have known I could see her reflection in my monitor.

"Did you have a nice lunch, Jane?" I could taste the syrup in my voice.

Jane grunted and tromped back to her desk.

The phone rang, ending our game of one-upmanship. "Barton, Barton, and Barton," she answered, morphing into the consummate professional.

Barton, Barton, and Barton. I cringed whenever I heard her say it. The first Barton was Barry's father, semi-retired now, who had founded the firm when Barry was a child. I'd only seen the elder Barton in the office a few times—an older, rosy-cheeked version of Barry, with longer, disheveled gray hair, who walked with a cane. The only cases he handled these days were from long-time friends.

The second Barton was Barry, the most important Barton, who carried the bulk of the workload. The only one who truly deserved to have his name on the door—no disrespect intended for Barry's father and his legacy. It must be an unwritten rule that law firms had to contain multiple names in order to be taken seriously.

The third Barton grated my nerves: Victoria. During their eighteen-year marriage, the Bartons had been a powerhouse couple, pillars of the Pecan Point community. Adding Victoria to the family law firm had expanded their business to encompass real estate and corporate contracts.

Their break-up had been messy, not only personally, but for the business. Victoria's career had taken a new direction toward real estate sales, which she'd found more lucrative than family law. The couple still battled over clients they'd left with divided loyalties. The firm maintained active case files that involved Victoria; Barry was gradually closing them. His ex-wife and former partner hadn't completely cleaned out her office, but it was usually dark. Sometimes, I wondered why Barry didn't box up her things and set them on the curb. He had taken Victoria's name off the door and the company logo, but he had not yet removed her from his life.

Although she no longer worked for Victoria, Jane refused to acknowledge the woman's departure from the firm. Jane reiterated her position every time she answered the phone and uttered three Bartons.

I was so busy fuming over Victoria's ubiquity, I didn't hear Jane approach my cubicle.

"Delores." Her voice had softened, its animosity gone. "The nursing home director is on line one."

Panic seized me even before I heard Jane say, "It's about your mother."

Chapter Six

I grabbed the receiver, punched line one, and listened to the director's voice.

"What do you mean my mother is missing? You're supposed to be taking care of her." I tried to sound outraged, but my voice quivered with fear.

Thoughts raced too fast for me to process the apologies and excuses coming from the other end of the phone.

My mother was missing. A surge of desperation returned as I relived the last time she'd taken off, from her senior independent living complex in midtown Atlanta. She'd wandered out in the middle of winter, barefoot, wearing only a flannel nightgown. Desiree and I had found her hours later, dodging traffic a mile away; her thin arms were icy to the touch. Afterward, she'd come down with a terrible cold that had turned into pneumonia. We'd almost lost her.

That incident had precipitated my decision to move her to the Pecan Point Memory Care facility, where they were supposed to keep her safe.

"How could you let this happen?" I repeated.

The woman on the other end of the line kept talking, but her words didn't make sense. They were English, but she might as well have been speaking a foreign language. Then the name "Demi Myer" filtered through the garble, and the story began to gel. Demi Myer was my niece.

"I'll be right there. Don't let Demi leave." I hung up without waiting for a response and grabbed my purse.

I rushed out of my cube, past Jane's desk. "I have to go."

"I'm so sorry." Jane actually sounded sympathetic.

Barry and Catherine emerged from the conference room as I reached the front door. "It's my mother," I called.

"Do you want me to drive you?" In a few quick strides, Barry caught up with me.

I shook my head. "Not necessary. Demi's there."

"Oh." He had met Demi. "What happened?" He followed me outside and across the parking lot to my car.

"Mom's missing." I clicked the key fob and opened my door.

"What?" His face contracted with disbelief. "But she's—"

I slid behind the wheel, closed the door, and lowered the window a few inches. "I'll text you when I hear more." He'd recommended that nursing facility, and the confused look on his face begged for reassurance that I wasn't blaming him.

"If you need a search party, Jane and I will help."

I nodded my thanks, rolled up the window, and headed out. In my rearview mirror, I saw him linger, watching me drive away, before going back inside.

* * *

Pecan Point Memory Care was a modern, red brick building with courtyards, gardens, and fountains to create a peaceful atmosphere for its residents. The individual quarters were spacious and clean; we'd customized Mom's room with family photos and favorite trinkets like her elephant figurine collection and wall rack of commemorative spoons. Skilled caregivers staffed the facility around the clock. I'd researched it thoroughly after Barry recommended it and had been favorably impressed.

Until now.

I pulled up to the front entrance and slammed the door as I sprang from my car. Primed for a fight, I marched into the director's office.

"Delores, I'm so sorry." The plump, gray-haired woman in a tailored business suit rose from behind the desk when I entered. "But she's on the guest list."

Demi cowered in a chair across the room, her six-foot frame contorted like a Great Dane trying to curl up on someone's lap.

I glared at my niece. "How did you lose my mother?"

Fear replaced her usual cocky expression. Apropos, under the circumstances. "Aunt Delores—"

Demi was a year older than I and a head taller, and she hated calling me "Aunt Delores." Since we were children, I'd slipped that tidbit into conversation every chance I got.

She was more like a sister to me than Desiree and David, my much older siblings—along with all the hair-pulling, name-calling, tattle-tale sibling rivalry. When I was born, Desiree was a sixteen-year-old single mom; her daughter, Demi, was barely a year old. Desiree lived at home with our parents until our father died of cancer. Then, our mother met Al and remarried soon after. Desiree clashed with our stepfather and took off when I was in kindergarten. Demi lived with us periodically, when Desiree's lifestyle didn't accommodate parenting.

Our brother David cut all ties with the family over twenty years ago when he came out and moved to San Francisco. Al had called him a pervert, and David didn't even ask the rest of us how we felt before disowning us. I thought he might reach out after Al died, but that never happened.

At least Demi and Desiree stayed in touch with Mom and me, although they usually stirred up trouble whenever they came around. Like today.

When Demi didn't answer my first question, I prompted, "What were you thinking?"

She straightened. "I just went to the ladies' room, and then I ran into someone—"

"Mom has Alzheimer's! You're not supposed to leave her alone. Not even for a minute."

"But she's never done this before."

"Before? What do you mean 'before'?"

Hand on her hip, Demi shot me a defiant look. "She's my grandmother. I can take her out for lunch if I want."

35

"She's my mother! It's my job to keep her safe." As far as relationships went, *mother* trumped *grandmother*, but Demi didn't get it. Just because her own mother hadn't always been there for her didn't mean she could appropriate mine.

She glared at me, which sparked a twinge of guilt. Truth be told, Mom had been more of a mother to Demi than Desiree had, and despite my resentment, I understood their connection.

I wasn't letting her off the hook, though. Yes, I'd put Demi and Desiree—and even David—on the visitor list, but the staff hadn't mentioned anyone visiting, much less taking my mother off the premises. "Who's looking for her while you sit here feeling sorry for yourself?" Surely, the staff had dispatched someone.

"I came here after I searched the restaurant and the grounds and couldn't find her." Demi ran her fingers through her short, frizzy curls. "I thought she got tired of waiting for me and came back to her room like she did last—"

My mouth dropped. "Last time? She's done this before? And no one told me?"

Demi dipped her head between her shoulders.

Good God, no one's looking for Mom. "Where did you take her?"

"Leonardo's," Demi squeaked.

I'd been to the restaurant several times with Barry. It was over a mile away, too far for Mom to walk back on her own. The rustic, Tuscan villa-style building, perched on the highest hill in Pecan Point, overlooked a nature reserve. It served expensive, highly rated Northern Italian cuisine, probably more Demi's taste than my mother's. When the temperature was mild like today, customers loved to dine *al fresco* and enjoy the view of the forest. Where my mother was most likely wandering…

"Let's go," I said. "I'll drive."

"Steve will go with you," the director said, pointing to a burly orderly who had just entered the office.

* * *

36

We arrived at Leonardo's during the lull between the lunch service and the early dinner crowd. Soft classical music played in the background. The young woman at the hostess station touched her hand to her mouth as she recognized Demi. A butterfly tattoo peeked from under her long white sleeve. "You didn't find her yet?"

Demi shook her head. "She never came back in here?"

The hostess threw up her hands. "We've looked everywhere. The restrooms, the kitchen, the storeroom."

"Only place left is the greenbelt," I said. "Let's fan out so we can cover more area." I looked at Demi. "Is your cell phone charged? And on?"

She nodded.

Steve held up his phone. "What's your number? I'll send you a text if I have news."

After exchanging cell numbers, the three of us separated, each taking off in a different direction. I hadn't worn proper shoes for hiking through brambles, but when I got dressed that morning, I'd had no idea I'd be searching for my mother in the woods. I was going to ruin my new leather pumps.

The trails were irregular and not well-traveled. Branches hung low across my path. I almost tripped over a fallen sapling. Thorns from a Cherokee Rose snagged the fabric of my slacks. Gnats swarmed around my face. "Mom!" I called.

I inhaled the sweet aroma of wild honeysuckle. If I weren't so worried about my mother, and gnats weren't flying into my nostrils, I would have appreciated it more. "Mom, where are you?"

The terrain sloped steeply toward Pecan Creek. The stream wasn't deep, but I knew a person could drown in just a few inches of water. What if she'd fallen in?

A rustling in the brush caught my attention. No doubt there were venomous snakes here. It was only a bird gathering nesting material. "Mom!" I called, louder this time.

Farther down the trail, I sensed I was being stalked. A few feet away, I met the unblinking gold eyes of a dark tabby who resembled Big Mack, camouflaged in the bushes. In a flash, he sprinted after a small rodent. As he dashed away, I noticed he had a tipped left ear. Like Big Mack would have by now.

I came to a clearing near the water's edge. There was my mother. Sitting on a log, talking to a strange man.

"Mom!" I rushed to her side. "We've been looking all over for you."

She turned at the sound of my voice, and a smile broke out across her face. "Well, hello, dear. Here I am."

"Has she been here long?" I asked her companion, who was dressed in a loose khaki shirt and an Indiana Jones hat like he was going on safari. The fortyish man had thick, straw-colored hair and a solid build. "She's my mother, and she's been missing all afternoon. Thank you for keeping her safe." I had to assume that was what he was doing; he looked trustworthy enough. I took my phone out of my pocket and sent a quick group text to Demi and Steve. Then, a separate one to Barry.

The man held out his hand. His eyes crinkled when he smiled; his leathery skin told me he spent a lot of time outdoors. "Nick Norton. Director of the Pecan Creek Nature Foundation. Your mother and I were having a little chat."

"I thought I'd see the cat lady," my mother interjected. She turned to Nick. "What happened to the cat lady?"

Chapter Seven

I stared at my frail mother, who'd made herself as comfortable on the fallen, moss-covered log as if she were sitting in my living room. "The cat lady? Who's the cat lady?" Catherine Foster was the first person who came to mind. But how would my mother know her?

By my mother's confused expression, I might as well have asked how many cats roamed the earth.

Nick looked at me, his amber eyes warm. "She's talking about Azmina Patel, the owner of Black Cat Books. Maybe you haven't heard: Azmina was killed last night in her store."

Not only had I heard, I found the body. "That's awful! But how does my mother know Azmina?"

I'd been about to ask him if he was a friend of Azmina's, but his watering eyes gave me my answer. "I was telling your mother the news when you walked up. Azmina came down here a lot to feed the feral cats in the reserve." Something about the way he spat the words "feral cats" led me to believe he did not share Azmina's fondness for them.

I gazed up the hill. The shopping center that housed Black Cat Books was less than a mile away, on the other side of the creek, in the opposite direction from Leonardo's. "Yes, but—" I turned to my mother. "You've walked in these woods before?"

Her expression was blank. She had checked out of the conversation.

Nick nodded. "Azmina and I saw her here last week."

Demi. "Mom, how often does Demi take you to lunch?" And why couldn't my niece keep track of her? And why did no one from the memory care facility bother to tell me she'd been missing before? If they even knew.

My mother perked up and looked at Nick. "The food in that place is awful, so my granddaughter takes me out to lunch."

"That's wonderful," Nick said. He turned to me. "Last week, we saw your mother out here and gave her a ride back to Pecan Point Memory Care. Azmina recognized her from when she visited the facility with her therapy cat."

"Her therapy cat?"

"Yes, the black cat who lives at her bookstore. Manny's super-friendly, and the residents love him. Stroking an animal's fur can be therapeutic."

I supposed if I were confined to a nursing home, petting an animal might cheer me up, too. So, my mother knew Azmina and Manny? Small world. Or rather, small town.

"Manny took off after Azmina was killed," Nick continued. "Poor animal, he was probably terrified. God only knows what he witnessed."

I flashed back to last night, when we'd found Manny outside the bookstore. Catherine, who knew the cat, had sensed his distress, and we'd soon learned the reason. But something about Nick's statement seemed off. Did the police know Manny lived in the bookstore? Catherine and I had not mentioned Azmina's cat to Officer Friendly. "How did you know Manny took off?"

A pallor crept over Nick's face.

But he recovered before the wheels of my mind could churn him into a suspect. "Azmina and I had scheduled a meeting at the bookstore this morning, and when I arrived, the crime scene investigators were there. They found the food bowl and litter box but no cat."

About to reassure him that Manny was safe at Catherine's house, I stopped; I'd have placed myself at the scene of the crime. I turned to Mom. "Shall we go? People are worried about you."

Nick helped me escort my mother up the trail to Leonardo's, where we reunited with Demi and Steve. They were chatting and laughing with the hostess and servers as if there had never been a crisis.

Demi threw her gangly arms around Mom. "Gram, you scared me half to death! I told you I'd be back in a minute."

I held my tongue. I'd already reamed her for leaving my mother unattended. Now that Mom had been found unharmed, Demi would no longer be open to learning from her mistake.

Chapter Eight

Back at Pecan Point Memory Care, Demi flirted with Steve and gushed over his dubious assistance with our search. My assessment of the facility had dropped a notch.

I walked my mother back to her room. Her feet shuffled across the tile floor, showing her exhaustion.

As I helped her into bed, a black smartphone slipped from her pocket. I caught it before it hit the floor. "Did Demi buy you a phone?" Before dementia set in, Mom had refused to carry a cell phone, claiming they were a threat to her privacy.

Mom reached for the device. "My picture."

I handed it to her. "You've learned to take pictures with your phone?"

She shook her head. "The man." She tapped on the screen, but it remained dark. Her brow wrinkled.

"Here, let me." I pressed a button that illuminated the screen.

A text included a photo of my mother, face beaming, holding Manny. In the picture, several other seniors hovered behind her, awaiting their turns to pet the cat. The text was from Azmina, and Nick was the recipient. "What the…?" My heart fluttered. "Mom, we need to return this phone to that nice man."

Surprised we hadn't been asked for a password, I scrolled through Nick's phone, searching for a way to contact him. Seeing the text from Azmina gave me chills.

And then I noticed another text exchange, sent at eight-thirty last night. My curiosity overruled respect for his privacy.

Nick: We need to talk. Please!!!

Azmina: The deal is off.

Nick: You can't back out now!! Hear me out.

Azmina: There's nothing more to discuss.

Nick: I'm coming over.

I set the phone down on Mom's bed. Had Nick gone to Azmina's store last night? Before or after she was killed? And if so, why hadn't he mentioned it? When I'd asked him how he knew Manny took off, he said the police had told him this morning.

While I scrutinized the contacts, my mother leaned back against the pillows and shut her eyes. I covered her with the rainbow-colored afghan she'd knitted years ago, when she still remembered how to knit. She snuggled against the wool and began to snore lightly.

With Nick's phone in hand, I kissed my mother's forehead and tiptoed out of her room.

Demi had already left. The director was on the phone, and I didn't feel like waiting to speak with her, although I wanted to clarify the ground rules. Maybe I should ask Barry to help me draft a strongly worded letter. But now, Detective Paul Ross expected me at the police station.

* * *

The Pecan Point police station occupied a one-story, gray-brick building constructed in the late twentieth century. It stood next to the county jail, which reminded me of that awful night when Officer Un-Friendly arrested me for D.U.I.

More like an entryway than a lobby, the police station's small waiting room held four straight-backed chairs that did not invite guests to linger. In two of those chairs sat an elderly couple struggling over a form attached to a clipboard. A uniformed police officer hovered nearby, helping them fill it out. The room smelled faintly of Lysol.

I crossed the gray tile floor to the craggy-faced, middle-aged receptionist, who worked behind a plexiglass window with a pass-through tray at the bottom. "May I help you?" she drawled into a pencil-thin microphone.

"Delores Myer to see Detective Paul Ross." I flashed the business card the detective had given me.

The receptionist eyed me over her wire-rimmed glasses. "Do you have an appointment?"

"He asked me to stop by this afternoon to make a statement. It's about the...uh," I lowered my voice, "the death of Azmina Patel last night."

That clarification triggered more interest. Raising a finger, she picked up a desk phone. "Just a minute."

After a brief, muffled conversation, she pressed a buzzer and pointed to an interior door opening into the lobby. I walked past the senior citizens, pulled on the knob, and let myself into a narrow hallway.

Detective Ross came out of his office and extended his hand. "Ms. Myer, thanks for coming." He ushered me inside the office and closed the door. On the wall hung an autographed poster of an Atlanta Braves player most people would recognize.

The chair facing his desk was padded and larger than the lobby chairs. I sank into its leather cushion. Something in the air gave me a sudden urge to cough.

He studied my face for a moment. I wondered what Officer Friendly had told him about last night. Had I walked into a trap?

"Would you like some water?" he asked.

"Yes, thank you." Not how I expected our interview to begin.

He pressed a button on his desk phone. "Abby, can you please bring us two waters?"

I covered my mouth and suppressed another cough. "Excuse me."

The door opened, and the receptionist leaned in with two plastic bottles of a generic brand of water. Lukewarm. I accepted one and passed the other across the desk to the detective.

We twisted off the caps. The liquid soothed the tickle in my throat.

He took out a notepad. "I appreciate your coming forward, Ms. Myer."

"DeeLo, please." Why had I said that to a cop?

"DeeLo," he repeated. "What brought you to Black Cat Books last night?"

"I'm a volunteer for the Pecan Point Humane Society." Sipping my water, I gauged his reaction to my use of the term "volunteer" before continuing. "Another volunteer—Catherine Foster—and I were there to TNR some cats for Azmina and—"

"Excuse me, what? TNR?" His brow had furrowed almost enough to swallow the pencil he tapped against his forehead. "What is that?"

I might have asked the same question yesterday, but today, I was the expert. "TNR stands for 'Trap-Neuter-Return.' Technically, it's now called TNVR, 'Trap-Neuter-*Vaccinate*-Return.' Studies have shown the best way to control the overpopulation of free-roaming cats is to humanely trap them, take them to a clinic to be spayed or neutered and vaccinated, and then return them to the area where they were captured. That way, they can live out their natural lives, keeping the rodents at bay, without reproducing to nuisance proportions." I knew I was veering off course. He'd asked me here to discuss a murder, not recite Catherine Foster's speech about cat overpopulation.

"Hmmm, I never knew that." He tapped his notepad. "You and Ms. Foster were there to trap cats for Azmina Patel. Did you see Azmina?"

"Not alive. As I told you, we found her body." To avoid his penetrating green eyes, I took another sip of water.

"Did you talk to Azmina before you started trapping?"

Was he trying to trip me up? "Catherine talked to her earlier in the day; Azmina knew we were coming. We assumed she'd gone home when the bookstore closed around seven."

"What time did you get there?"

"A little after nine."

He wrote in his notepad. "What made you go inside?"

"We'd just set our traps when Azmina's cat wandered up." I rubbed the cap from the water bottle between my thumb and forefinger. "I found out today he's a therapy cat."

The detective stopped writing. He probably wondered what a therapy cat had to do with murder.

"Manny's an indoor-only cat," I continued. "He was outside."

Detective Ross did not react.

"Catherine knew something was wrong because the cat was outside. And then I noticed the back door to the bookstore was open."

"Go on."

"It was dark. There was a musty smell—not the usual incense and tea and new books that hits you when you enter the store. Catherine turned on the light, and there was Azmina, lying on the floor." I pressed my fingers to my forehead and closed my eyes. I'd never get the image of her body out of my head. Those bruises...

The detective was silent for a moment. "I'm sorry. That scene must have been upsetting." But then he was back to business. "Did you touch her? How did you know she was dead?"

That part was a blur. Especially since I'd planned to change it up a little, so Catherine and I wouldn't look guilty. What if she was still alive, and we'd left her there to die when we could have helped? "No. It was such a shock."

He changed tactics. "What was the body's position?"

"Sprawled on her back, head twisted." I winced. "Dark bruises on her neck. Her eyes looked like polished glass marbles." Like dead people on TV or in the movies, but much more gruesome in 3D with all the senses experiencing the scene.

Detective Ross consulted the folder on his desk. Was he matching up my story with that of Officer Friendly? "Did you move her?"

"No. I started to call nine-one-one but couldn't..." I was going to say I couldn't get a signal, but maybe he wouldn't buy it. "We heard a noise, and Catherine thought the killer might still be in the building, so we rushed out."

"You went outside to call nine-one-one?"

"Well, Catherine thought we should drive to the police station to make a report in person." That story didn't sound as credible as it had last night, now that I had dropped the "no signal" part. "In case the killer was still inside."

He nodded, eyebrows raised.

"But then Officer Friendly drove up, and we told him about finding Azmina's body."

"Didn't he ask you to stick around to give witness statements after he checked out the scene?" Detective Ross tapped the side of his mouth with his pencil.

"No, he told us to leave."

"He told you to leave?" The pencil fell from his hand.

"Seemed strange to me, too, but I don't think he believed we'd found a dead person. He accused us of trespassing." In our defense, I added, "Catherine asked if we should make a statement, and he told us no." Well, maybe we'd interpreted his hateful look as a "no."

Detective Ross wrote several paragraphs, then reviewed what he had written. I sipped more water and tried to appear relaxed and truthful.

"Let's get back to the noise you heard inside the bookstore. Can you describe it?"

I hadn't heard a noise, and now I had to fabricate one. I gulped. "Maybe I heard the trap door closing."

"The trap door?"

"Yes, when we got outside, we found we'd caught Big Mack."

He suppressed a smile. "Big Mack?"

"Some caretakers name the cats."

"And from inside the bookstore, you heard the trap door snap shut?" His eyes searched my face.

We'd been outside when Big Mack tripped the sensor. I focused on the poster of the baseball player instead of the detective's face. "I'm not sure what I heard."

"Let me get this straight: you went outside after finding a dead body and hearing a strange noise, then checked the traps to see if you'd caught a cat?"

He made us sound so insensitive.

"Well, the trap was right outside. We heard the door clink shut. You have to go cover the trap so the cat doesn't go berserk."

"You took care of the cat in the trap before heading to the police station?"

I pulled at the plastic label around my water bottle. "It only took a few minutes to pick up the rest of the traps."

"How many had you set?"

"Four."

He wrote more. Then, "You didn't call nine-one-one from inside the bookstore because you were afraid the killer might be lurking there. But instead of hurrying to the police station, you stopped and picked up traps?"

"We didn't know how long we'd be gone. It's not humane to leave a trapped cat unattended."

"And you didn't think to call nine-one-one while you were picking up traps?"

I should have stuck with the "no signal" story.

He gazed at me for a moment, then shook his head. "Did you see anyone while you were collecting your traps? Someone leaving the bookstore?"

"No, but while we were carrying traps to the van, I saw a light go out at José's Mexican restaurant. Then a motor started, and someone drove away. The building blocked my view of the entrance and the parking area, so I can't tell you what the person or the car looked like."

"If you couldn't see the entrance, how could you tell a light was on at the restaurant?"

I cupped my chin, trying to visualize the scene. "We were around back, by the dumpster. I could see light through the window over the back door. It must have been in the kitchen or an office."

"What time was that? When the light went out, and the person left the restaurant?"

"Around ten, maybe ten-thirty."

"And when did Officer Friendly arrive?"

Was he testing me? Officer Friendly should have written the time in his report. "Just after that. When we were leaving. To go to the police station."

"Right."

He didn't believe me.

"How well did you know Azmina Patel?"

"I've shopped in her bookstore a few times, and we've chatted about reading recommendations. Like me, she loves—loved—mysteries."

"Can you think of anyone who'd want to hurt her?"

I shook my head. "I've never heard a bad word about her."

With a nod, he reread his notes. "Those are all the questions I have for you today, Ms. Myer. Can you think of anything else that might be important?"

The paper in Azmina's hand, with the logo from Barton, Barton & Barton. What if it said something incriminating about Barry or his firm? "She had a document clutched in her hand. I have no idea if it's important."

"A document?" He opened a folder and picked up some photographs. "You're sure?"

"It caught my eye because of the logo from Barton, Barton & Barton. The firm where I work."

"You could read the logo?"

"I recognized the intertwining Bs of coral and cobalt. Our old logo." What a big mouth I had. I hoped it was nothing incriminating.

He stared at the photographs. "I have pictures of the crime scene. There's nothing in her hand." He held up a photo. I leaned over his desk, drawn to the horror but repelled at the same time. Azmina's hand lay at her side. Empty.

My heart hammered against my chest. I'd told this detective the truth about that part, and now it sounded like a lie. "I don't know what happened to the paper. I didn't touch it."

He slid the photo back into the file. "I'll check with the coroner and the crime scene investigators. Maybe it will turn up." He set the file aside. "I'll need to speak with the other woman who fled the scene."

Fled the scene? My eyes popped.

"Your friend Catherine Foster. Do you have her number?"

"Friend?" Catherine was hardly a friend. She was the reason I was being accused of fleeing the scene of a crime. I reached into my purse, and my hand touched Nick's phone.

The detective watched me fumble too long through my purse.

I pulled out my cell, found Catherine's number, and held it so he could copy the information.

While he was writing, I produced Nick's phone. "Uh, I found this."

Detective Ross looked at the device I had yet to relinquish. "When? Where?"

"Not at the crime scene. But there might be a connection." I pushed it toward him. "This afternoon, I met a guy. Long story, but I ended up with his mobile by mistake."

"Have you tried to reach him through one of his contacts? Or is it password-protected?"

"No password. One of his contacts is Azmina Patel." I watched the detective's eyes widen. "I believe you spoke to the gentleman this morning. Nick Norton from the Pecan Creek Nature Foundation. You must know how to contact him."

Detective Ross accepted Nick's phone from me. "Thanks. I'll get it back to him."

I paused. "I saw something that might be relevant to the case. By accident; I swear I wasn't snooping. I was searching for a way to contact him. Maybe you'll want to look at it."

"Is it something I need a warrant for?"

I shrugged. "I don't know what the rules are for that."

He raised his brow.

"Some texts," I said. "With Azmina, the night of her death. You might want to ask him about them." I rose and opened the door, leaving the detective to puzzle over my revelation.

As I was almost outside his office, he called, "Ms. Myer, please make yourself available should we have more questions."

Chapter Nine

Barry and I opted for a home-cooked dinner at his apartment that evening. When I arrived, he'd changed into Bermuda shorts and tennis shoes with no socks. He still wore his Oxford, but the shirttail hung out, and he'd undone the top few buttons.

He fired up the gas grill on the deck for salmon steaks marinated in teriyaki sauce while I assembled a green salad and made my mom's vinaigrette. Cooking together gave us a chance to unwind and discuss our day.

And we had a lot to discuss.

I filled Barry in about how Demi had managed to lose Mom this afternoon. And about the stranger I'd found her with, whose phone Mom had inadvertently taken—a man who'd exchanged suspicious text messages with Azmina the night of her death.

"There must be a reasonable explanation for those texts," Barry assured me. "A business deal?"

The story of Azmina's murder had been all over the local news; Barry already knew about that. However, he didn't know Catherine and I had found her body.

Even though he and Catherine Foster had spent half the day shut in a conference room together, she had not uttered a word about our grisly discovery, as if she was in denial about the murder and our connection to it. Except for the part where she'd thought she could embarrass me in front of my boss. Her smug look had faded once she realized Barry and I were a couple, and he already knew about my D.U.I. *Priceless*.

Barry gasped when I told him about finding Azmina. "You must have been horrified. Why didn't you call me?"

"I did, but it was late, and my call went to voicemail." Lowering my eyes, I noted the regretful twitch of his mouth, how he scrutinized me for cracks in my armor. "I'd never seen a dead person before. Not counting funerals, where the body is all prettied up. Death isn't like the movies when it's fresh and in person." I continued to slice the tomato for our salad, its red juice oozing onto the cutting board.

He took the paring knife from my hand, set it on the counter, and wrapped his arms around me. "It's a hard image to get out of your head." He pushed a strand of blond hair behind my ear. "You must have been up late, talking to the police."

"No." I looked into his earnest brown eyes. "Catherine didn't want to call the police."

"What?"

"I tried to dial nine-one-one, but she grabbed my phone and said we had to get out of there."

"You're kidding." He dropped his arms and stared at me with a startling intensity. "You left the scene of a crime?"

"Not technically. Before we could drive away, Officer Friendly—that nasty cop who arrested me—drove up and started harassing Catherine about trespassing."

"Trespassing?"

"Catherine told him we had permission to trap cats on the property, except she couldn't verify it because Azmina was dead."

Barry got that look on his face when he pondered a complex problem. He fiddled with the temple of his glasses. "So, you *did* report the homicide?"

I bit my lip. "He didn't believe us."

"The officer didn't ask you to stay and give a statement? After you found someone dead?"

"No. He told us to leave, so we did." The more I recounted my story, the crazier it seemed.

Barry rolled his eyes at the ceiling. "DeeLo."

I touched his hand. "It's okay."

"How's it okay?"

"Today, when I went to pick up our lunch at José's, I ran into the detective investigating the case, Paul Ross." I hoped my smile would erase the worried expression on Barry's face. "I told the detective everything. He asked me to make a formal statement, so I stopped by the station this afternoon."

"Why didn't you call me? I'd have gone with you. This was more than just a witness statement. You left the scene of a murder."

Having a lawyer present hadn't crossed my mind, but it should have. Barry could have helped me navigate the detective's trick questions. "You were busy. I figured I could handle it myself."

He put his arms around me again. "I'm never too busy for you, and even innocent people can use legal counsel."

"You know," I tilted my head, "Azmina had a piece of paper in her hand. With a Barton, Barton & Barton logo."

He knitted his brow. "A document with our old logo?"

"Was she a client?"

The timer sounded, and he released me to turn the salmon. The smell of grilled fish wafted into the room as he slid open the glass door to the deck.

I thought he'd dropped the subject, but when he came back inside, he added, "Azmina came to the office a few months ago to update her will."

My breath caught in my chest. Could she have been holding her will? Why?

"She also had a business deal going on with Victoria."

"Victoria still uses our logo?"

"I've asked her to stop. She works for Whitehead Realtors now, and they have their own logo." Barry's pale neck reddened as it often did at the mention of his ex-wife.

"What did Azmina have to do with Victoria?" I pressed.

"Azmina's husband owned the undeveloped land surrounding the shopping center, and he dreamed of building a subdivision. But after he died last spring, she decided to sell it."

I whistled. "That plot must be worth a lot."

"Victoria's firm is working with those movie executives who've been trying to buy land in Pecan County for a new studio. They have their eye on Azmina's property." He opened a cabinet and pulled out a serving platter. "Did you notice any writing on the document?"

"No. I didn't get that close. And when I told Detective Ross about it this afternoon, he showed me pictures of the crime scene. There was nothing in her hand."

Barry shrugged. "Strange. Maybe they'd already removed the paper when they took the photographs. Although the usual procedure is to take the photographs before anyone touches the body." He headed back to the deck to take the salmon off the grill.

I set the small butcher-block table and brought the salad bowl from the kitchen counter. When he came inside with the salmon, we sat down to eat.

Barry's apartment exuded a transient feel, even though he'd occupied it for almost a year. Unpacked boxes stood in the corner. No pictures hung on the walls; no knickknacks adorned the mantle. He'd once owned one of the ritziest mansions in the best neighborhood in Pecan Point until Victoria won the house and most of its contents in their divorce. Even though he was the wronged party, Barry hadn't fought for a more favorable settlement. Too bad his friend Tony, my divorce lawyer, didn't practice in Georgia.

Victoria put that ostentatious monstrosity on the market but hadn't received a single offer; she'd reduced the price several times. There was some justice in the world.

Sometimes, I wondered whether Barry's living situation stayed temporary because he hoped Victoria would take him back. If she said the word, he could pack up and vacate the apartment in an hour. They could even reclaim their mansion. But I'd seen them argue during her visits to the office and concluded reconciliation would never happen.

Maybe Barry was too busy shouldering the bulk of the work for Barton and Barton to bother making an oasis away from the office, like a traveling salesman sleeping in random hotel rooms. The office must have felt more like home than his apartment.

I also wondered if Barry expected to move in with me. Tony had milked my louse of an ex-husband. Besides paying for my mother's memory care facility and a new Lexus, my settlement had enabled me to purchase a renovated Craftsman-style house in a gentrified Pecan Point neighborhood and hire a decorator to create my sanctuary. My house wasn't flashy like the Barton place, but it had style. Despite it being big enough for two, I wasn't ready to share my space with anyone.

Even if he was a good cook.

"The salmon is perfect," I congratulated Barry, sticking my fork into the flaky pink fish.

He beamed. "The salad is delicious."

It didn't take much skill to wash lettuce and chop vegetables, but being appreciated felt good. Compliments from my ex-husband had been rare. "Thanks."

We ate in silence for a few minutes, savoring the buttery texture of the salmon infused with teriyaki. Then I asked, "What were you and Catherine Foster up to for so long today? If telling me doesn't violate client confidentiality."

Barry set down his fork. "You're indexing my files, so you'll read about her case anyway." He clinked the ice cubes in his water glass. "Catherine received a large insurance payment and punitive damages in a wrongful death lawsuit three years ago. Afterward, she became a client of our wealth management services. We're structuring her assets so she can create a nonprofit foundation with enough money left for her to live comfortably."

Catherine Foster, a philanthropist? "A nonprofit foundation? To help cats?"

Barry nodded. "To fund spay and neuter programs. She didn't mention it when you worked together last night?"

"She didn't share much about her personal life. And after we found Azmina..." I blinked, trying in vain to dispel the image. "Catherine doesn't strike me as someone with a lot of money."

"The award was huge, and her investments have done well." I suspected Barry was too modest to admit he'd been the one to choose and manage Catherine's investments. "But you're right. She likes the simple life."

"What was the award for?" I took another bite of fish.

Barry looked down at his plate. "Such a tragic accident. A drunk driver killed her husband and four-year-old daughter."

The mouthful of fish caught in my throat, and I coughed.

Barry leaned over to assist, but I waved him away. I regained control and then took a swig of water.

"Are you okay?"

I nodded, but my heart still raced.

"So sad," said Barry. "The driver worked for a major trucking company, and he was on duty at the time. The money is consolation, but money can't replace someone you love."

Tears welled in my eyes. "No wonder Catherine was mortified when I told her my reason for doing community service was a citation for D.U.I."

Barry reached across the table and patted my hand. "I should have warned you about her."

I should have called an Uber. Or passed on the wine. I squeezed his hand, which felt warm and reassuring.

My phone vibrated on the kitchen counter. Sliding my hand from Barry's, I rose and went to answer. Catherine Foster's name appeared on the screen. Had she bugged the place?

"Hello, Catherine."

"Where are you, D.D.?" Her voice was shrill. "You were supposed to meet me here at eight-thirty."

I held the phone away from my ear. "We're still trapping tonight? I thought after last night—"

"I told you we need to catch that pregnant female before she pops out a litter."

"But—" With Azmina dead, did we have permission to trap cats on the property?

"Don't tell me you're quitting already. How are you going to finish those community service hours?" Her voice morphed into a sneer around the words "community service hours."

With a resigned look at Barry, I replied, "I'll be right there."

* * *

Catherine had set up most of the traps before I arrived, but she saved two for me to prove I'd paid attention last night. I passed the test.

"Good," she said, inspecting my work. "Too bad you're a short-timer."

I guessed that was as close to a compliment as I'd get from her.

"Did you talk to the detective investigating Azmina's murder?" As we headed for our lookout spot, I wondered if Detective Ross had tried to contact her yet.

"Why should I?"

"Don't you want to help find the real killer and take the suspicion off us?"

She snorted.

Taking her cue, I changed the subject. "What does this momma cat look like?"

"Tuxedo with a white splotch on her black nose." Catherine surveyed the woods with the small pair of binoculars she'd draped around her neck. "I named her Smudge, but Azmina called her Octomom." She gave a sad chuckle. "That cat had eight kittens in each of her last two litters. I don't know how she managed. Such a tiny thing."

"Is eight a lot?"

"The average litter is about four. With more, the mother can't produce enough milk to feed them all. But Octomom's kittens were healthy."

"Was Big Mack the father?" I remembered how she'd touted his virility last night.

"Possibly. Or the father could have been one of her sons from the first litter."

"Her son?" Incest in cat colonies?

Catherine peered over her binoculars. "Cats don't care." She shook her head. "Reminds me of a time some ignorant people adopted a brother and sister from us, before we started using the LifeSaver for pediatric surgery."

"Pediatric surgery?"

"Veterinarians used to tell you to wait until your pets were six months old," she explained. "But by then, they may have already had a litter. We've since learned surgery can be done safely once the animals have reached two pounds—when they're eight or nine weeks old."

"Oh." This revelation was news to me, but I saw no need to broadcast my ignorance to Catherine.

"Anyway," she continued. "We gave the adopters certificates for free spay and neuter at a local veterinarian, but they never used them. Then the idiots wondered why they had kittens four months later."

I smiled and nodded but might have wondered the same thing. After only four months? Weren't the cats still babies?

"'But we never let them outside,'" Catherine mimicked the maligned adopter. "'They're brother and sister!'" She shook her head. "That's why I hate working adoptions. People are stupid. I get along better with cats."

I spotted movement near the trap. A tuxedo cat. "Is that Octomom?"

Catherine lifted the binoculars. "No, that's Mittens, her daughter from the first litter."

"How can you tell?"

"Mittens has white paws. And an ear tip." Catherine leaned forward and cried, "Mittens, don't you dare go into that trap."

We held our breaths as Mittens sniffed the wire contraption, then got distracted by rustling in the brush.

"I saw another ear-tipped cat in the reserve this afternoon," I said. "Must have been one you and Azmina had fixed." Despite the unimpressed expression on Catherine's face, I continued, "This afternoon, I left the office early because my mother went missing from her memory care facility."

Still no reaction from Catherine. I don't know why I expected her to care about my mother's dementia.

"I found her in the reserve talking to a man named Nick Norton. He's with the nature foundation and claims to be a friend of Azmina's."

Catherine's eyes widened.

"Do you know Nick?" I asked.

"Unfortunately," she huffed. "He's a jerk, but Azmina liked him."

"As in, dating?"

"Maybe. But he's a decade younger than Azmina. I suspect he was hitting on her so she'd sell him her property."

"Nick was trying to buy her land?" Those text messages on his phone...

A trap door clanked.

"It's Octomom! D.D., you're a good-luck charm." Towel in hand, Catherine rushed across the parking lot and into the brush. I followed. "Careful, she's a Houdini."

A thin tuxedo cat thrashed against the wire, rocking the cage from side to side. Catherine cried, "Oh, no. She's already had her kittens." Panic flashed in her eyes. "We have to find them. They can't survive on their own."

"Should we let her go back to them?"

Catherine shook her head. "She'll never venture into a trap again. I'll take them all to my house and let her raise the kittens in my basement until they're weaned, and then we can get everyone fixed. That was the plan with her last litter, but a careless volunteer let her escape." She gestured to me. "Get a flashlight out of my van and search the woods for those kittens. They can't be too far away."

Another clink.

"Mittens, you stinker! We don't have time for this." After covering Octomom and securing the entrance door to prevent her escape, Catherine hurried to where Mittens had been loitering.

Blue lights flooded the parking lot as a police car pulled up. Officer Friendly. What did he want? More harassment? I pushed the record button on my cell phone.

The cop jumped out of his car just as Catherine lifted the trap door to free Mittens. "Cat Foster, you're under arrest. Section Six of the Pecan County Animal Welfare code: Animal abandonment."

She put her hands up but flexed her middle finger as he approached.

I stepped forward. "That's ridiculous! You can't—"

"Careful, Missy," Officer *Fiendly* snarled. "Or I'll arrest you for interfering with a police officer." He placed handcuffs around Catherine's wrists.

"You jerk," she spat, putting up no resistance.

"I'll do you a favor and pretend I didn't hear that." He marched her toward the police car while I gaped in astonishment, powerless to stop him, but recording the whole event.

"I'll phone Barry," I called to Catherine. "He'll straighten this out."

"My keys are in the van." She allowed Officer Friendly to push down her head as she slid into the back seat of his patrol car. "Get those kittens and take them to my place. And hurry, DeeLo. They'll die if we don't find them soon."

I stared at the departing vehicle. Catherine had called me DeeLo.

Chapter Ten

Through the camera lens on my cell phone, I watched Officer Friendly drive away with Catherine slumped in the back seat of his squad car. He turned on his lights and siren, which I thought was overkill.

Kittens. I put my phone back in my pocket, picked up the trap containing Octomom, and carried it to the van. "Where are your kittens?" I asked her.

Octomom just hissed at me.

"You're no help," I told the fertile cat. I'd considered carrying her around while hunting for the babies, thinking she'd call to them, but the trap was too bulky. Opening it was out of the question. I would not be the second "careless volunteer" who let Octomom escape.

My cell phone pinged with an incoming text from Barry. "How's it going?"

I hit the telephone icon. Barry picked up on the first ring.

"Catherine's been arrested. You have to get down to the police station and bail her out."

"What happened?"

I related the tale of Officer Friendly's harassment and my search for Octomom's kittens. I didn't mention my recording of Catherine's arrest or my plans for it.

"Want me to come help?" Barry asked.

"Go to the police station first. Catherine shouldn't be in jail on such absurd charges. She has cats to take care of." And I didn't want that responsibility to fall on me.

"On my way."

How was I ever going to locate those kittens? Octomom would have been smart enough to find a proper hiding place. I grabbed Catherine's flashlight from the van's floor. It had a steady, bright light—a good-quality tool. I scoured the perimeter of the parking lot, shining the light into nooks and crannies that might make suitable nests for kittens, and found nothing.

While continuing to look for the kittens, I collected the rest of the traps and loaded them into Catherine's van. I wasn't making another trip to the LifeSaver in the morning if I could help it. Octomom spit and hissed as I stacked the empty traps next to hers.

"I'm trying to help you," I rebuked her.

Tramping through the brush, I heard rustling. I cringed. There were probably snakes in these woods. I shone the flashlight in the direction of the sound.

A possum emerged and scurried past me, its pointed snout hovering close to the ground. Better than a snake. It was the first live opossum I'd seen in years; I was used to seeing them crushed beside the road. Would it hurt the kittens?

At least a half hour elapsed before I heard a meow. I shone the flashlight into the bush ahead and picked up the glow of cat eyes.

Framed in the spotlight, Mittens held something in her mouth, perhaps a mouse or a vole. I hesitated to interrupt her dinner but then looked more closely at her prey.

The creature in her mouth wasn't a rodent; it was a tiny kitten. And she wasn't eating it; she was bathing her young sibling with her tongue. I shone my light downward, exposing eight thumb-size kittens snuggling against Mittens, trying in vain to suckle her.

"Good girl, Mittens. Stay there." I withdrew my high beam and backed away.

I raced to the parking lot, hoping the cat wouldn't try to move the babies before I returned. From the dumpster behind Azmina's bookstore, I retrieved an empty cardboard box. Then, I grabbed a clean towel from Catherine's van and sprinted to collect the kittens.

Relieved, I found them right where they'd been.

I tiptoed closer, cooing as I walked. "Nice kitty. No one's going to hurt you." The feral cat tracked my approach and guarded the kittens with her body. "I'm just going to take these babies to their mommy. Promise, I won't hurt them." I was standing over them now. Mittens hadn't budged.

I extended my hand. *Please don't bite me, Mittens.*

I picked up the kitten farthest away, and Mittens didn't react. Gently, I placed the baby in the box and reached for another. They were so tiny and silky, with their ears folded into their heads and their eyes pasted shut. Their little claws flexed, searching for a warm nipple.

One by one, I loaded the newborns into the box under the watchful eyes of their older sister. I counted eight. With a sweep of my flashlight, I checked the area to ensure I hadn't left anyone behind. Mittens blinked.

"Thank you, Mittens. Good girl." I was tempted to pet her but didn't want to push my luck. After all, she'd been deemed too feral to be adoptable.

Careful not to drop any kittens, I made my way through the brush and into the parking area, then placed the box in the front seat of Catherine's van. I retrieved my purse from my vehicle and relocked it.

Before starting the van's engine, I sent Barry a text to let him know I was leaving the shopping center for Catherine's house.

An ammonia odor lingered inside the van. I hated driving other people's cars. Octomom yowled while I adjusted the seat and mirrors. The kittens squirmed in their box. Could they hear their mother's cries?

Easing out of the parking lot, I tried to get a feel for driving the unfamiliar vehicle. The steering wheel was difficult to turn, and the transmission slipped.

Obeying all traffic laws, I came to full stops, used my signals, kept under the speed limit, and reached Catherine's house without incident. I pressed the button on the garage door opener clipped to the visor.

I'd never been inside her house and felt like an intruder. The dishes stacked in the sink and opened mail strewn across the kitchen table weren't meant for a stranger's eyes. A bored, long-haired white cat lounging on the back of the living room couch looked up at me, yawned, and went back to sleep. Surprisingly, Catherine's house didn't reek like her car.

At least, Catherine would have cat supplies.

After two false tries—a closet and a pantry—I located the door to the finished basement, flipped the light switch, and made my way down the hardwood stairs.

Catherine's basement contained a bathroom, a kitchenette, and several storage rooms, one piled high with bags of cat and kitten food. Another stashed folding cages, cat litter, and other supplies marked for the Pecan Point Humane Society. In the kitchenette at the base of the stairs stood a full-size refrigerator stocked with animal medications.

I found an empty utility room suitable for the little family and set it up with cat beds, a litter box, and big bowls of dry food and water for Octomom—all of which I obtained from the supply rooms. Catherine seemed prepared for all contingencies. Once I'd readied the room, I went back upstairs to bring the new residents to their quarters.

First, I removed the box of kittens from the van. They had gathered themselves into a heap, and I worried the bottom ones might suffocate. Juggling the box, I opened the door with one arm and maneuvered down to the basement.

"Your momma's coming," I cooed, placing the babies into the nest of towels I'd arranged for them. One black-and-white kitten sucked on my finger as I moved it from the box to its new bed. "This will be better than living in the woods."

Kittens unloaded, I returned to the van to retrieve their mom. The clunky wire trap banged against the doorjamb, earning me another hiss.

Once I got the mother cat inside the room and set down the trap, I closed the door. There was a hopper window on the outside wall, but I'd already checked the lock. Holding my breath, I lifted the trap door.

Octomom shot out in a blur of howling black and white fur. She rammed against the walls, pawed at the cabinet, sniffed the floor and the space under the door, and jerked her head from side to side, seeking escape. Then she spotted her kittens. Blind, they gravitated toward her, squeaking and mewling.

I watched, gratified, as the family reunited. Octomom snuggled into the towels and let the kittens crawl to her swollen nipples. She seemed to be counting heads as she licked each baby and pushed it against her breast.

She gave me a slow blink, not exactly in thanks, but maybe in forgiveness. Relieved to see the family reunited and safe, I slipped out of the room and closed the door behind me.

Upstairs, I fed Catherine's pet cats, even though she hadn't asked me to. Something hairy rubbed against my legs. I looked down to find Azmina's therapy cat, Manny. As I stroked his head, he stretched his paws to my knees, begging to be cuddled. I obliged. His thick fur felt soft as velvet. He had a small, white spot on his throat, shaped like a perfect five-pointed star, that I hadn't noticed before. I'd thought he was solid black.

The doorbell startled me. Should I answer?

With Manny in my arms, I peered out the window. Barry stood on Catherine's front porch, alone.

I opened the door. "What happened at the police station? Where's Catherine?"

He shook his head as he came inside. "They won't hold a bail hearing until tomorrow."

"That's ridiculous. She shouldn't have been arrested. Can't we change that idiotic law?"

Barry bit his cheek to suppress a chuckle. "You want to change a county ordinance?"

Was that so crazy? "Why not?" Manny, purring loudly, nuzzled my neck and demanded attention. "We can keep this from happening again. How does someone go about getting a law changed in this county?"

Barry adjusted his glasses, no longer so amused. "You'd get a lawyer to rewrite it with the revisions you're proposing, gather support from key stakeholders like rescue groups and Animal Control, and then present it before the Board of Commissioners for a vote."

I stroked Manny's fur in thought. "You're a lawyer. Will you help me?"

Barry gulped. "I'm not sure I have time."

"What if I write it? Then you can edit it for proper legalese." I set Manny down and sidled up to Barry. In a sultry voice, I purred, "I can make it worth your while."

He rolled his eyes toward the ceiling and smiled at me. "All right."

* * *

Barry drove me back to the shopping center to pick up my car. He waited until I started the engine and exited the parking lot.

When I was almost home, an unfamiliar dark-colored sedan, headlights on high beam, appeared from a side street. It quickly accelerated until it was following less than a car length from my bumper. From my rearview mirror, I watched its lights flick on and off. My pulse quickened. Was it a stalker? Dare I go home, or should I drive to a public place?

I made a turn, and the car kept the pace, creeping even closer. I reached for my phone.

The car zoomed around me and sped off into the night. As my pulse slowed to normal, I wondered why anyone would follow me. Maybe they were kids out joyriding, looking for someone to torment. Maybe I was paranoid because I'd found a dead person.

Upon my arrival at home, I checked to ensure all my doors and windows were locked, and no one lurked in a closet or behind a curtain. Exhausted, I fell into bed.

And then I lay awake thinking about cats and jails and stupid regulations.

Unable to fall asleep, I fired up my laptop and googled the animal ordinance for Pecan County. It was only a few pages long; I printed it out and read through it. From what I could tell, no one had updated it since the 1970s.

I found the problem passages Catherine had cited. The definition of "owner" should be modified. And missing was a description of "feral cat," or "community cat," as Catherine preferred to call them since all unowned cats weren't necessarily feral.

Pecan County's ordinance assumed all domestic cats had owners. But, because feral/community cats were unowned, the restrictions regarding owned pets should not apply to them; the law lacked that distinction. It also contained rules about restraint and the number of pets a person could own; that section should be modified to exempt community cats and their caretakers.

Officer Friendly had cited the abandonment clause. If we added an exception to that rule for community cats and those who cared for them, there would be no legal reason to arrest someone like Catherine for TNVR activities.

I made some notes before the words began blurring on the page, reminding me to go back to bed.

This time, I fell asleep.

* * *

Barry was in the conference room with a client, and Jane was away at a doctor's appointment the following morning when Victoria Barton marched into the office, dressed in a form-fitting red business suit and frilly blouse with a scooped neckline. I bent over my computer and pretended not to notice her.

She stood outside my cubicle, hands on her hips.

I kept typing. Victoria's too-sweet, floral perfume reminded me of a funeral parlor.

She cleared her throat. "Hey, Surfer Girl."

"Surfer Girl" was her nickname for me, probably because I was from California and looked the stereotype: long, sun-lightened hair and an easy-to-tan complexion. Looking like a surfer didn't mean I was one, though. My older brother, David, had taught me when I was ten, but I wasn't much good at it. And after he left home, I never picked up a board again. Victoria's tone assured me the moniker wasn't a compliment; she could have easily substituted "Barry's Bimbo."

I paused in thought, then continued typing.

"Excuse me." She stepped inside my cubicle, invading my space.

I looked up. "Oh, hello, Victoria. I didn't see you come in." As usual, her bubble-cut auburn hair was plastered in place, á la American Girl Barbie, and her make-up thick enough for a TV appearance.

"I need a file," she said.

"Did you look in your office?" I flashed a sugary smile.

She tightened her plum-red, collagen-infused lips. "Some of what I need might be in Barry's files."

I leaned back in my swivel chair. "Did you ask Barry?"

"Look, Surfer Girl, I don't want to argue with you. Get me the file, will you? Maybe it's one you've already converted to electronic."

I turned back to my computer. "What's the client's name?"

"Azmina Patel."

My fingers froze on the keyboard. "Azmina Patel? The woman who was murdered the other night?"

Victoria swallowed and distorted her facial features enough to redistribute her Botox.

Before she could respond, Barry and his client came out of the conference room. They shook hands, and the visitor headed for the exit.

Detective Paul Ross. What was he doing at our firm? Was the detective a client, or did he want to ask Barry about the paper I saw in Azmina's hand at the crime scene?

"Victoria? Why are you here?" Barry ushered his former wife into his office. As soon as he closed the door, I did another computer search for Azmina's file, in case I'd missed it yesterday. Still no record in my database. Of course not. I would have been the one to put in the information.

I walked to Jane's desk, glad she was out of the office so I didn't have to rummage through the boxes around her feet. The cartons were labeled alphabetically, but I'd discovered the files were not always returned to their rightful place. Nevertheless, I figured L through P would be my best starting point for Azmina Patel.

Cramped from my stooped position, I hoisted the box of dusty file folders to the top of Jane's desk.

Though I thumbed through the folder names twice, there was nothing between Pastor and Peterson, and no files in that container seemed out of order. I tucked the box back under the desk.

Perhaps Jane had filed Azmina's paperwork under her first name. I grabbed the A through E box. A few of those files were out of place, but I dug through all of them and couldn't find any names resembling "Azmina."

I paused. Could Barry have the file? Last night, he'd said Azmina had recently updated her will.

Barry's office door opened, and Victoria stormed out. Her body language suggested their conversation had not been cordial.

She scowled at me as she passed. "What are you looking at?"

Before I could think of a snarky retort, Victoria stomped to the exit.

Barry walked to Jane's desk, where boxes surrounded me.

"I can't find the file she wants," I explained. "Azmina Patel. It's not here."

Barry nodded. "I told her it's not here. The police took it this morning."

"They took the original?" I set down the folders I was sorting. "What about copies of the documents?"

"I told Victoria I'd have Jane look for them later."

Obviously, his response had not satisfied Victoria. "Why did Detective Ross have a warrant for that file?" I asked.

"We prepared Azmina Patel's will, and they need to know who benefits." Barry helped me lift the box of folders from the top of Jane's desk and stash it underneath.

"Jane hasn't given me any of these files yet." I gestured toward the boxes. "I'd get started digitizing them but don't want to mess up her system."

He sighed. "We might have to give Jane a push. She's slow to get on board with change."

"I've noticed."

We walked back to my cubicle. "Do you have plans for lunch?" Barry asked.

"I'm going to work on my draft of ordinance changes."

His eyebrows shot up.

"By the way," I ventured. "Did Detective Ross know anything about Catherine's status? Hopefully, someone more reasonable than Officer Un-Friendly threw out the charges."

Barry shook his head. "They're still holding her. She's a person of interest in the murder of Azmina Patel."

"You're kidding. Catherine?" I grabbed the cubicle wall to brace myself.

"She's named in the will."

Chapter Eleven

I stared at Barry. "Catherine is a beneficiary in Azmina's will? Because of the foundation she's starting?"

He nodded. "It's normal to question anyone who stands to benefit from a victim's death."

"Question, of course. But can they keep her in jail?"

"In Georgia, they can hold someone for forty-eight hours without charges. And she's not cooperating."

"Why would Catherine kill Azmina?" I eyed him in disbelief, wondering why he didn't seem more outraged at the injustice done to his client. "She has enough money to start a foundation."

Barry adjusted his glasses. "I'm not privy to the police investigation."

"Don't suspects need opportunity as well as motive? If being a beneficiary is considered a motive." We stood awkwardly outside my cubicle. I'd have invited him to sit down, but I'd piled folders on my guest chair, dangerously close to the Starbucks sack containing the remains of my pumpkin-pie-spice latte. Out of the corner of my eye, I spotted Jane entering through the front door, back from her doctor's appointment.

"The police don't have an exact time of death," Barry said. "I know you assume Catherine couldn't have done it because you were with her Sunday night, preparing the traps at her house, but she could have gone to see Azmina earlier."

"But—" I recalled the text messages from Azmina on Nick's phone. They'd been sent around eight-thirty the night of the murder, while Catherine and I had been together. Detective Ross should have read that exchange and

71

realized Catherine had an alibi.

Before I could remind Barry about the texts, my cell phone rang.

"I'll let you get that." He headed back to his office, and I ducked into my cubicle.

The caller was Jill Hernandez, my reporter friend at the *Pecan County Daily News*. My niece had introduced us shortly after I moved to town, but I liked to think Jill preferred me to Demi. I'd sent my recording of Catherine's arrest to Jill last night with no explanation.

"DeeLo, what the—?"

"You liked my video?"

"Where did you get it?" she demanded.

"I took it."

"Explain." Jill's rising pitch told me she was too busy for guessing games.

"I thought you'd sympathize. Your favorite charity is Alley Cat Allies." I twisted in my chair. "You didn't know it's illegal to conduct Trap-Neuter-Return in this county?"

There was a pause. "How is it illegal?"

I nodded as though she could see me. "Look up the animal ordinance. I can send you a link if you like." I turned to my computer and, with one hand, typed "Pecan County Animal Ordinance" into Google. "If you want to get technical, the Trap and the Neuter are okay, but they can arrest you for the Return."

"Unbelievable." I heard Jill clear her throat. "How did you get involved in this?"

I hadn't talked to Jill since the night of her engagement party. The night I'd been stopped for D.U.I. after the party. I'd been too ashamed to tell anyone besides Barry, who only knew because he picked me up at the jail and helped me get my car out of the impound lot. "Uh... I started volunteering for the Pecan Point Humane Society."

Giggling. "DeeLo? Volunteering?"

It was hard to lie to Jill; she'd been a reporter too long, and she'd dig for the truth until she found it. "On my way home from your party last month, I got pulled over."

"What?" Her giggling stopped.

Lowering my voice to prevent Jane from eavesdropping, I related the whole humiliating tale. "Don't tell Demi. She'll never let me live it down."

Jill uttered an expletive. "I thought you were okay to drive."

"So did I."

"I should have warned you, though. In high school, we used to call this town 'Police Point' because the cops didn't have any real crimes to investigate, so they'd lie in wait for young drivers and cars from out of the county."

"I learned my lesson the hard way, as usual." I put Jill on speaker while I typed an email to her. Although the police now had a real crime to solve, I wasn't ready to share my involvement in Azmina's murder investigation with the press, friend or not. "Just sent you a link to the animal ordinance."

I heard her computer ding. "Got it," she said. "What do you want me to do with it?"

"Write a story. Aren't you glad I'm sending you content to make your job easier? You're welcome." I couldn't see her but sensed she was rolling her eyes. "Seriously, can you help? This is a stupid law, and once the public is aware of how ridiculous it is, we can get it changed. Barry's going to help me rewrite the necessary passages and present it to the Board of Commissioners."

"Those rednecks?" Jill was laughing again. "DeeLo, you're hilarious. Sentenced to community service, and now you're going to change the world."

"Not the world. Just one stupid law." I sighed. "Will you help?"

She paused. "I have work to do."

"But it's a story. Your editor likes when you find new stories of interest to the community."

"About an animal ordinance?"

"That's why I sent you the footage of Catherine Foster's arrest for violating that section. You can add drama."

"All right." She dragged her words of consent into three syllables. "Scott gets to craft headlines about our county's first murder mystery, and I'm writing a below-the-fold story about an obscure animal ordinance."

As I hung up from my call with Jill, Jane darkened my doorway. "Have you been going through my stuff?"

I spun in my chair to face her. "I'm supposed to be converting Barry's files to a digital database."

She put a hand on her hip. "Only after I give them to you."

"Relax, Jane." I suppressed the urge to laugh at her self-righteous pose. "Victoria asked me to find the file for Azmina Patel. I didn't have it, so I thought it might be in one of those boxes under your desk. We'd have asked you, but you weren't here."

Jane's nostrils flared.

"Turns out the police took it this morning. Barry said they had a warrant. You must have copies, but I didn't know where else to look."

"A warrant?" Jane's eyes widened. "Whatever for? Victoria applied for all the right permits."

It was my turn to look confused. "What kind of permits? Azmina Patel is dead."

If Jane was sorry or surprised about our client's demise, her face did not reflect either of those emotions. With a huff, she turned on her heels and stomped back to her desk.

A few minutes later, Jane rose from her chair, and her heavy shoes clomped across the tile floor. The lights in Victoria's office flicked on. To get a better view, I strolled out of my cubicle to the break room in search of a bottle of cold water.

I waited until Jane came out of Victoria's office carrying a thick manila folder. She headed back to her desk, stashed the file in the second drawer, and locked it with a key. Then she placed the key in her top drawer, which I knew did not have a lock.

Coast clear, I returned to my cubicle.

Called to a last-minute meeting with a client on the north side of Atlanta, Barry announced he'd be gone for the rest of the day. Before he hurried out, he handed me a stack of briefs to file at the courthouse. "No need to come back to the office after you're done. Just bring the stamped copies in the morning. I know you need to check on Catherine's cats."

* * *

It was a crisp, sunny day, and I was glad for the chance to get outside, breathe fresh fall air. The errand at the courthouse went smoothly, as Barry had assured me it would. The wait was short, and no one questioned me, which was a good thing since I didn't know anything about the papers I was filing. I collected my copies like I knew what I was doing. As I walked back toward my car, I passed several local government offices on the square. The sign for the Pecan County Board of Commissioners caught my eye, and on a whim, I went inside.

A heavy-set, dark-skinned woman with short black curls looked up from her desk. "May I help you?" The badge on her navy jacket read, "Amanda."

I shifted my feet from side to side, not sure where to begin. But the forty-something woman looked approachable, so I decided to test the waters. "Hi, Amanda. What's the process to present an ordinance change to the Board of Commissioners?"

"An ordinance change? What ordinance?" I saw it as a good sign that her expression was serious rather than mocking.

"The county's animal laws." When Amanda nodded as if inviting me to continue, I plunged in. "I'm a volunteer for the Pecan Point Humane Society," (I was) "and we'd like to see the wording changed to protect our people who practice Trap-Neuter-Return." I watched her brow crease as I explained TNR, more accurately TNVR. "TNVR has been proven to be the most effective, most humane method of controlling the free-roaming cat population."

"Interesting. I never knew that." Amanda drummed her fingers on her desk; her nails were painted a bright red. "The best way to get a change like that on the agenda is to work with one of the commissioners. If they sponsor it, the vote at the public meeting is usually just a formality." She picked up a flyer. "Have you ever been to a B.O.C. meeting?"

I shook my head.

She handed me the flyer. "They're meeting tonight at seven, and it's always open to the public. Might be a good way to get a feel for county government in action."

I examined the flyer. "Which commissioner do you recommend I approach? Do any of them like animals?"

"Roy Don sure does love his hunting dogs. Maybe he'd be a good one to talk to." Amanda looked at her watch. "He's in his office now if you want to meet him."

Roy Don Whitehead, the man who broke up Barry's marriage to Victoria. What would Barry say about us working with him on the ordinance? I'd worry about that later. I wasn't prepared with a completed draft of my proposed changes, but I'd read enough to know what the current law said, and what needed to change. I couldn't pass up the opportunity to set the wheels in motion.

Apart from tobacco-stained teeth, Roy Don wasn't an unattractive man; he didn't fit the ogre description I'd painted in my mind. He looked to be in his late forties, a few years older than Barry, with a ruddy, weathered face. His neatly trimmed mustache was heavy on the salt when compared with his thick head of salt-and-pepper hair. As I entered his office, his hazel eyes swept my body from head to toe, lingering on certain feminine parts longer than on others. Checking me out.

I extended my hand and introduced myself, strictly business.

"What can I do you for, little lady?" His voice rasped like a pack-a-day smoker. "Have a seat."

I sat in a straight-backed chair, crossed my legs, and pulled my skirt down over my knees as far as it would stretch. "I'd like to talk about making some changes to the county's animal ordinance. I'm a volunteer—"

He slapped his knee. "I knew I liked you off the bat. Our animal shelter was built back in the nineteen-sixties, and it's way too small for our county. I've been trying for years to pass a bond to build a new one. They need twice as many dog runs as they have now. I'm glad you folks at the Humane Society are in favor of this."

I gulped. "I'm sure the county could use a new animal shelter. But that's not what I wanted to talk about today." I began my explanation of TNVR and noted the sections of the ordinance needing change. I pretended I didn't notice his eyes stray from my face to my chest while I was talking.

He scrunched his features. "Let me get this straight. You got wild cats running around the county. You trap them. And then you want to just let them go?"

"Trap-and-kill doesn't work; it creates a vacuum. More cats will move in and breed as long as there's a food source."

"Well then, we remove the food source and shoot 'em. Problem solved."

A wave of nausea rose from the pit of my stomach. What an ignorant jerk! This was a waste of time. I started to rise.

He let out a throaty cackle and slapped his knee. "Gotcha! If you coulda seen the look on your face." He motioned for me to sit back down.

"Commissioner, I—"

"There are people in this county who feel that way, but not me. I'd never hurt an animal. I was just messing with you." Still chuckling, he wiped his eye, proud of his sick joke. "I'll admit, I never was much of a cat person. My ex-wife had one, and that thing was mean."

I wondered if the cat-owning wife was the one who dumped him after he took up with Victoria Barton. The cat was probably a better judge of character than its mistress.

"Commissioner, the current ordinance doesn't protect people who are trying to control the free-roaming cat population—at no cost to the county, by the way. If I bring you some proposed changes, will you help me get them on the agenda in front of the Board?"

He sobered. "Tell you what, little lady. You bring me a document with your proposed changes, and I'll run them by some of the other commissioners." He glanced at the calendar on his desk. "When do you think you can be ready?"

I straightened. "Next week." I'd have to push myself—and Barry—but I couldn't waste the momentum. As we settled on a date and time to meet, a knock vibrated his doorjamb. A familiar, nauseating perfume wafted into the room, reminding me of a flower-filled funeral parlor.

Roy Don grinned. "Just a minute, Darlin'. I'm finishing up here." He winked at me. "Thank you for coming in, Ms. Myer. We'll talk at you next week."

I rose and extended my hand again, which he held a second longer than necessary. Victoria's face hardened.

As I slipped past her, I couldn't resist wrinkling my nose. "Ooh, who died?"

Chapter Twelve

When Catherine didn't answer the doorbell, I used her key to let myself in. Manny greeted me with a headbutt and followed me through the house. Everything looked the same as I'd left it; Catherine must still be in jail. What was taking so long? It seemed like harassment for the police to keep holding her.

Her other cats showed slightly more interest in me than yesterday, now that I'd come to refill their almost-empty bowls.

Upstairs cats taken care of, I headed down to the basement to check on Octomom and her kittens.

Slowly, carefully, I opened the door to their room, sticking my foot in first to prevent the mother cat from bolting. It didn't work. I'd barely cracked the door when a black-and-white blur of fur shot past me.

Octomom bounced from door to door like a moth against a porch light, searching for an escape. I'd closed the doors to all the other rooms, so there weren't many places in the basement where she could go. I didn't know whether to chase her or wait for her to return to her kittens. Should I take advantage of her absence to replenish her kibble and water and scoop her litter box? And perhaps cuddle a kitten or two. How far could she go before she gave up and came back to food and maternal responsibility?

Before I could get started, the feral mother bounded up the stairs. I gasped. The door from the main house to the basement hadn't closed securely behind me, and now she'd popped it open. How would I ever catch her?

A low growl pierced the air. Claws scraped against hardwood flooring as Octomom reversed her trajectory and scrambled back down the stairs.

At the top of the flight perched Manny, his thick, black hair puffed to make him look twice his normal size, playing "King of the Mountain."

Skittering across the basement floor, Octomom darted toward the room where her kittens napped. I jumped out of the way so she could race past me to her secure space. I closed the door behind her, then remounted the stairs to cut off access to the rest of the house.

Manny had almost shrunk back to normal. I patted his head. "Good boy, Manny. You kept Octomom out of your territory." A purr replaced the growl. I gave him another pat before closing the door and heading back downstairs to service Octomom's quarters. This time, I was extra careful not to let her escape.

Before leaving Catherine's, I phoned the memory care facility to check on my mother. "She's been sad," confided the nurse. "She keeps asking about the Cat Lady. Your mom loved that therapy cat."

"What do you tell her?" Manny brushed against my legs.

The woman lowered her voice, "I understand Azmina Patel was murdered. We've tried to explain to the residents—without alarming them with too much detail."

"Should I come by?"

"Maybe tomorrow. Your mom's in a group session now."

After I hung up, I stroked Manny's head. "Manny, what do you think about visiting some old friends tomorrow?" How hard could it be to play custodian of a therapy cat? Maybe I could cheer up my mother.

The melodic chime of Catherine's doorbell startled me. I pushed aside the drapes and peered out the front window. A pimply-faced, twentyish courier stood on the step, holding a legal-size brown envelope. He spotted me and motioned toward the door. I opened it.

"Catherine Foster?" He thrust the envelope into my hands before I could speak. "Certified letter."

"I'm not—"

He held up his hand. "Spare me. I'm just the messenger."

"But—"

"Sign here." He held out the clipboard and handed me a pen.

I scribbled my own name. Without looking at my signature, he hurried down the walkway to his car.

Manny meowed as I closed the door, envelope in hand. I stroked the cat's head again. "What do you think, Manny? Should I open it?" *Open Catherine's mail! Am I crazy?* But Barry was Catherine's lawyer. If this were a legal matter, she'd take it to him. If it were something important, he'd need to see it right away. As Barry's employee, I had a duty to determine if it required his attention.

I walked into the kitchen where I put the rest of Catherine's mail on the table. Manny followed. I fingered the envelope. It wasn't sealed. Maybe if I undid the clasp, peeked, then put it back, I could check if it was relevant to what she was working on with Barry.

Then I noticed the sender—Nick Norton, Pecan Creek Nature Foundation—which piqued my curiosity. I looked at Manny. "Are you going to tell on me?"

Manny rubbed against me and purred.

Gently, I bent the clasp so I could lift the flap and slide out the paper. The letter was one page, short and to the point. "Dear Ms. Foster, it has come to my attention that you are planning to set up shelters for feral cats again this winter in the Pecan Creek Nature Reserve. This activity will not be permitted. You are hereby prohibited from feeding, trapping, or otherwise encouraging this invasive species to thrive on public property per Pecan County ordinance. Failure to heed this friendly reminder will result in trespassing charges being filed against you."

Friendly reminder? The tone was about as friendly as the misnamed Officer Friendly. The letter was signed by Nick Norton, purported friend of Azmina Patel. Had Azmina known how Nick felt about the community cats she loved?

The undeveloped lot beside the strip mall Azmina owned abutted the Pecan Creek Nature Reserve. The cats she fed did not respect arbitrary boundaries. Had Nick sent a letter like this to Azmina? Would she have been willing to sell her land to Nick under the circumstances? Was that why she'd texted, "The deal is off"?

Had my mother and I been alone in the woods with a killer?

I looked at my watch. Jane always left promptly at five. Barry had said he might have dinner with his client to wait out the Atlanta traffic, so the workplace should be empty. Victoria didn't have a key anymore.

I drove back to the office and parked around the side of the building.

Sure enough, the place was dark, so I let myself in and locked the door behind me. By the flashlight app on my cell phone, I made my way to Jane's desk.

The key I'd seen her stash was still there. I used it to open the drawer where she'd locked the folder she'd taken from Victoria's office earlier. The file's label read, "Azmina Patel." I'd guessed correctly.

I opened the folder and started to read. "An Offer to Purchase..."

Before I could finish reading, a key turned in the front door, and the overhead light flicked on. My pulse quickened, and my stomach vaulted to my throat.

"DeeLo," said Barry. "What are you doing here in the dark?"

"Barry! I thought you were having dinner with a client." Caught red-handed, I clutched the folder to my chest.

"We finished our business early, so I tried to beat the traffic." He headed toward me. "Why are you still here? Did you make it to the courthouse?"

Face to face now, I met his gaze. I had nothing to fear, nothing to hide, not really. "After Victoria left, I told Jane about the police taking Azmina Patel's file, and then I saw her get this folder out of Victoria's office."

Squinting, he touched his glasses.

"You know how Jane doesn't like me to touch her stuff, so I waited until she left to see if this file had anything to do with Azmina. I was afraid it might be something the police should see, and I didn't want you to get in trouble for withholding evidence." I thought I sounded convincing.

"And?"

"I'd just opened it when you came in."

"It's about Azmina Patel?"

I nodded.

"You're probably right. I'll make sure the police get it." He held out his hand, and I had no choice but to relinquish the folder. "I don't know what else they're looking for, but we have to cooperate."

A page fell to the floor, and we both dived for it. He picked up the paper before I could see what was written on it.

He put Azmina's file in his briefcase; its contents remained a mystery to me. "You said Victoria was helping Azmina sell some land," I ventured. "Did she have an offer yet?"

Barry fingered the folder. "There was interest, but the tenants of the shopping center were concerned about what might happen to the surrounding land. The owners of that new movie studio—Oakwood, I think is the name—and Nick Norton, the guy who manages the nature reserve, had both made offers."

I leaned on Jane's desk. "What will happen to the land now that Azmina is dead?"

"We'll have to sort out her estate once the police return the files." He picked up his briefcase. "Want to get some dinner?"

"I can't. I'm headed to the Board of Commissioners' meeting."

"You are?" His briefcase banged against Jane's chair as he turned around. "Why?"

"I want to get a feel for the playing field before I present my proposed revisions of the county's animal ordinance. Come with me. Help me strategize."

"I'm not up for it tonight." He clenched his teeth. "But you go. It'll do you good to see what you're up against. It won't be as easy as you think. You might change your mind."

"I don't think so." As we kissed goodbye, I didn't mention I'd already had a private meeting with Roy Don Whitehead, his least favorite person.

* * *

The crowd at the public meeting room was larger than I'd expected. A Boy Scout troop, all the clean-cut youngsters in tan uniforms, occupied the front three rows on the left side of the aisle. Proud parents hovered in the rows behind them. Were they working on a merit badge in civics? Milling among the Boy Scouts and their leader was a sandy-haired man in safari attire. Nick Norton. Possible murderer. Confirmed cat hater.

Emboldened by the presence of the Boy Scouts, I strolled up to Nick. His eyes flickered with vague recognition as if he were trying to place where we'd met.

I extended my hand. "Delores Myer. Thanks again for helping my mother yesterday when she was lost in the woods."

He smiled and shook my hand. "Of course. How is your mother? I trust you returned her to the facility safely?"

"She's fine." People were taking their seats, and a sergeant-at-arms walked toward the lectern. "Did you get your phone back?"

He gave me a quizzical look and reached into his pocket, but before he could respond, the sergeant-at-arms called the meeting to order. "Ladies and gentlemen, please join me in the Pledge of Allegiance."

Everyone not already standing rose and faced the large American flag in the corner of the room. Hands over our hearts like schoolchildren, we citizens of Pecan County recited the Pledge of Allegiance, a few adults stumbling over the phrase "under God," as if unsure whether it was still politically correct.

When we finished the pledge, the crowd was invited to sit. I tried to squeeze into the row with Nick and the Boy Scouts. But it was like a game of musical chairs, and I was the odd player out. Shoulder to shoulder, without a space among them, no chivalrous Boy Scout yielded his seat, forcing me to relocate across the room.

I spied my friend Jill Hernandez bent over her laptop, her raven-black hair cascading down her back. I'd forgotten she'd told me she covered the Board of Commissioners meetings for the newspaper.

"DeeLo," she exclaimed as I slid into the chair behind her. "What are you doing here?"

"Research," I replied, watching the five commissioners—all middle-aged white men—take their seats on the dais.

"Did you get an agenda?" Jill whispered. When I shook my head, she handed me a piece of paper with an outline of meeting topics. "They have them at the entrance."

"Thanks." I studied the page. Call to order. Pledge of Allegiance, check. "Invocation?"

Jill put her finger to her lips, and I looked up as Roy Don strutted to the lectern. He bowed his head reverently. "Let us pray."

Head bowed I finished reading the agenda.

The next item was a proclamation recognizing Boy Scout Troop 257 for their work cleaning up the Pecan Creek Nature Reserve last weekend. Nick Norton presented each boy with a certificate and hung a medal around the scout leader's neck.

Everyone clapped. After a few photos, the boys and their families paraded down the aisle and out the front door, almost emptying the room. Nick followed. So much for my plan to inquire about the text messages between him and Azmina.

I turned to Jill. "Tell me about these Commissioners. Which ones are the most reasonable to work with? I've already met Roy Don."

Jill chuckled. "Ask me after the meeting. I want to hear your impressions."

They were talking about a restaurant's request for a liquor license. Application granted.

Next was a request from the president of a homeowners' association that the speed limit be lowered in his subdivision. Grilling him was a silver-haired commissioner with a square jaw and linebacker shoulders who looked like his glory days had been in high school when he was captain of the football team, dating the homecoming queen. Vince Connors, according to the wooden placard on the table in front of him, was unable to trip up the prepared HOA president, who provided answers to every question fired at him. Plea granted.

The meeting droned on. Another liquor license. A business owner's request for a zoning variance. A request from the fire department to purchase more personal protective equipment.

My ears perked up when Roy Don introduced a land-use variance proposed by Oakwood Studios for a pending purchase.

"We're going to have to table that because of the death of the current landowner," said the fat, bald commissioner in the center of the panel—Eric Graham, Chairman—whose double chin wobbled when he spoke. He looked like the model the Hasbro toy company had used to make Mr. Potato Head.

I felt a chill. They were talking about Azmina Patel.

"She already signed the papers," said Roy Don.

"Oakwood Studios can re-submit the request at a later date," said Chairman Graham. "We'll wait until we know what's going to happen to that land."

With a grunt, Roy Don dropped the matter.

When they moved to "old business," Roy Don said, "Last month, we didn't have a quorum when this issue came up for a vote. I'm going to let the little lady tell you all about it. Can we bring up Sandra Larson, the new director of the Pecan Point Animal Shelter?"

"I hear she's very progressive," Jill whispered to me. "She moved down from Wisconsin last summer to fill the vacancy after old Fred Sullivan died. You should talk to her about TNVR."

Sandra Larson was a large, freckled woman with spiked red hair and a booming voice. I wondered how she felt about Roy Don referring to her as "little lady." She talked about how animal overpopulation was exacerbated by people who adopted intact animals from the shelter and then, instead of having them spayed or neutered as per their adoption contract, let them run loose. Staff spent many hours following up on spay/neuter commitments, often learning the animal had run off before being fixed. "I propose that we have all cats and dogs spayed or neutered before they leave the shelter."

The bug-eyed commissioner—Randall Sparks, according to his nameplate—held up his hand. His haircut resembled one of those bowl-over-your-head home jobs. "Excuse me, ma'am, why are we forcing people to get their pets fixed? Seems we're interfering with individual liberties here, and that's a dangerous path to go down."

Sandra cleared her throat. "Sir, we already require people to spay or neuter any pet adopted from our shelter. I'm asking to remove that burden from the adopter and do it for them since we don't have 100% compliance. It will save my staff time so they can focus on investigating animal cruelty cases and reuniting lost pets with their owners. And it will ensure the animals don't breed and leave more homeless puppies and kittens to be brought into our shelter."

"I understand pet overpopulation is a problem, and I'm all for spay and neuter," said the nerdy commissioner with thick horn-rimmed glasses and a sallow complexion—Phillip Gates, his placard read. He looked like he'd rather be playing video games in his mother's basement than conducting county business. "But why should the county pay for it? You should have come to us last year when we were preparing the annual budget."

Randall shook his head, his straight bangs fanning his eyebrows. "I still don't get why we're making people deliberately maim their pets. Deny them the ability to procreate, one of the most sacred, God-given rights. What if we fixed all the pets in the county? Pretty soon, there'd be none left to adopt."

What? Emitting a guffaw of mirth mixed with horror, I almost tumbled from my chair. Jill covered her mouth and focused on her laptop. "That's going in the paper, right?" I murmured.

A forest of eyes spotlighted my outburst. I looked around at the other concerned citizens in the audience, but none seemed amused. Was I the only one who found Randall's statement ridiculous? I quickly straightened in my chair and adjusted my expression to a more somber mien.

"I'm ready to take a vote on the motion before us." Chairman Graham leaned back in his chair and stroked his Buddha belly like a pregnant woman in her eighth month. "Any other questions?" When no one spoke, he continued, "All in favor?"

Roy Don and Vince said, "Aye."

"Opposed?"

Eric, Randall, and Phillip voted nay.

"Three votes to two. Motion is denied."

"Sorry, little lady," Roy Don called as Sandra stalked out.

I looked at Jill in alarm.

"See what you're up against?" she said.

Chapter Thirteen

D reams of facing the Board of Commissioners—transformed from a group of backwoods lawmakers into a panel of judges—haunted my sleep. I was derided and shot down for daring to suggest the county sanction TNVR; Randall Sparks's bug eyes stared at me as he cried, "How dare you ask people to neuter their pets?"

And then Officer Friendly appeared with handcuffs.

I'd set the alarm but awakened before it went off. My plan was to stop by the animal shelter on my way to the office. Sandra Larson had been the most rational voice at the meeting last night, and I hoped to enlist her as an ally in my battle to update the Pecan County animal ordinance. *Battle*. I hadn't thought of it that way before. I was Georgia's Joan of Arc.

The animal shelter wasn't much bigger than the LifeSaver clinic, and it probably hadn't been renovated since the twentieth century. I could see why Roy Don thought Pecan County needed a new one.

The reception counter was unattended, so I made my way to the director's office. Sandra sat behind her wide, metal desk, nursing a cup of coffee, reading a file in a manila folder. The dark, military-style uniform of an animal control officer made her look more masculine than last night, when she'd been wearing a hot pink pantsuit. Her freshly gelled vermillion hair stood at attention. No way was that shade her natural color; the lines over her brow made her look old enough to have some gray mixed in, and there wasn't any.

Hovering in her doorway, I cleared my throat to get her attention. "Ms. Larson?"

She looked up, hand still on her coffee mug.

"I'm Delores Myer, a volunteer for the Pecan Point Humane Society, and I'd like to talk with you about our county's animal ordinance. I was hoping we could work together to update it to allow—"

She set down her mug. It had a big red heart on it but I couldn't read the name of the city or object for which the heart was proclaiming love. "You're with the Pecan Point Humane Society? And you want to work with Animal Control?"

I shifted my stance. There was a chair across from her desk, but she had not invited me to sit. "We have common goals. We all care about animal welfare and controlling pet overpopulation—"

"Who are you? Does Deb Holt know you're here representing them? Proposing to work with 'animal killers'?"

Deb Holt was the president of the Pecan Point Humane Society. I'd only met her once, when she'd introduced herself to the new volunteers at my orientation meeting. She'd paid little attention to me, viewing me as a short-timer, certainly not someone she would authorize to represent the organization.

The look on my face must have betrayed my lack of authority.

Sandra shook her head. "I didn't think so." The phone on her desk rang. She lifted the receiver and gestured with it toward the door. "You can show yourself out."

Defeated, I turned toward the exit. Catherine hadn't mentioned animosity between the Humane Society and Animal Control. But then, Catherine was a rogue volunteer who played by her own rules. Something we had in common.

A uniformed animal control officer now stood behind the previously unattended reception counter in the lobby. "Have you been helped, Ma'am?" he asked. I glanced over my shoulder at the director's office, where Sandra had just hung up the phone. I nodded to the officer, pivoted, and headed back for a rematch.

Jaw clenched in irritation Sandra looked up from her desk. "Did you forget something?"

I sat down in the chair facing her. "I recently moved here from California, and I'm a brand-new volunteer. I don't have the authority to represent the Pecan Point Humane Society, and I'm not familiar with any drama going on between your two groups." I paused and met her icy gaze. "I was at the Board of Commissioners meeting last night."

Sandra protruded her bottom lip and blew out a puff of air. "Condescending jackals."

"'Little lady,'" I mimicked.

She stifled a grin. "I didn't realize spay and neuter would be a controversial topic in the twenty-first century. When I met with Roy Don and Vince, they thought the policy change was a no-brainer."

"You only lost by one vote. Any thoughts about which commissioner would be most likely to change his mind?"

Sandra sighed. "I thought the chairman would have been more reasonable. But he listens to that idiot, Randall Sparks. I hear they're hunting buddies."

"That budget guy, Phillip Gates, might be persuaded to come around." I stroked my chin. "We'd have to approach the issue from a financial standpoint. Introduce the proposal again during the annual budget discussion, as he suggested. Let him know how much money the county can save with this program. Which is the same argument we can use for changing the animal ordinance to allow—"

"We?" Sandra raised a copper-colored eyebrow.

"Don't you want public support?" I pasted on my sweetest smile.

Sandra ran her tongue along her large teeth. "You mentioned the animal ordinance. What about it should change?"

I leaned over her desk and opened my folder so she could see my printed copy with the notes I'd made. "The way it's written, a person could be arrested for practicing Trap-Neuter-Vaccinate-Return. Look at the definition of 'owner.'"

Without even a glance at my paper, she gave a dismissive wave. "That's ridiculous. I'd never enforce that law. The last director didn't. It's like carrying wire cutters in Texas. The law is still on the books from cattle-rustling days, but no one would ever be arrested for it."

"But—"

She looked at me, her blue eyes earnest. "I don't have a problem with TNR. I was a big supporter in Wisconsin. It's the best way to keep feral cats from entering the shelter, where they rarely make it out alive." She shook her head. "I don't like to kill animals. Most animal control officers hate it. Worst part of our job! But feral cats aren't adoptable, and most go nuts confined in a cage. Euthanasia is the kindest thing for them. Keeping them out of the shelter in the first place is better. And it leaves us more space for the adoptable animals. So yes, go forth and practice TNR. You have my blessing."

"Maybe you wouldn't enforce this law, but a new director could. And local police officers do now." I sat back in my chair. "That's why we need to change the wording of the ordinance."

Her head jerked up. "You're kidding me. Some redneck police officer has read this outdated ordinance and takes it literally?"

I nodded. "Catherine Foster was arrested the other night when she released a community cat that had sprung one of her traps."

"Cat Foster?" Sandra huffed. "That woman's a piece of work. I get a lot of complaints about her. I usually end up taking her side, but she makes it hard because she's so disagreeable." She narrowed her gaze. "Cat got arrested? They must have given her a slap on the wrist and let her go. I've heard one of those patrol officers has it in for her."

"No, he took her to jail, and they're still holding her. I was there. We were trapping cats behind Black Cat Books."

At the mention of Black Cat Books, Sandra flinched. "It's so awful about Azmina Patel."

"Catherine and I found her body."

Sandra clasped a hand to her cheek. "Did you see what happened? There hasn't been much information in the news."

"No, we got out quickly, and then the cop showed up." I closed my eyes but could not erase the gruesome memory of finding Azmina's body on the bookstore floor.

"I hope they question José Garcia from the Mexican restaurant next door.

He and Azmina were always at each other's throats. I lost count of how many times he called me to pick up those cats Azmina was feeding, or to complain when Catherine helped her get them fixed." Sandra tapped her pencil on her desk. "Last week, I wrote José a citation for animal cruelty after Azmina caught him putting out poisoned meat. Luckily, we removed it before any cats got sick, but José was hotter than a chili pepper. I heard him threaten to kill Azmina. And now she's dead."

My jaw dropped. "He threatened to kill her? Do the police know?"

Sandra shrugged.

"You should talk to them." I remembered watching the light go out at the Mexican restaurant and hearing a car leave just after we found Azmina's body. And the nervous way José had acted the next day at the restaurant. Maybe he was the killer. So focused on suspecting Nick, I'd forgotten about José. "Did you ever have dealings with Nick Norton?"

"Guy who runs the nature reserve?" Sandra rolled her eyes. "He's another one who complains about Catherine Foster and the feral cats. He thinks they're killing too many birds. He's asked me to remove all the cats from the reserve and relocate them—like that's going to solve his problem."

"Do you think he could have killed Azmina?"

She knitted her eyebrows. "Well, no, they were dating."

"Dating?" When I'd met Nick in the reserve with my mother, I'd concluded he and Azmina were friends. But dating? Catherine suggested he might be feigning interest in Azmina to get hold of her land.

"I thought so, but maybe not." Sandra scrunched her face. "Why are you so interested? Are you Agatha Christie? You don't think the cops can solve this murder mystery?"

"What about you? You just told me your theory about José, but you haven't told the cops what you know."

"Touché." She took a sip of her coffee, which I figured was cold by now. New York. I "heart" New York, the mug said. "I don't believe Nick did it. No motive."

Except maybe a land deal. "The police suspect Catherine. That's why they haven't released her yet."

"Catherine!" Sandra sputtered, and drops of coffee rained on her folder. She blotted it with her sleeve. "No way. Azmina and Catherine were friends. Well, as close as Catherine could get to being a friend." She shook her head. "I don't buy it."

The phone on her desk rang again. Sandra glanced at the caller ID. "Look, I have to take this, and I'll be a while." She handed me one of her business cards. "Call me later, and we'll talk more about the ordinance."

* * *

I arrived at work to find Victoria's red S-Class Mercedes convertible straddling the two parking spaces closest to our building. If I were a vindictive person, I'd have keyed it.

Loud voices reverberated from behind Barry's closed office door.

Jane glared at me as I walked past her desk. "You stole my file."

"Stole?" I stopped and turned to face her.

"You saw me get it from Victoria's office, and you waited for me to leave, and then you took it." She gritted her teeth. "You had no right!"

"Relax, Jane. What do you mean I stole your file? All the files are the property of Barton and Barton. Which one are you talking about?"

Her eyes blazed. "Don't play stupid with me, Miss Priss. You know what I'm talking about. The one you stole from my desk drawer."

I pretended to concentrate. "Oh, the file for Azmina Patel? Our deceased client?"

"You know that's the one I'm talking about."

"Barry has it." I motioned toward his office. "Ask him."

Before I could reach my cubicle, Barry's office door banged open. In a cloud of pungent floral perfume, Victoria stormed out, a manila folder clutched against her chest. Moisture glistened on her thick mascara.

Barry stood in the doorway and pounded his fist against the frame. "You and your boyfriend are going to the devil!" His voice cracked on his last word.

Jane and I watched Victoria stomp across the room to the exit.

In a moment, she revved the engine of the Mercedes and peeled out of the parking lot.

I turned toward Barry, who was still clenching his fist and glaring after his ex-wife. His neck was fiery red, and his face looked drawn and beaten. I wanted to give him a hug, run my fingers through his hair, and tell him everything would be okay. As I took a step in his direction, his eyes met mine. With a shake of his head that signaled, "Leave me alone now," he ducked back into his office and closed the door behind him.

Jane gave me a smug look. "He's not over Victoria, you know."

Knowing she was right, but not about to admit it, I spun on my heels and headed into my cubicle so she wouldn't see my face.

Chapter Fourteen

I t was past one, and Barry's door was still closed. He had not even come out to use the restroom or get himself a cup of coffee.

I knocked and took his mumbled response as an invitation to enter. "Going to grab a bite and run some errands. Can I bring you back lunch?"

He pushed his glasses up the bridge of his nose. "No thanks." His usually neat desk was covered in papers and file folders.

"Any news about Catherine?" I hovered at the entrance, hesitant to intrude into his space. "They should let her post bail."

"She hasn't been arraigned yet. The prosecutor is out with the flu." He stared at one of the papers in front of him.

"Can they do that? Deny her due process? Habeas corpus?" I tried out the new vocabulary I was learning in my paralegal lessons.

He contemplated the paper in his hand instead of my face. "It's a small town, and Catherine's not well-liked. She hasn't been cooperative."

I glanced at my watch. "She's been in jail almost forty hours. This is America."

He sighed. "I called my friend George—you know, the criminal attorney in Atlanta? He tried to talk to Catherine, but she sent him away."

"What?" I pushed against the doorframe. "I'm going to stop at the jail and visit her. Do you have any objections?"

I interpreted his nonreaction as acquiescence and slipped out, closing the door behind me.

* * *

Catherine occupied the same dreary cell where I'd been taken the night of my arrest. Barry had quickly facilitated my release, so I hadn't had to sleep on that metal cot fastened to the plaster wall.

She paced the concrete floor like a tiger in a cramped zoo enclosure, dressed in the same clothes she'd worn the night we'd been trapping. They hadn't even issued her a county jail jumpsuit. Foundation caked in the creases of her crow's feet and frown lines; her smudged mascara had created raccoon eyes. I hadn't realized Catherine wore make-up. And her deodorant had worn off a long time ago.

She glowered at me. "What do you want, D.D.?"

"Is that the way you greet the person who's been taking care of your cats while you're a guest of the county?"

Her expression softened. "Thanks."

"You're welcome, I guess." Trying to cheer her up, I announced, "I'm working on getting that stupid animal ordinance changed. Barry's going to help. And I think—"

"Is that how long I'll have to wait to get out of here?" She rolled her eyes at the grease-gray paint peeling from the concrete ceiling.

I should have known Catherine wouldn't be impressed with my efforts on her behalf. "What have they told you?"

"Nothing."

With both hands, I gripped the iron bars of her cell. "Barry said they want to question you about Azmina's murder, and you won't cooperate."

She shrugged.

"He sent you a defense attorney. Why won't you work with him?"

"The guy acted like a jerk. He obviously thought I was guilty."

"Catherine, he could have gotten you out of here." I frowned. "We're trying to help you. Why won't you cooperate? What do you have to hide?"

She remained silent.

"They have to let you go if they can't charge you with a crime. Do they think you committed murder?"

Catherine tucked her head between her shoulders like a pound pit bull who'd given up on freedom.

"You and I were together when we found her. Why do they think you did it?"

She sighed. "Azmina and I argued earlier that day. José Garcia and a couple of the bookstore customers overheard us."

Sandra suspected José. Interesting that he'd try to point the finger at Catherine. "An argument hardly constitutes a motive for murder. What did you argue about?"

"Nick."

I raised my eyebrows. *My* favorite suspect. "Go on."

She blew out a puff of air. "Azmina couldn't see it. He courted her so she'd sell him that land which would allow him to expand the nature reserve and make a big name for himself. He wanted to get rid of the cats! Azmina refused to believe it."

I should tell Catherine about the cease-and-desist letter Nick had couriered to her yesterday afternoon—but how to admit I'd opened her mail? I recalled the text exchange with Azmina on Nick's phone. Could it be about the cats? "Do you think you got through to her?"

"I hope so." Catherine pushed an oily strand of hair off her forehead. "Azmina wanted to sell the land. She needed cash because she wasn't earning enough on the rents from the shopping center and sales from her bookstore. The settlement from her husband's life insurance had run into some delays. Nick's offer wasn't as good as the one from the movie studio, but she liked the idea of the land remaining undeveloped, which wouldn't happen if the movie people bought it."

"Were there other offers?"

"Not that I'm aware of."

"Did you know you're a beneficiary in Azmina's will?"

Catherine's raccoon eyes widened, and I could make out the blue of her irises in the dim light of the cell. "For real? She never told me."

I nodded.

"So, he was right." She licked her chapped lips.

"Who?"

She waved her hand. "That jerk, Stan *Fiendly*. The cop who arrested me.

He said Azmina was leaving me money, and I didn't deserve it."

"How did he know?" I also wondered why Officer Un-Friendly hated Catherine so much. I sensed it went beyond her basic unlikability.

"He said she was holding a copy of her will when he went into the bookstore and 'discovered' her body."

I'd recognized the Barton, Barton & Barton logo, but the document I'd seen in Azmina's hand had only been one page, not multiple pages like most of our Last Will and Testament packages. Officer Friendly must have removed the paper before the crime scene investigators photographed the body. But why? Did Detective Ross know? Was the patrol officer confident no one would call him out for tampering with evidence and then gloating to Catherine about it?

"The will makes me a suspect, doesn't it?"

I forced a smile. "Not necessarily."

Catherine changed the subject. "Did you get Octomom's kittens?"

I held up eight fingers.

She pressed her hand against her forehead.

"Living in your basement. Octomom's taking care of them."

"She's always been a good mother. But we need to shut down the kitten factory. Don't let her escape this time."

I didn't tell Catherine about Octomom bolting from the room the first time I went over to feed her. Manny had saved me. "What's going to happen to Manny?" With a smile, I pictured him following me around, head-butting my legs and begging to be picked up. "Will he be adopted through the Pecan Point Humane Society?"

"Probably," she replied. "Depends on what Azmina's sister wants to do. She's the only relative. Kyra lives in an apartment in New York City, so she might not take him."

I tried to sound casual. "Did you know Azmina had been bringing Manny to the memory care home as a therapy cat?"

Catherine raised her eyebrows.

"My mother stays there, and she's grown attached to Manny and Azmina."

I thought I detected a hint of sympathy streak across Catherine's face.

But not for my mother and the other seniors suffering from dementia; her emotion must be for Manny, who'd lost his person and been uprooted from his home.

"Is it okay if I take Manny to the memory care center to visit my mother and the other residents? Let him continue his role of therapy cat?"

She gave me a quizzical look. "You know how to work with a therapy cat?"

Before I could answer, a jailer walked in and signaled that my visit was over. I nodded my farewell to Catherine as he escorted me out of the cell block.

* * *

I marched next door to the police station to find Detective Paul Ross. Maybe he could tell me why they wouldn't release Catherine.

Finding him was easier than I'd expected; we almost collided in the lobby. He was taller and more muscular than I remembered, and the green flecks in his brown-and-gray tweed jacket highlighted the color of his eyes.

"Detective Ross," I addressed him.

Recognition flickered. "Ms. Myer. What brings you here?"

"Can I talk to you about Catherine Foster?"

He motioned toward the hall leading to his office, then opened the door and allowed me to pass through.

"Why is she still in jail?" I asked, taking a seat.

Rounding the desk, he replied, "The prosecutor and the judge have both been out with the flu. There's no one to bring formal charges, no one to set bail."

"Seriously? No one can fill in for them?" I squinted in disbelief. "You can't keep holding her without charges. Technically, she didn't break the law. The cat she released was already living on the property. She went into the trap by mistake, and Catherine let her out."

He frowned. "What are you talking about?"

"The county animal ordinance. The reason Catherine was arrested. Didn't you read the report?"

"Catherine Foster is being held as a person of interest in the murder of Azmina Patel."

"Why? She didn't do it."

His mouth twitched. "What makes you so sure?"

"Catherine and I found the body, remember?" Did he not recall taking my statement?

"Finding the body doesn't exonerate someone. On the contrary..."

Here I was, talking to the police again without a lawyer present. Barry would not be happy. Was the detective going to arrest me, too? "I was with her all evening."

He picked up a pencil and tapped it on the desk. "We're not sure of the time of death. Azmina Patel could have been killed earlier."

"What about those text messages?" The exchange between Nick and Azmina should clear Catherine. At the time the texts were sent, she and I were together at her house loading traps.

"What text messages?"

"On Nick Norton's phone." I leaned forward. "Didn't you read them?"

"Oh. Stan Friendly talked to Mr. Norton again, and he had an explanation. He was happy to get his phone back, so thank you for turning it in."

"But the timestamps! Didn't you look at the timestamps on the messages?" I gripped the edge of his desk. "Azmina was still alive at eight-thirty on Sunday evening when she sent those texts. Catherine and I were together then, and the rest of the evening, until we found the body." I shook my head vigorously. "And if Catherine Foster had killed Azmina, she wouldn't have let Manny outside."

I couldn't tell if the look on the detective's face was mocking or reflective.

"Officer Friendly is not your most reliable witness," I continued. "You said the crime scene investigators didn't find a document in Azmina's hand, and I told you I saw one. Ask Officer Friendly what happened to it."

"Okay, Jessica Fletcher. Believe me, the police have this case under control."

Jessica Fletcher. Agatha Christie. Was I being a busybody? No! I had a stake in this case. I bit my lip to keep myself from unleashing a snarky retort.

His tone changed. "But, Ms. Myer, there is something you can help me with."

I straightened in my chair.

"We live on three acres backed up to woods. My wife has been..."

Wife? Even though he didn't wear a wedding band, I shouldn't have been surprised.

"...feeding some stray cats. It was just one until she had kittens under our porch last spring." His eyes met mine, and I tried to keep my expression neutral. "I remember what you were telling me about Trap, Neuter, whatever. We don't mind feeding those cats. Lisa has grown fond of them. But we don't want them to multiply into... what was it you said... a colony?"

"And that will happen if you don't get them all fixed. As soon as possible." I was back in comfortable territory. "We use a low-cost clinic called The LifeSaver—"

He shook his head. "Lisa can't pick them up."

"She might have to use a humane trap."

"Can you help?"

I raised a hand to my hip. "Catherine Foster is the expert. If you release her, I'm sure she'll be glad to help." Well, maybe not glad.

"I told you we can't release Catherine Foster yet."

"She has rights. Habeas corpus."

"We can hold her for up to forty-eight hours without charges."

I pointed to my watch. "You're coming up on it."

He gave me a sharp look. "Even if Catherine Foster were released, Lisa doesn't want to work with her."

I almost asked why not, but I could guess the answer.

"Will you call her?" Rummaging in his desk drawer, he produced a business card and handed it to me without waiting for my reply. "She works at Connors Insurance, which is located next to Black Cat Books."

I had no choice but to accept the card: Lisa Ross, insurance agent.

"Thanks, Ms. Myer." He rose, signaling our meeting had ended. "I'll make sure the hours you spend helping her will count toward your community service."

Chapter Fifteen

When I returned to the office, my in-basket was still empty. I picked up the desk phone and punched in Lisa Ross's number before I had time to dread the call.

Although her voice reminded me of Minnie Mouse, she sounded approachable as I recounted my conversation with her husband and suggested Trap-Neuter-Vaccinate-Return as a solution to her cat problem. "If you don't mind them living on your property, it's the kindest thing you can do. Getting them fixed and vaccinated will make them healthier, and you won't have to deal with more kittens to feed."

"Sounds great," she squeaked. "Thanks so much for your help."

"Don't thank me yet; I'm new at this." I switched the receiver to my other ear. "I don't own any traps, but maybe I can borrow some from Catherine Foster."

"Oh, Paul told me you didn't have any equipment, so I got one from Animal Control," Lisa said. "When can you come by? I'm usually home by six." She rattled off the address.

I gulped. Lisa didn't waste time. Had Detective Ross told her about my community service sentence, too? "Will tomorrow night work?"

"Perfect. See you then."

"Wait, Lisa."

"Yes?"

"Don't feed the cats tonight. We want them to be hungry when we bait the traps, so they'll go in."

There was a long pause, and I thought she'd hung up. "Don't feed them?

Isn't that cruel?"

"They'll survive." That's what Catherine said.

"Fine." Her tone had lost some of its perky friendliness.

"It will be an unpleasant, traumatic day or two for the cats," I admitted. "But for the rest of their lives, they'll be better off."

As I hung up the phone, I glimpsed Jane slinking toward her desk. While I was talking, she'd dropped a thick manila folder into my in-basket to be archived. I rolled my chair across the carpet to retrieve it—the Catherine Foster file.

I spent the afternoon sifting through papers representing the pieces of Catherine's life, scanning documents, and organizing them into an electronic file. It was like watching a suspense movie after someone had blurted out the ending. Barry had already told me about the car accident that killed her family, the wrongful death settlement from the trucking company, and the feline foundation Catherine had created with the proceeds, so there were no surprises.

The file contained financial statements from half a dozen investments. Barry had put them into a trust with Catherine as trustee and her newly formed foundation as the beneficiary. The trust documents were long and tedious.

A page from the transcript of the trial over the wrongful death of her family slipped to the floor while I fed the rest of the document into the scanner. I bent to pick it up, and the name of one of the defense witnesses caught my eye: Stan Friendly.

Officer Stan Friendly! I skimmed the transcript. His testimony wasn't as a police officer or witness at the scene of the accident; he had vouched for the good character of the drunk truck driver who'd killed Catherine's husband and daughter.

I leaned back in my chair to catch my breath and digest the new information.

* * *

After researching the accident on Google, I phoned my reporter friend Jill Hernandez. Some of the news stories about the trial and Stan Friendly's role had been archived by the paper where she worked, and I needed her to access them.

"What's up, DeeLo?" She'd recognized my caller ID.

"Does the name Catherine Foster ring a bell?"

"Your friend who got arrested the other night?"

Friend? "Remember a terrible accident on County Line Road about four years ago? A truck ran the stop sign and hit a family driving a sedan. Killed the man and his daughter."

Jill gasped. "That Catherine Foster? The one whose husband and child got killed?"

I nodded, though Jill couldn't see me. "I gather it was a big story. Wasn't the truck driver drunk? And on duty?"

A keyboard clicked. "It was our headline for months. Every day, new information surfaced," Jill said. "Wrongful death suit. Some bigwig ambulance chaser from Atlanta took the case. Catherine Foster got a huge settlement from the trucking company. Not that she didn't deserve it, of course. But the award exceeded their liability insurance, and it put them out of business." She paused, reading. "Catherine's attorney was relentless."

"Can you email me some of those articles?" I looked down at Catherine's file. "I'm especially interested in the trial."

"Sending." More clicking. "The trial went on for months. The truck driver tried to deny being drunk, insisted the accident wasn't his fault. Catherine's lawyer nailed him, bringing in witnesses to dispute those claims. The driver broke down and cried on the stand when he realized he'd been caught in a lie. Even the heartfelt testimony from his cop brother-in-law couldn't help him."

Cop brother-in-law? "Do any of the articles include the name of that witness?" I crossed my fingers, hoping I'd struck gold. My computer dinged to announce incoming mail.

"Stan Friendly," Jill read. "He wasn't at the scene, but the defense brought him in as a character witness. Didn't do much good since the defendant demonstrated his poor character by lying on the stand."

"Why was Stan Friendly so anxious to protect his loser brother-in-law?" The squirrelly Officer Friendly didn't strike me as someone who would stick his neck out for anyone.

"Oh." Jill stopped typing. "This is so sad. I'd forgotten all this."

"What?"

"After he got fired, and sued by his employer, the truck driver committed suicide. The life insurance company denied his wife's claim because suicide wasn't covered. He left her penniless, with two little children."

"That's awful."

"She lost her home and had to move in with her brother."

"Stan Friendly," we said in unison. No wonder he hated Catherine. Her quest for retribution over the loss of her family destroyed his.

* * *

After work, I stopped at PetSmart to purchase litter and a box, cat food, and bowls, then headed to Catherine's house to pick up Manny. Technically, he wasn't mine yet, but I figured Catherine wasn't anxious to add him to her menagerie. Azmina's sister in New York might want him, but I'd deal with that later.

Because there was still no sign of Catherine's return, I fed her cats. They were growing friendlier toward me now that they recognized my power to dole out the kibble. The big, fluffy, white one even competed with Manny for attention. Circling my legs as I walked through the kitchen, the two of them almost tripped me.

After taking care of the upstairs cats, I headed down to the basement to check on Octomom.

Her food bowl was empty and her litter box lumpy, but no sign of the feline family.

I stared at the hopper window just below the ceiling. It was too small for a human to crawl through; a cat would have no trouble. But there was no way to reach it unless she climbed the wall. Eight times, with babies in her mouth? I inched closer, inspecting the painted wood for scratch marks. None. I looked up again. The window was still closed, undisturbed.

Where could she have gone?

My eyes shifted to a built-in cabinet against the opposite wall. The upper shelves were exposed; the lower ones hidden behind wooden doors. I bent and pulled open one of the doors.

Octomom blinked as the light hit her eyes. She stared at me like a sphinx while thumb-size kittens jockeyed for position against her abdomen. Why she preferred the cedar-plank shelf to the soft cat bed I'd prepared for her mystified me, but I wasn't going to argue with an experienced feral mama.

Gently, I closed the cabinet door. After scooping the litter box and replenishing Octomom's food and water, I slipped out of the room with a baggy of her waste. The saying, "Dogs have owners, cats have staff," came to mind.

* * *

Manny was a lovebug on his terms—when he followed me around the house begging for head scratches or when cuddling on my lap. But it was a different story when I tried to stuff him into a cat carrier. His piercing cries sent the other cats scattering. I hoped the neighbors couldn't hear. "Nice kitty," I clucked. "No one's going to hurt you."

His howling continued as I schlepped the hard plastic cage down the walkway to my car. The carrier rocked when Manny agitatedly changed positions, thrust his body against the sides, and rattled the bars of the door. A woman raking leaves across the street looked up, startled by an earsplitting yowl. I smiled and nodded, hoping she didn't think I'd torture Catherine's cat.

I set the carrier on the front seat beside me. Manny stared with soulful gold eyes, full of betrayal, and let out another plaintive cry.

"It's okay, Manny," I murmured. "You've been to this place before, with your mommy Azmina. You like these people."

Manny glared like he didn't believe a word I said.

The cat was still wailing when I arrived at the memory care facility. A middle-aged couple, on their way out, gawked at the bouncing carrier as the man held the door for me. I nodded my thanks with an apologetic smile.

"It's Mr. Manny!" cried the young woman at the reception desk, jumping up to greet us. She smiled at me. "You brought Manny. I thought we'd never see him again."

I set down his carrier. "Sorry he's making such a racket."

"You don't like being cooped up, do you?" The woman bent to address Manny.

She escorted us to the common area where my mother and other seniors lounged. "Ladies, look who's here!"

My mother lit up like Times Square on New Year's Eve, and then her eyes swept from me to the cat carrier. A puzzled expression crossed her face.

I opened the gate. Manny hesitated for a second, then shot out—straight into my mother's lap. Several elderly women gravitated toward the cage, but they changed course as the cat made a beeline for Mom. She opened her arms to caress his furry body.

The howls were a distant memory, replaced by outboard motor purrs. Shaky, shriveled hands reached for his silky, black fur. Manny was a ham.

I applauded myself. There was nothing to this "therapy cat" gig.

Cold, bony fingers gripped my arm, and a wizened woman stared into my face, so close I could smell her sour breath. "Azmina! You came."

"I'm not—" I stopped. No matter that I looked nothing like Azmina. The handler was inconsequential; the cat was the star. The woman let go of me and shuffled toward Manny, who sat on my mother's lap—a queen and her prince consort holding court.

"It's Manny!" I heard Demi's squeal before my niece sauntered around the corner. What was she doing here? Again? She strode toward my mother and bent to give her a peck. "Hi, Grandma." She looked around. "How did Manny get here? I thought his owner—" She covered her mouth and then patted the cat on the head. He rubbed his cheek against her hand.

"Hello, Demi." I kept my voice calm. It irked me that my niece apparently already knew Manny. What else about this place did I not know?

"DeeLo!" Her hazel eyes swept to the empty carrier at my feet. "You brought Manny? What—?"

I held up my hand. "It's a long story."

My mother nuzzled Manny and then graciously sat back to allow her friends to caress him, too. The cat maintained his patient pose and endured the seniors grabbing at him like toddlers.

Demi sidled up next to me. "Jill and I are going out for a drink later. Want to join us?"

I remembered what had happened the last time I'd been drinking with the girls. Flashing lights in my rearview mirror. The helpless feeling of being locked behind bars. "Can't. I have to take Manny home."

Demi's face fell.

For a moment, I felt sorry for her. Demi had that "I need to talk" look from back in high school when she'd broken up with a boyfriend and elevated me to confidante. "Tell you what," I relented. "Why don't you and Jill come over to my place? I have a bottle of wine. We can drink responsibly."

Demi gave me a look that said, "What have you done with my Aunt DeeLo?" but before she could ponder my proposal, her eyes darted to the door that opened to the courtyard. "Incoming," she whispered, jabbing my side with her elbow to direct my attention to the new arrivals. "Ooh…he's hot."

Accompanied by the nursing home director, a silver-haired ex-football type pushed an older, shrinking version of himself in a wheelchair. "And this is the common area," the director said, gesturing around the room with her clipboard. "As you can see, Mr. Connors, your father will have plenty of company here."

There was something familiar about the man. As soon as the director addressed him as "Mr. Connors," my memory clicked: Vince Connors, Pecan County Commissioner. One of the two commissioners who'd voted in favor of Sandra's spay and neuter program. Serendipity. A potential supporter for my TNVR proposal.

Still staring, Demi whispered, "Never mind, he's with somebody."

Trailing a few steps behind the group, Victoria Barton stepped over the transom. *Seriously? Must she turn up everywhere I go?* "This is perfect, Vince," she chattered. "And once Dad's admitted, I'll put his condo on the market."

Dad?

Vince's eyes swept the room, brushing past me and stopping on Demi. Like a tailor taking measurements, they followed her willowy legs up her shapely physique to her fine, café-au-lait facial features and welcoming smile displaying thousands of dollars of orthodontia. I was accustomed to watching men stare straight past me—the sweet but mousy girl next door—to drool over my Beyoncé-look-alike niece.

The deadpan expression on Connors Senior's face came to life, and he pointed at Manny like a child in a toy store.

My mother rose and offered a turn at holding the cat to the new arrival.

"Dad, don't touch that cat. You know you're allergic." Vince took a step toward his father and blocked my mother's advance with Manny. Victoria rushed in to run interference.

A low growl emanated from Manny's throat, and then he hissed like a tomcat in an alley brawl. His thick, black hair stood on end as he bared his teeth at the newcomers. He dove from my mother's arms and ducked behind a table.

Vince turned to the director. "Who brought that vicious animal here? It's a danger to these residents."

Victoria pointed an accusing finger at me. "Her!"

Flabbergasted, the director turned toward me. "Out! Get the cat out now!"

Chapter Sixteen

Pandemonium ensued. Residents scattered. Staff dove after Manny, who scooted under tables and chairs, bolting to a new hiding place as soon as anyone got close.

One woman tripped over her walker and tumbled into Demi's arms.

Another woman burst into tears.

Victoria continued to glare at me.

"What is this varmint doing here?" bellowed Vince Connors. "Get it out!"

An old man pressed both hands to his ears.

Vince's father's face had become blank, like a TV channel that had gone off the air.

My heart stopped. The door to the courtyard gaped open. Chair legs scraped against the tile floor as patients and staff moved furniture around and chased the poor cat like hounds after a fox.

"Someone, close the door!" I screamed as a flash of black fur zipped toward the exit.

A man in a wheelchair rolled by, oblivious to the brouhaha, and cut off the cat's egress. Manny changed course and scurried under another table.

I grabbed the plastic carrier and placed it on the other side of the table where he was hiding. Then I opened the grate and sprinkled a few cat treats inside.

The feline's gold eyes flitted from his angry pursuers to his detested prison cage/familiar shelter, evaluating the consequences of his next move like a chess player. Tentatively, he crept toward the carrier. With a glance at me, he crawled inside and gobbled the treats. As soon as his body had moved beyond the entrance, I pushed his tail in and latched the door. I expected him to start his caterwauling, but he was too busy chewing to make a fuss. "Sorry." I nodded to the group. "I'll be going now."

My mother's mouth hung open, and a tear formed in the corner of her eye. I wanted to go to her side, but Demi was already comforting her. I picked up Manny and slinked out to my car.

* * *

Manny cowered quietly in his carrier on the seat beside me. In one terrible moment, we'd gone from basking in the limelight to being outcasts, no longer welcome at the facility.

Instead of meowing on the ride home, he stuck his paw through the bars, a look of shared guilt on his furry face.

My phone vibrated. A glance at the screen told me the call was from Barry, but I made no attempt to answer while driving. In a moment, it went to voicemail, followed by a text message.

He called again as I pulled into my garage. I hesitated, then let voicemail take another message.

I set up the litter box in my laundry room and filled the new cat bowls with food and water. Next, I brought Manny inside to show him his new digs. He sniffed around the room, took a bite of kibble, and then followed me into the main part of the house.

Barry phoned again. This time, I answered. "Hi, Babe. Just got home. I saw you'd called, but I was driving." I sank onto the couch, and Manny hopped onto my lap. He head-butted the hand holding my phone and purred loudly. Our harrowing experience at the memory care facility had been forgiven.

I moved the phone closer to my ear, away from Manny, as Barry said, "DeeLo, I'm sorry I've been so distracted today. I hope you didn't think I meant to be rude to you earlier."

"It's okay." *At least he's aware*, I thought. "Victoria pushes your buttons."

"Can we get together for dinner tonight?" he suggested. "I promise I'll make it up to you."

I stroked Manny's head. "I've already made plans."

"Plans?" His voice grew wary.

I knew he wanted to ask me about my "plans" but wouldn't because it would sound jealous or controlling. He'd heard me complain about how my ex-husband had been both, and he was ultra-sensitive about crossing that line. I appreciated that trait about him.

When I didn't elaborate, he murmured, "For the whole evening?"

"Demi and Jill are coming over for a glass of wine. A modified girls' night out. I don't know how late it will go, but we're doing it here, so it won't turn out like last time."

"Oh," he responded.

Manny reached up to put his paws on my shoulder, his signal that I wasn't paying him enough attention. I rubbed his back and then spoke into the phone. "See you at the office in the morning?"

"What about dinner tomorrow night?"

I gave Manny another pat. "Let's talk tomorrow." When I didn't hear Barry agree and terminate the call, I added, "My guests will be here soon. Gotta run."

He took the hint. "Good night, DeeLo. Sleep well."

After I hung up, I wondered why I'd been so short with Barry, my best friend, the person who'd helped me the most with my transition through multiple major life events. It wasn't as if I'd never seen him act like a wounded puppy whenever Victoria wagged her finger, and I'd endured daily barbs from Jane, the head cheerleader for their reunion. I knew better than to kid myself that he and his ex-wife were over, or that I was more than a rebound relationship.

Sometimes, it hurt that we were in such different stages of post-divorce trauma. There was zero chance I'd ever go back to my ex-husband. It helped that he lived on the other side of the country, and our paths never crossed. But Victoria wouldn't stay away from Barry. She twisted the bayonet in his heart every chance she got, if only to prove she still could.

And she could. That's what disturbed me the most.

Although I usually confided in Barry about everything, today, I'd balked at disclosing my absolute failure: bringing Manny to the memory care facility as a therapy cat, attempting to continue the role Azmina had filled. What was I thinking? I had no license, no business pretending to be a therapy cat handler. And I'd alienated Vince Connors, one of the county commissioners I'd hoped to recruit to support my ordinance changes. Not to mention making a fool of myself in front of Victoria. What an over-confident idiot I'd been! I couldn't bring myself to admit it out loud yet, even to Barry. I knew I'd tell him sometime, but only when I could laugh about it. I wasn't there yet.

The doorbell rang. I moved Manny off my lap and went to answer.

Demi stood awkwardly on the stoop, an almost full bottle of red wine in hand. "DeeLo."

I opened the door and stepped aside to admit her. "You didn't have to bring wine. I told you I had some."

"You said, *a* bottle," she reminded me. "I didn't want us to run out."

"Thanks." I took the bottle and led her into my living room. "Looks like you've already started."

"I had to see if it was any good."

"Can I get you a glass?" I offered. "Or should we wait for Jill?"

"Why wait?" She examined my beamed ceilings. "Nice place. Are you going to give me the grand tour?"

I'd forgotten Demi hadn't visited me here yet. "Sure. This way."

The house wasn't large, so the tour didn't take long. I'd expected Demi to make one of her usual catty comments about my taste in décor—lavender and white color scheme, plantation shutters, bedroom sponge-painted to look like wallpaper. Or at least make a snide remark about my move to a "hick town" instead of an up-and-coming Atlanta neighborhood like hers. But she didn't. "Nice," was all she said, and her tone sounded sincere.

When we returned to the living room, Manny was perched on my bookshelf. I thought about removing him but then decided the shelf must make him feel more at home, like he was back in Azmina's store.

Demi eyed Manny, then me. "Are you going to tell me why you have this cat?"

"It's a long story. Let me get some glasses."

We settled at opposite ends of my couch, wine glasses in hand, and I told Demi about finding Azmina's body on the floor of her bookstore after seeing Manny roaming loose in the parking lot.

Demi clasped a hand to her mouth. "How awful! A dead body! DeeLo!"

I nodded grimly. "Not something you can ever unsee."

"Wait a minute." She set down her glass. "Why were you trapping feral cats behind the shopping center?"

"I started volunteering with the Pecan Point Humane Society." I tried to keep my expression nonchalant.

"You? Volunteering?" She picked up her wine again and took a big slug. "Since when do you have time?"

"It's… uh…" I sipped my wine. "Community service."

"Community service! You mean like those people picking up trash along the highway?" Amusement crept onto her face. "What did you do, DeeLo?"

So, then I had to tell her about my D.U.I. Which made her laugh so hard she spewed a fountain of Merlot onto my new beige carpet. "But you're such a lightweight," she giggled. "Too funny it was you and not me!"

I set my glass on the coffee table and dashed into the kitchen for the stain remover and a rag.

The doorbell sounded while I was on my knees, applying pressure to the wine splatter as if it were a hemorrhaging wound.

"It must be Jill." Demi rose to answer. "Girl, you're a glass behind," she slurred.

An aroma of chili, melted cheese, and deep-fried tortilla chips wafted through the room. "Sorry I'm late," chirped Jill. "But I brought nachos and guacamole."

I'd planned to put out cheese and crackers, but cleaning up Demi's spill had derailed me. I'd already lost control of this party anyway.

Jill entered the living room, and we spread her offering on the coffee table. She was dressed in a pale blue business suit, and her dark hair was tied back with a matching bow.

Manny sniffed the air, licked his paw, and then settled back to his nap on the bookshelf. Apparently, spicy Mexican food didn't entice him.

"Thanks, Jill, but you didn't have to bring anything." I set plates and napkins on the coffee table so we could be halfway civilized while we munched, and then settled into my wing chair.

Jill sat in the spot I'd vacated on the couch. She slipped off her jacket and untied her hair, letting it flow over her shoulders. "I had to go to José's to cover a story." She picked up a nacho, took a bite, and gave us a conspiratorial look. "This story's a juicy one."

Demi dipped a chip in the guacamole. "Do tell."

We watched Jill chew her nacho in slow motion, her cheeks churning like a chipmunk's, closing her eyes as if savoring every morsel.

"Maybe the story isn't that good," I said.

Jill finished chewing. "José Garcia was arrested on a domestic violence charge."

"What?" I had a hard time picturing tiny, round José beating his wife, who was almost twice his size. She could pick him up and toss him like a beachball.

"Sylvia claims he tried to strangle her." Jill picked up her wine glass.

"Why? What were they fighting about?" Demi poured herself more wine.

Jill frowned. "Does it matter?"

Demi took a sip, and I held my breath, waiting for her to spill her wine, but she managed to keep her glass level. "Maybe she provoked him."

"To strangle her? That's not okay." I narrowed my eyes at Demi.

She took another swig of wine.

"I interviewed Sylvia at the hospital before I went to the restaurant to talk to the staff," Jill continued. "Their argument was stupid. She'd given some scraps of meat to the feral cats behind the dumpster, and José went ballistic. The choke marks on her neck..." She shivered. "Like the ones on Azmina Patel."

I touched my mouth. "You saw the marks on Azmina?"

"Scott left pictures on his desk." Jill pulled her cell phone from her pocket. "Here. Take a look at Sylvia's neck."

I leaned over to view the gory photo and shuddered. "Reminds me of

Azmina."

"Who?" asked Demi before taking another drink of wine.

"You know, the bookstore owner who was killed a few days ago." Jill dished some guacamole onto her plate.

"The one with that cat?" Glass in hand, Demi gestured toward Manny. At least the wine level was low enough that nothing sloshed out.

Jill nodded, then did a double take as she noticed Manny for the first time. She gave me a questioning look.

I mouthed, "Long story."

Jill continued, "José is a suspect in the murder investigation." She shook her head. "This arrest doesn't help his case."

I recalled my conversation with Sandra at Animal Control concerning her suspicions of José. And I'd seen someone leaving the restaurant the night we found Azmina. Maybe Sandra was right. "Did you know they're holding Catherine Foster in the county jail? She's a suspect, too. Which is ridiculous, because she was with me all evening."

"Unless you did it together," laughed Demi, filling her wine glass again.

"Not funny." I glared at my niece. "You've had too much wine already. Slow down."

"Catherine Foster wasn't in jail when I stopped by," said Jill. "They let her go."

"It's about time," I said. "She was arrested on bogus charges." I'd thought Catherine might call me when she got released, but then why would she? We weren't friends.

"They didn't have any real evidence against her for the murder," said Jill.

Out of the corner of my eye, I watched Demi head to the kitchen. The wine bottle on my coffee table was empty. "Do José's employees think he's guilty?" I asked.

"They're loyal, so they'd never say it, even if they're suspicious," Jill replied, reaching for her glass. "Some servers said he'd seemed depressed lately, but they were surprised he tried to strangle his wife. He's usually mild-mannered around them."

But he hadn't been so mild-mannered around Azmina and Catherine.

"Does José have an alibi for the night of Azmina's murder?" I put two nachos and a dab of guacamole on a plate.

"I don't know," said Jill. "Scott's covering that story, and he has a lot more details than I do. But I'll get him to share since now his story overlaps with mine."

Demi returned from the kitchen with a newly opened bottle of Cabernet—one I'd been saving to enjoy with Barry. She topped off Jill's and my glasses, which were only a few sips down, and then refilled her own. She plopped back onto the couch and took a deep drink.

I eyed my glass, wondering how the newly created red blend would taste.

Jill glanced at Demi, who was cradling her drink and staring into space, then turned back to me. "Did you get everything you needed today about the wrongful death suit and Stan Friendly's involvement?"

"Yes, thanks." I stole a peek at Demi, slumped into her trademark pouting position. A tear slid down her cheek, and she pounded her fist onto the coffee table.

"Demi," I asked. "What's wrong?"

She sniffed.

Jill put down her glass and turned toward her friend. "Hey, girl, what's the matter?"

Demi chugged more wine. "I don't want to bring you guys down."

I rolled my eyes. Demi loved being in the spotlight, and now that she had it, she was going to play the diva. "That's good. I'd rather hear more Pecan County gossip from Jill."

Jill scooted across the couch to Demi. "You wanted to have a drink tonight and talk. Let's talk. What's up?" She placed a hand on Demi's shoulder.

"Carl went back to his wife!" Demi blurted, then burst into tears.

For the next hour, Jill and I listened to a blow-by-blow account of Demi's relationship with Carl, last name unimportant, a software executive at least a decade her senior. Eight months ago, he'd been a full-fare, first-class passenger on a flight she was working, and they'd exchanged contact information. Afterward, they'd arranged secret, romantic, assignations in exotic locations; every time, he'd showered her with flowers and jewelry.

And then, last week, Carl had become distant. Stopped calling, didn't return her texts. The inevitable breakup had happened last night.

Demi's relationships often ended like that, mainly because she chose men who were unattainable—married, gay, geographically undesirable, or just emotionally immature. After my own marriage failed, I stopped judging her so harshly.

And now I was dating a man who had deluded himself into thinking he was over his ex-wife.

I tried to discreetly remove the wine bottle, but Demi grabbed it and refilled her glass. She was determined to get drunk and was well on her way. When depressed, she tended to use alcohol to drown her sorrows, but it only served to sharpen her pain.

And turn her into a slobbering mess.

I spotted Demi's purse on the kitchen counter. While Jill consoled her through one of her crying fits, I pulled out her car keys and slipped them into my pocket. My niece wasn't driving anymore tonight.

"Demi." I nudged her heaving shoulder. "I made up the guest room for you. Maybe you should get some rest." I nodded to Jill and patted the car keys in my pocket. "You're welcome to stay, too, Jill. There are nightgowns and T-shirts in the chest of drawers."

"I have to go home." Demi rose from the couch and wobbled toward her purse on the counter. She fumbled through it, strewing half the contents on the floor. "Where…where are my k…keys?" Her eyes swept the room, unable to focus. "DeeLo, have you seen my k…keys?"

"Sorry," I told her. "Let's look for them in the morning. You can sleep here tonight."

She waved a finger at me. "You took my keys, *Aunt* DeeLo. Give them back!"

"Tomorrow," I said.

"Come on." Jill put an arm around Demi's waist. "We're having a slumber party. It'll be fun." She winked at me as she led Demi into the guest room.

The click of the latch as the door closed muffled Demi's rant. "You win, Aunt DeeLo. Aunt DeeLo knows best."

Manny watched me clean up after my guests and then followed me into the master bedroom. He jumped onto my bed and made himself comfortable while I undressed.

I turned off the light, climbed into bed, and snuggled under the covers. In a moment, loud purring buzzed in my ear, and a furry face pressed against my cheek. I stroked Manny's head and drifted to sleep.

Chapter Seventeen

The aroma of fresh-brewed coffee, along with sounds of kitchen cabinets opening and mugs clinking, awakened me. Manny was nowhere to be found. Had I only dreamed I'd unofficially adopted Azmina's cat?

I wrapped myself in a pink terrycloth robe and padded out to the kitchen in my stocking feet. Jill was back in her business suit, as polished as when she'd arrived, preparing to leave for work. I glanced at the kitchen clock. I should be doing the same. "How is she?" I gestured toward the guest room.

"Sleeping it off," said Jill, car keys in hand. "How are you?"

"Much better than Demi."

We both chuckled.

"Last night was fun," she said. "I'd stay and chat over coffee, but I've got an early staff meeting." With a wave, she headed out. "Thanks again for your hospitality."

The door to the guest room stood open. Demi lay in the double bed, her face pale, her eyes tiny slits. The only indication of life was a slight rise and fall of her chest underneath the comforter. I imagined she'd awaken with a terrible headache. Jill had already placed a tall glass of water and three aspirins on the nightstand.

Next to Demi sat Manny, kneading her arm as if he were making biscuits. *The traitor.*

I poured myself a cup of coffee, showered and dressed, refilled Manny's bowls, then checked on my niece again. Like a still-life painting, the scene had not changed. I set her car keys on the counter, along with a note encouraging her to help herself to coffee and whatever food she could scrounge.

* * *

I'd expected to spend my morning archiving Catherine Foster's file. Yesterday's research into the animosity between Catherine and Officer Friendly had slowed my work. When I arrived at the office, the folder was missing from my desktop.

Jane buried her face in a stack of papers and pretended not to notice me as I approached. Before I could say anything, my phone dinged with a text message from Lisa Ross. "I have an errand to run after work this evening. Can we make it six-thirty instead of six?"

I slapped my forehead. Barry was expecting me to join him for dinner tonight, but I'd forgotten my commitment to help Lisa trap cats. For my community service. "Fine," I texted back.

Resuming my walk toward Jane's receptionist station, I caught sight of Catherine's folder on her desk. I grabbed it.

Jane's head shot up from her reading. "You can't—"

"I wasn't finished with this yet." I clutched the folder against my chest.

"But Victoria—"

At that moment, Barry walked into the office, briefcase in hand, a questioning look on his face at the sound of our raised voices.

I eyed Jane. "Surely, you're not going to tell me Victoria needs Catherine Foster's file? It has nothing to do with real estate."

The feigned innocent expression on Jane's face revealed that was exactly what she was about to tell me.

I turned to Barry. "Are we sharing Catherine Foster's legal documents with Victoria?"

"No!" His eyes bulged. "Jane, please don't give Victoria any more of our files before checking with me. She is no longer a partner in this firm, and sharing our client information with her violates confidentiality."

Jane shot me a dagger-like glare before hunching her shoulders and muttering, "Yes, sir."

I bit my bottom lip to keep a smirk from creeping onto my face as I sashayed back to my cubicle.

* * *

Just before noon, Barry stopped by my desk. "I thought you'd like to know Catherine Foster was released from jail last night."

I swirled around in my chair to face him. "I heard. It's about time."

"Apparently, her alibi checked out." Smiling, he leaned against the padded wall of my cubicle.

Had Detective Ross taken my advice and checked the timestamps on Nick's text messages? "Great news."

"And now they're talking to another person of interest in custody," he added. "The owner of the Mexican restaurant in the Patel Shopping Center: José Garcia."

I didn't mention that I'd already heard about José's arrest from Jill. "What evidence do they have?"

Barry shrugged. "The police didn't share anything with me."

"Do you think José did it?"

"It's not my place to speculate." He removed his glasses and wiped them with a tissue.

"It's human nature to be curious." I sensed Barry was done with that conversation. "Does Catherine need anything?"

He shook his head. "I offered, but she said she had it covered. She was anxious to get home to a warm bath, a good meal, and her own bed. Anyway, now you don't have to go feed cats and scoop litter boxes after work."

I shot him a thumbs-up. "And I was getting so good at it."

"Did you give any more thought to dinner?"

"I forgot I promised Detective Ross's wife I'd help her trap the feral cats on their property this evening."

"On your own? Without Catherine?" He frowned. "You feel comfortable doing that?"

"Detective Ross said I could count it toward my community service hours." Barry shuffled his feet and looked down, as if hesitant to leave.

"It's true," I felt compelled to insist.

His sigh sounded almost like a moan. "I feel like I'm losing you."

I almost slipped from my chair. His remark rolled in like a rogue wave, catching me off guard. "Why?" Where did the neediness come from? Was he resentful I'd started building a life in this town that did not completely revolve around him? Or was he afraid I'd witnessed too many of his emotional interactions with Victoria and was ready to give up on him?

The look that flashed across his face showed a mix of frustration and sadness. I wanted to give him a reassuring hug, but not in public. I said softly, "I'm free for lunch if you are."

* * *

Barry took me to Leonardo's, one of our favorite dinner venues. I started to argue that the service was too leisurely for lunch, but he was the boss; I didn't question his time-management decision.

It was a warm, glistening autumn day, and we asked for a table on the patio overlooking the nature reserve. I couldn't help thinking about the last time I'd been here, after Demi had taken my mother to lunch and lost her. And how I'd found Mom in the reserve—talking to Nick Norton, the cat hater. And possible murderer.

The waitress brought us menus and two big glasses of ice water. I took a sip and eyed Barry, who pored over the menu. "Thank you for giving Jane more direction about the files. I knew we shouldn't be handing over documents to Victoria whenever she demanded them."

He set his menu down. "When Victoria was at the firm, she and Jane worked closely together. Now, my ex-wife takes advantage of that loyalty. Jane doesn't understand the repercussions of violating our client confidentiality."

"If she's so loyal, why didn't Jane go with Victoria?"

"Whitehead Realtors didn't have a spot for her."

"What does your former partner want with Catherine Foster's file?" I folded a linen napkin across my lap. "From what I've read in the paperwork, Catherine had no transactions involving real estate, no legal matters that involved Victoria."

Barry sighed. "You remember Catherine is one of the beneficiaries in Azmina Patel's will?"

"Yes, but what does that have to do with Victoria?"

"As I said, Azmina was planning to sell a large plot of undeveloped land surrounding her shopping center."

"And Victoria was her realtor." I picked up my water glass again and took a big swallow, trying to quench my thirst from last night's wine fest.

Barry nodded. "Azmina had several offers, with various terms and conditions. She kept going back and forth about which one to take. Just when Victoria thought she'd made up her mind, something would happen to create an objection. At one point, Azmina wanted to take the property off the market and donate it to the animal foundation Catherine Foster was creating."

I set my glass down too quickly, and some of the water splashed onto the tablecloth. "Now that Azmina's dead, who gets the land?"

He picked up his menu again as the waitress returned to take our orders. "It's complicated."

I chose a seafood primavera I'd tried before. Barry ordered the beef lasagna.

Once the waitress left, I asked, "How complicated?"

"Victoria claims the sale to Oakwood Studios should go through—that Azmina had already signed the contract."

"I don't get it. Either the contract is signed, or it's not. Unless..."

His eyes blazed. "Victoria's sleazy boyfriend is the buyer's agent for Oakwood Studios, and Whitehead Realtors stands to earn a large commission if this transaction goes through. Conflict of interest, if you ask me."

My eyes widened. "Roy Don Whitehead? The county commissioner?" I tried to remember his reaction at the BOC meeting the other night when someone referenced the stalled sale.

Barry pursed his lips. "There's something shady about the way they're trying to force that land deal, and Victoria should know better." He gripped his fork as if he wanted to stab someone with it. "She changed so much after she took up with Roy Don."

I kept my eyes on the fork he was brandishing, not wanting to become a casualty of his wrath against Roy Don and Victoria. "Why does she want Catherine Foster's file?"

He set down the fork, which made me breathe easier, even though I knew Barry would never stab anyone. "Victoria knows about the foundation we're setting up. She's searching for a loophole, some reason the document isn't valid. Something to negate Catherine's right to the land. Which leads me to believe Victoria doesn't have a valid contract for the sale."

"Who gets the property if not Catherine's foundation?"

"Azmina had a sister and a nephew. There's also a stepson who might contest the will since Azmina didn't leave him anything."

"Do you think he'll contest it?"

Barry adjusted his glasses. "I advised Azmina to leave him something, even a token bequest, but after they had a major disagreement, she cut him out completely."

I wondered if the police had checked his whereabouts. "Who's the executor?"

"Azmina's older sister, a stockbroker in New York City. She's coming down later this week."

"So, if it takes months to probate the will, the sale of the land will be stalled for a long time." I signaled the waitress to refill my water glass. "If the sale even happens."

"Not what Victoria and her boyfriend want to hear." He rolled his thumb over his forefinger as if handling dollar bills.

What if one of them went to Azmina's shop to persuade her to sign the contract, and the conversation turned ugly...

The call of "Here, kitty, kitty" interrupted my reverie. At the sound of giggles behind me, I abandoned my fantasy of Victoria in handcuffs and turned to see two teenage girls tossing scraps of meat over the rail and

126

taking videos with their cell phones. "Do you think your dad would let you have one?" one asked the other.

"What the—" I rose from my chair and leaned over the barrier to observe three young brown tabbies devouring the morsels the girls had tossed. The kittens appeared to be about six months old, and none had ear tips.

The waitress brought our food and noticed me eyeing the felines. "Those cats live in the reserve, and the woman who feeds them got killed. They've been coming here for the past few days, and people have been feeding them. Poor things."

"Is the restaurant owner okay with people feeding them?" We didn't need another cat hater like José.

"Not sure he knows." The waitress gestured toward our steaming plates. "Enjoy your lunch."

As she left, Barry grinned. "A new project for you and Cat."

"For me and Catherine?" I speared a shrimp and twirled some pasta around it. "Because we get along so well?"

"You two have more in common than you realize."

"Please!" I rolled my eyes.

"You both care about the cats."

Out of the corner of my eye, I glimpsed Roy Don and Victoria venture onto the patio, then stop and retreat inside. Barry had his back to the door, so he hadn't spotted them. Seeing Roy Don reminded me of my plan to revise the county's animal laws. "Speaking of cats, I'm almost through with the changes I'd like to make to the ordinance. Can we go over them tomorrow?"

Chewing, Barry nodded.

"Great." I took another bite of pasta. No need to ruin his lunch by telling him his ex-wife and her boyfriend were there.

Chapter Eighteen

I stopped at the grocery store on my way to Lisa's and purchased a package of fresh mackerel like Catherine Foster used to bait her traps. It cost as much as my own dinner.

The Ross family lived about a mile outside the Pecan Point city limits off a two-lane highway. At the end of a long, pine tree-lined driveway stood a 1960s-era ranch house with a covered porch outfitted with rocking chairs. I hoped Detective Ross wasn't home; I didn't feel like dealing with his skepticism.

Lisa opened the front door as my tires crunched gravel, and I came to a stop at the head of the driveway. She looked a lot like I'd pictured her. Her pint-size body and brown Shirley Temple curls fit her squeaky Southern voice.

I got out of my car and walked up to the porch. One of the wooden steps creaked under the weight of my foot.

"You must be DeeLo," she greeted me. She'd changed into jeans and tennis shoes as I'd instructed but still wore her pearl necklace. "Thanks so much for coming."

I glanced around. "You said you had traps?" I was beginning to wish I'd stopped by Catherine's for advice and to borrow whatever equipment we were missing.

Lisa motioned toward a small animal trap. The rusty contraption was similar to the ones Catherine used, but a different brand. I hoped I'd be able to figure out the mechanism. "You just borrowed one trap from Animal Control? How many cats are there?"

"Four—a mom and her three almost-grown kittens. I have this carrier, too." Lisa pointed to a plastic crate large enough to hold a small dog. "It's big, so we can fit two or three cats in there."

"Are these cats tame enough to pick up and put in a carrier?" I remembered her husband telling me they weren't.

"No, but I thought if we catch one, we can move it to the carrier, so we can trap the next one." Her curls bounced as she talked.

I shook my head. "At the clinic, they require each feral cat to arrive in its own trap or wire transfer cage. They say it's easier to administer anesthesia through the bars of a trap than to reach into a cat carrier. Besides, you get a better price on the surgery if they're feral as opposed to a pet."

"Why's that?"

Before my visit to the LifeSaver, I might have asked the same question. "Because feral cats don't have owners. The people who run the clinic give a break to Good Samaritans who spend their own money to help control overpopulation. The feral package includes a rabies vaccination, a distemper shot, and an ear tip along with the surgery."

"An ear tip?" Lisa's blue eyes widened.

"That's how you can tell they've already been fixed."

"Won't it hurt them?" She grimaced.

"They do it while the cats are under anesthesia."

"Do they have to cut their ears?" The look on her face remained horrified.

I put my hand on my hip. "Are you going to move them inside?"

"I can't. My son's allergic to cats." She wrung her hands. "When the kittens were born, I asked the Pecan Point Humane Society to help me find them homes. A woman said I'd have to bring them inside and foster them as house pets until they could be adopted. As much as I would have liked to, I couldn't do that."

"Then it's better to get them fixed as ferals if they're going to live outside." Two orange tabbies chased a squirrel across the driveway during our discussion. I pointed. "Are those the cats we're talking about?"

Lisa nodded. "Two of the kittens. Or maybe one was the mom. I can't tell them apart now that the kittens are big."

"All of them are orange tabbies?" When she nodded again, I laughed. "If we catch one tonight and get it fixed, you'll save everyone a lot of trouble if it gets an ear tip. You don't want to keep hauling the same cat to the clinic." I inspected the trap, mentally reviewing the lessons Catherine had taught me. "You didn't feed them, right?"

"Not since breakfast."

"Breakfast? I told you not to feed them starting last night. We want them hungry, so they'll go into the trap."

Lisa stared as if I'd recommended torture. "Well, they haven't had their dinner yet."

With a sigh, I walked to my car to retrieve the mackerel.

When I returned, Lisa asked, "What's that?" Her lip curled at the smelly fish.

"Mackerel, for baiting the trap. Cats love it."

"If you say so."

We found a sheltered spot to set up in an area the cats frequented. I hadn't thought to bring a ribbon to tie around the entrance door, like Catherine did with hers, but the trap was close enough to the back patio for us to monitor the activity around it.

Lisa didn't offer to help me bait the trap, so I was the one who had to handle the slimy, stinky fish. And I'd forgotten to bring rubber gloves. Since we only had one trap, I couldn't use Catherine's teaching technique—making Lisa do the next one herself.

"What's next?" she asked after I finished setting the trap.

"We wait." Gesturing toward the patio, I suggested we sit there, where we'd have a good view of the operation.

The large brick patio, containing an outdoor grill and a firepit, overlooked a swimming pool and a wooden-encased hot tub—the perfect set-up for outdoor entertaining. While Lisa disappeared into the house, I washed my hands in the pool house bathroom.

A few minutes later, Lisa returned with a tray. It held two glasses of lemonade, two plastic straws, and a plate of Thin Mints Girl Scout cookies. She poked a plastic straw into one of the lemonades and handed it to me, then set down the tray and took a seat across the glass table.

I removed the straw and sipped my lemonade. It was sweeter than I liked but refreshing. "Is your insurance office in the Patel Shopping Center? By José's Mexican restaurant and Black Cat Books?"

Nodding, Lisa stirred her lemonade with her straw. "Terrible what happened to our landlord."

"Did you know Azmina well?"

"She was okay." Lisa sucked lemonade through her straw.

Her answer didn't match my question. I attempted to clarify, "Okay, as a landlord?"

"For the most part. She was getting greedy lately."

"Greedy? How?"

Lisa set down her glass. "After her husband died, the whole shopping center started to fall apart. Azmina couldn't afford to keep up with the maintenance. To save money, she fired the landscapers who used to take care of the plantings around the parking lot. She was slow to get anything fixed. And then she refused to give us a break on the rent."

"Do you think—" I stopped, put a finger to my lips, and watched as an orange tabby approached the trap. He circled it, stuck a paw inside, sniffed, then walked away. In a moment, a second cat did the same thing.

"Poor babies. They know it's time for their dinner." In the shrubs on the edge of the patio, two more felines loomed, warily eyeing me.

"We want them to be hungry, so they'll go into the trap for food," I reminded her.

We watched for a few more minutes, listening to a symphony of insects in the surrounding woods. Despite their hunger, none of the cats went into the trap.

"Azmina was feeding some strays who lived behind the bookstore." Lisa slurped her drink. "Do you like the lemonade?"

My answer was a smile and another sip.

"I made it myself. You don't think it's too sweet?"

"It's fine." I drank more as proof. "You know, Catherine Foster helped Azmina get those cats fixed. Like we're trying to do with yours."

Lisa sniffed. "That Catherine Foster's a piece of work."

"Why don't you like her?" I picked up a Thin Mint cookie from the tray. It was still frozen.

"She's so…" Lisa looked skyward as if the word she needed could be found among the twinkling stars starting to appear. "Condescending. Argumentative. Bless her heart."

I found it comforting to hear others complain about Catherine's demeanor. At least her disdain wasn't reserved for me. "She's not a people person."

"You got that right."

The ping from an incoming text startled the orange tabby who'd been sniffing near the patio, and the feline bolted back into the woods. I groaned; I'd meant to silence my phone.

The text was from Catherine. "What happened to Octomom, D.D?"

"What do you mean?" I typed. "Is she hurt?"

"SHE'S GONE!!!"

I typed, "Did you look in the cabinet?"

"WHAT CABINET?!!"

I pressed the telephone icon. As soon as I heard Catherine's breath at the other end of the phone, I launched into my explanation, "I put her in the room next to the laundry—"

"I looked already. She's not in there anymore. The kittens are gone, too. Did you lose her, D.D.?"

"Did you look in the cabinet?"

Footsteps tromped across the tile floor, and I sensed Catherine was going back to Octomom's room.

"See that built-in cabinet against the wall? Open the bottom left door."

"This one?" There was a long pause. Followed by muffled cooing. Catherine must have located Octomom and her kittens. "Why did you put her in here? She can't get out."

"Has her litterbox been used? Is her food dish empty?"

Another pause. "Yes."

"She gets in and out on her own."

Catherine hung up without saying goodbye.

Chuckling, I typed a text message, "I trust the rest of your cats are okay." And then, before she could berate me again, I added, "I have Manny."

Her response was a thumbs-up emoji. I set the phone down on the table and muted it.

"Have more, please." Lisa pushed the plate of cookies toward me. The edge of the plate clipped my glass, knocking it over and spilling lemonade onto the table. "Oh, I'm so sorry. How clumsy of me!" She jumped up, grabbed a handful of napkins, and began dabbing at the pool of liquid.

While Lisa buzzed about like a hummingbird, I moved my phone and shifted my position to avoid getting wet. "It's okay. Don't worry about it." I picked up a napkin and blotted the area in front of me.

Crisis averted, Lisa sat back down and righted my glass. "Would you like more lemonade?"

"No, thanks."

"Just let me know if you change your mind." She fingered her pearls. "Those poor cats in the greenbelt behind the store. I don't know what will happen to them, now that Azmina's gone. I'll feed them if we stay."

"Are you going somewhere?" I took another frozen Thin Mint.

Lisa sighed. "Who knows what's going to happen to the property? Now that Azmina's...you know...dead."

"Probably nothing will happen with it right away. Not until her will gets sorted out." Out of the corner of my eye, I watched the cats again circle the trap as if reconnoitering an alien spaceship, but then retreat.

Lisa looked at her watch. "How long does this trapping stuff usually take?"

"Depends on how hungry they are." I couldn't resist mentioning, one more time, my instructions to withhold food.

"I don't think they like that smelly fish."

"Mackerel? Catherine uses it all the time."

"I've never known these cats to eat anything but Meow Mix. Last time Paul went fishing and brought home a catch, we tried to give some fillets to the cats as a treat. They turned up their noses."

Lesson learned: find out what the cats like to eat. "Let's put a bowl of Meow Mix in the trap and see what happens."

Lisa fetched the bag of kibble and poured some into a plastic bowl while I disabled the trap and removed the mackerel. "Do you remember how to set the trap?"

"No." She threw me a panicked look.

I placed the bowl of Meow Mix beyond the trip plate and reset the trap.

We headed back to the patio. A mosquito landed on my arm, and though I swatted it away, moments later, I felt a welt rising where it had been. The weather hadn't turned cold enough yet to kill off the little pests.

A tow-headed child of around four, showcasing a blend of his parents' best features, plodded outside to join us. Sucking his thumb, wearing what looked like pajamas, he stared at me without speaking.

"You should be in bed." Lisa rose to intercept her son. Bending over, she spoke softly to him and pointed toward the door. He squirmed and whined, and after a bit of cajoling, she persuaded him to go back inside.

"Your son?" I stated the obvious. I wondered if they'd named him Paul, Jr. She nodded. "He knows it's bedtime."

The trap sprang shut amid a flash of thrashing orange. I grinned at Lisa. "Guess Meow Mix was all it took."

While I grabbed a towel to cover the trap, Lisa jumped up and dashed toward the captured cat, two steps ahead of me, banging the cat carrier against her thighs. I hadn't realized she could move so quickly.

"Wait," I called.

Before I could ask her what she was doing, she opened the door to the cat carrier, shoved it against the trap door, and lifted the gate.

The terrified cat shot out of the trap, knocking the carrier aside and leaving a six-inch scratch on Lisa's arm as it raced into the brush.

"Ow!" she cried, clutching her arm.

"Oh, that looks bad." I took the clean towel and pressed it against Lisa's wound to control the bleeding. "Should I drive you to the urgent care clinic?"

"No, it'll be okay. I have some antiseptic and bandages in the house."

I eyed the bloody towel. "You're sure?"

Detective Ross drove up the driveway and parked his pick-up alongside my SUV. Lisa gestured toward her husband, who was getting out of his truck. "Paul will take me if we think it's that bad. You better get going." The detective didn't look our way, so I figured he hadn't noticed us against the background of dark woods. Lisa turned and headed into the house through the back door.

I closed the trap, placed it and the empty carrier on the patio, and managed to reach my car without crossing paths with Detective Ross. I had no desire to face an interrogation about my role in his wife's injury.

* * *

On the road back into town, I again saw in my rearview mirror headlights belonging to a fast-approaching car. In a moment, it was on my bumper. I tried to pull over on the shoulder so the car could pass, but the driver seemed content to hug my bumper and flick his lights. I sped up, but so did he.

I reached for my phone to dial nine-one-one, but then he whizzed around me and disappeared into the night. While waiting for my heartbeat to steady, I tried to remember details about the harassing vehicle. Could it have been the same driver as before? Was someone out to get me, or was I just a random victim of a sadistic motorist?

Once I got home, my pulse returned to normal. After a thorough security check, I fed the rest of the mackerel to Manny. He gobbled it down with gusto as if he hadn't eaten in weeks.

Afterward, he snuggled with me in bed, curling up close to my head. I had to turn my nose away from his fish breath as I listened to his rhythmic purr. I stroked his silky fur, grateful for the unconditional love from someone who didn't judge me, didn't care that I had failed at my first attempt to teach Trap-Neuter-Return.

Before I drifted off to sleep, I thought again about Azmina, Manny's former owner. Had she known her killer? Had she fought back? And what did her pet see? If only cats could talk.

Chapter Nineteen

Lisa Ross called me at work the next day. I was surprised she still wanted to speak to me.

"DeeLo, I know what I did was stupid. I promise I'll listen to you," she said. "Shall we try again tonight?"

I almost dropped the phone. I'd half expected her to present me with a bill for urgent care. "Hold on," I told her. "The spay/neuter clinic isn't open on Saturday. Why don't we trap Sunday night, and then if we catch some of the cats, you can take them for surgery Monday morning? No use making them stay in traps all weekend."

She hummed in resigned agreement. "And I guess we need more traps. Should I go buy some?"

Lisa was making me dizzy. She was so gung-ho in the planning stages of this project, but then not so much when it came to the execution. "I'll see if I can borrow the equipment from Catherine." I wasn't going there unprepared again, and leaving it to Lisa to line up everything we needed would not be wise.

"And I'll remember not to feed them," she added.

"Thanks. That will make it easier to catch them. With Meow Mix." I switched the phone to my other ear. "Is your husband still on board with this project?"

"Oh, yeah. He wasn't happy I let that cat escape after we trapped it."

"You told him it was your fault?" I found that hard to believe.

"Well, it was. After I messed up, I remembered you told me not to try putting the cat in the carrier."

Yes, I did. "How's your arm?"

"Much better. Looked like a lot of blood, but after I got it cleaned up, there was just a surface wound. A little antiseptic was all it took."

"Good to hear. I wouldn't want our local police detective to think I put his wife in danger."

She giggled. I wasn't sure how to interpret her laughter. Did she mean her husband wasn't concerned about her safety? Or that he trusted me enough to know I wouldn't purposely jeopardize it?

"Were you serious about feeding the colony behind Black Cat Books?" I asked her. "I don't think anyone's looking after those cats since Azmina—"

"I brought a bag of Meow Mix to work this morning and put out a bowl behind our office. And Natalie Wojcik from the dry cleaners feeds them sometimes. She did even when Azmina was alive." Lisa lowered her voice. "Paul's worried about me getting involved with those cats, though. He's afraid they're the reason Azmina got killed."

Nick. José. Both cat haters. "He thinks a scuffle over cats could be a motive for murder?" When she didn't respond, I continued, "Does your husband have any more leads?"

Lisa laughed again. It resembled a snort. Or maybe a whinny. "He doesn't talk to me about his cases."

"But it sounds like he has a theory, if he warned you about feeding the cats."

"I think he's considering lots of theories," she confided. "Everyone who works at the shopping center is a suspect. Even me."

"You?" I doubted tiny Lisa had the strength to strangle someone, even a small woman like Azmina. "What about José? I heard he got arrested for assaulting his wife, so he has a temper."

"Definitely a possibility," Lisa agreed.

"Why does your husband suspect Azmina's other tenants? Did anyone else quarrel with her?"

"Paul knew we dragged Azmina to a meeting last week—Vince, Natalie, José, and Mr. Kim from the Dollar Store. We were all angry when she refused to lower our rents to compensate for the declining condition of the property." Anger rose in Lisa's voice. "We had every right to be upset." Her voice quivered. "That's the problem with being married to a cop. He can twist seemingly inconsequential information to use against me, his own wife."

"Like what?"

"He keeps grilling me about that meeting. What we talked about, who was there. How was I to know someone would go and kill our landlord shortly afterward?"

"But not you. Detective Ross must know that."

"Vince had to lay off all our other employees," Lisa continued.

I wondered why she didn't immediately agree that her husband had no reason to suspect her, but maybe she was too absorbed in her tale to respond to my remark.

"Part of the problem is some bad investments Connors Insurance has made recently," she was saying, "But Azmina was completely unsympathetic about our cash flow issues."

"I'm sorry to hear that." Could a dispute over the rent be a reason to commit murder? What would it solve?

"I went to see her the afternoon she was killed," Lisa confessed.

My breath caught in my throat.

"Vince always had me deal with Azmina, woman to woman," said Lisa. "I usually had better luck than he did; he has a bit of a temper. But this time, she wouldn't budge. Said she couldn't afford to reduce our rent."

"What time did you go see her?"

"Around six. Right after we finished working."

"You were open on Sunday? That's the day she was killed."

"Not to the public. Vince and I went to the office that afternoon to catch up on paperwork."

"Vince knew you went to see her?"

"It was his idea."

Six o'clock. The text messages to Nick had been sent at eight-thirty. Detective Ross should know that. Unless he suspected Azmina was already dead by eight-thirty and someone else sent the texts.

138

"Like I told you last night, I don't know what's going to happen now," continued Lisa. "There's a rumor the whole shopping center might be bulldozed for a movie studio. You work for the lawyer who drafted her will. Do you know what was in it? Is there a mortgage? A beneficiary?"

"I don't know." I hadn't seen the file, and Barry hadn't shared many details. How did Lisa know which lawyer prepared Azmina's will?

Jane stood in front of my cubicle with a stack of folders in her arms and impatience on her face. Though I wanted to ask Lisa more about her last meeting with Azmina, I quickly terminated our conversation and promised to see her Sunday evening.

* * *

Kyra Chowdhury, Azmina's stockbroker sister from New York, arrived at our office Friday afternoon to meet with Barry about Azmina's will. Except for her Western-style dress, Kyra looked very much like her sibling: small-boned, with shiny black hair, large brown eyes, and smooth skin that could pass for forty, even though I knew she was in her fifties.

After they'd been meeting for about a half-hour, I poked my head into the conference room to ask if they'd like coffee or a cold drink. Jane had gone home early.

"No thanks, DeeLo," said Barry. "Ms. Chowdhury, can we get you anything?"

The smile on her lips was gracious, although her eyes looked sad. "No, thank you, dear."

"Just let me know if you change your mind." With my hand on the doorknob, I added, "I'm so sorry about your sister. Such a loss for our community."

The smile widened. "How nice of you to say that. You knew Azmina?"

"Not well. But I shopped at her store, and she gave me some great book recommendations." This wasn't the time to tell Kyra I'd found her sister's strangled body.

She dabbed a tear from her eye with a crumpled tissue. "She loved reading.

That bookstore was her little paradise."

I couldn't help myself. I was growing more attached to Manny every day, and I had to know if Azmina's sister would take him away. "Did she ever mention her bookstore cat? I mean, did she ask anyone to look after him if something happened to her?"

Kyra smiled through her tears. "Manny? He was such a sweetheart." She wiped away another tear. "The police told me he ran off. I wonder what that poor animal saw." She sniffled. "I keep asking myself what kind of madman could have done such a terrible thing to a kind and gentle woman."

Barry set down the paper he was holding and looked earnestly at Kyra. "The police will find Azmina's killer."

"I certainly hope so. Do they have any leads? They couldn't tell me much."

"I'm sorry." Barry shook his head. "They haven't shared many details with the public."

I looked down, then shifted my gaze to Kyra. "I have Manny. He's safe."

Kyra brightened. "I thought he was gone for good. All those woods. A busy parking lot by a highway…"

Why didn't I let her go on thinking that? Now, I'd lose my new pet. "Would you like to see him when you're done here?"

"Oh, could I? You're so kind. Manny's all I have left of my dear sister."

* * *

After we closed the office, Kyra Chowdhury came to my house to reunite with Manny. I arrived home a few minutes before Kyra pulled up in her rental car, followed by Barry. Before greeting my guests, I took a moment to cuddle Manny, who rewarded me with a steady purr.

With a glance at my new beige carpet, Kyra slipped off her shoes. "What a cute house," she said.

I ushered her into the living room and invited her to sit on the couch. "I was about to make tea. Can I get you some?"

"That would be lovely, dear."

Before I left the room to prepare the tea, Manny moseyed in. He rubbed against Barry, who was sitting in my wing chair, and then headed over to Kyra. He sniffed her feet and sidled up against her leg. She patted the cushion next to her, and he hopped onto the couch, then made himself comfortable in her lap. So much for my hope that they wouldn't take to each other.

"Oh, Manny, Manny, Manny," Kyra cooed, cupping the cat's face in her hands and practically touching noses. "What are we going to do without Mina?"

Barry and I exchanged glances. He started to rise to assist me in the kitchen, but I motioned for him to stay seated.

"Would you like to go back to New York with me?" Kyra whispered to Manny. His answer was a purr.

I got out my Wedgewood china tea service, a wedding present I loved but didn't use very often. I made a pot of Earl Grey with a box of loose tea I'd bought in Azmina's shop. Kyra should appreciate the tribute to her sister.

When the tea had steeped sufficiently, I carried the tray into the living room and placed it on the coffee table in front of Kyra. I set a cup on a saucer for her. "How do you like your tea?"

"Just plain, thank you. My, what a lovely tea set." She accepted the cup I handed her.

I poured a cup for Barry, then sat down and served myself.

"Mmm, Earl Grey was Azmina's favorite," said Kyra as she sipped.

"I bought this in her store."

Azmina's sister looked up from her teacup and smiled. Again, just the lips, not the eyes.

As soon as I'd settled onto the other end of the couch, Manny leaped off Kyra's lap and jumped onto mine. He purred loudly and rubbed against my arm, jostling my tea.

I set down my cup and yielded to his demand for petting.

Kyra took another sip and smiled again. "He loves you."

I stroked Manny's silky black fur as he curled up on my lap. "He loves everybody."

Kyra winked. "But I think he's partial to you."

I gave Manny another ear rub. "I suppose you'll be taking him back to New York with you?"

"That was the plan. But would you consider keeping him? He seems to have made himself at home here."

"For real?" I scratched Manny under his chin, which made him purr louder.

"DeeLo would make a great pet parent." Barry smiled, subtly pleading my case.

"It would save him a plane ride," said Kyra. "And I don't think he and my cat would get along in my tiny apartment. Sabrina's thirteen years old, and she's a diva." She gestured around the room. "Your place is bigger and so much cheerier. Manny can be the center of attention. You'd be doing us all a favor."

"I'd love to adopt him. I promise to take good care of him." I felt myself glowing.

"I have no doubt." Kyra smiled again, and this time her eyes participated.

"Thank you." I grinned at Kyra and then gave Manny a big kiss. *My cat.* Maybe I wouldn't be able to work him as a therapy cat at the memory care facility, as Azmina had done, but it would be wonderful to have a pet again. Both cats and dogs had been part of my family while I was growing up, but my ex-husband never wanted pets—which should have been a clue the marriage was doomed.

We finished our tea and chatted about New York, Pecan Point, and travel. Kyra shared stories about herself and Azmina, and she lamented that she hadn't spent enough time with her sister in the past few years. "Don't ever take the people you love for granted," she warned. "You never know how long you have."

I nodded, thinking about my mother. And maybe a little about Demi and Desiree. And my brother David, wherever he might be.

I had to remove Manny from my lap when it was time to bid goodbye to Kyra. "And please," she said as we stood in the doorway. "If you find out who killed my sister, call me right away."

"Of course," we both agreed.

Barry stayed overnight, and Manny reluctantly allowed him to share our bed.

Chapter Twenty

The aroma of French Roast seeped into my nostrils. I was in that space between deep sleep and awakening when feathery kisses brushed my forehead. Then, my eyes and nose, making their way to my lips. My eyelids fluttered open. Barry stood over me, and a steaming mug of coffee waited on my nightstand. Without his glasses, he looked more like Superman than Clark Kent.

"Sweet dreams?" he asked as he crawled back into the bed beside me.

Rubbing the sleep grit from my eyes, I propped myself up against the pillow so I could take a sip from the mug he'd brought me. The strong coffee was heavy on the milk, exactly the way I liked it. "No. I dreamed again about finding Azmina's body. Only this time, the killer was still in the bookstore."

He frowned. "Who was the killer?"

"I don't know." I shut my eyes, trying to salvage the images that had haunted my sleep. "I couldn't see his face. It kept changing: José Garcia, Nick Norton, that horrible Officer Friendly…"

Barry patted my hand. "The police will find the murderer. Let's talk about something else."

If only the police wouldn't ignore so many clues… "I could get used to coffee in bed." I smiled. "Thanks."

"I fed your cat. He kept weaving around my legs and trying to trip me while I was in the kitchen, so I figured he must be hungry."

As if on cue, Manny hopped onto the bed. Purring loudly, he made a circle and settled at our feet.

We spent a leisurely Saturday morning drinking coffee in bed, reading, and snuggling. Our conversation avoided Victoria, Jane, Azmina's murder, and anything to do with the office.

When we finally got up, Barry and I set to work on the ordinance changes. Manny watched us from the top shelf of my floor-to-ceiling bookcase.

Over the past week, I'd printed out sample verbiage from ordinances in other locales that had successfully implemented Trap-Neuter-Vaccinate-Return. Some documents spelled out many details and requirements, whereas others left the language vague, which I preferred. Not only would the latter require fewer changes to the wording of Pecan County's existing law, it would appear less intimidating to the commissioners.

While Barry marked up my draft, I compiled statistics and created a PowerPoint presentation showing how much money Pecan County could save by not capturing, housing, and ultimately killing unadoptable cats. Although I was encouraged by the number of feline lives TNVR programs across the country had saved, the resulting decline in cat intake and shelter deaths could be translated into cost savings for the county, which was what the commissioners cared about.

Late Saturday afternoon, I called Catherine and asked if we could come over. I couldn't wait to show her our mostly finished document, although she'd probably feign disinterest. Either that or she'd pick it apart.

After greeting us at the door, she thrust a letter in Barry's face. "What am I supposed to do about this?"

I recognized the cease-and-desist order Nick Norton had sent by courier while she was in jail—the one I had signed for and then peeked at. We both watched Barry read it, his lips moving slightly.

"Glad to see you out of jail," I said to Catherine.

"Smelled like a filthy litter box," she replied. "Couldn't sleep on that hard cot, and every meal tasted like cat food."

I didn't ask if she'd ever eaten cat food. "I'd want to sue someone. They had no right to hold you so long."

"It's Pecan Point." Her apathy surprised me.

Barry finished reading Nick's document and pushed his glasses up his nose. "Don't build cat shelters in the reserve. You can put them on your own property, or somewhere you have permission."

Catherine puffed out her lower lip. "I'll be glad when D.D. gets that new ordinance written."

"Here it is." I beamed, handing it to her.

"You're kidding. You rewrote the county's animal ordinance? Already?" Catherine squinted at Barry. "Does she even know what she's doing?"

Barry put a hand on my shoulder. "DeeLo has done a lot of research. I think you'll be impressed. But," he warned, "even if this ordinance passes, it doesn't supersede the laws against trespassing."

Catherine huffed. "It's public land."

"It's owned by the Pecan Creek Nature Foundation," said Barry. "They can restrict who goes on that property and make rules about what happens there."

With a harrumph, Catherine led us into her dining room. We sat down, and I drummed my fingers on the table while she perused our documents. Her long-haired white cat rubbed against my leg. I reached down and stroked its head.

Catherine looked up from her reading. "I can't believe Snowball lets you touch her. I'm usually the only one she'll come to."

"You were gone for a couple of days." I scratched Snowball's chin to prove she liked me. "The princess had to be nice to me if she wanted to eat."

Catherine went back to reading. "I see you didn't get rid of that stupid leash law for cats."

"One thing at a time," I explained. "We studied ordinances from cities and counties that have leash laws, as well as those that don't. While I agree it's stupid, we found some ordinances that allow TNR and still require owned pets to be restrained."

Barry chimed in, "We've added a definition for 'community cat' and exempted those cats and their caretakers from the leash law."

"Lots of people believe all cats should live indoors," I said. "Trying to get rid of the leash law might derail the whole proposal."

Barry nodded. "And the goal is to make TNVR legal, which you can do without tampering with any other hot-button issues."

Catherine finished reading, then stacked the papers neatly. "Good job. What's next?"

"Round up support." My excitement grew. "I know you hate the idea, but we need to explain to Nick Norton what we're trying to do." Ignoring Catherine's scowl as she fingered the foundation director's cease-and-desist letter, I continued, "Cats already live in the reserve. An ordinance isn't going to change that. But if he allows us on the property to trap them and get them fixed, their population will eventually dwindle, and they'll kill fewer birds."

"Yeah, good luck with that. Talking to Nick can be your job."

I'd expected her to say that.

Barry looked at me. "Are you okay with talking to him, DeeLo?"

I felt a chill. Nick might be Azmina's killer. I couldn't forget those text messages sent right before she died. But no one else seemed to take them seriously. "If you'll go with me, Barry."

"Sure."

I turned to Catherine. "Will the Pecan Point Humane Society speak in favor of these changes at the BOC meeting?"

"I'm not getting up in front of those Neanderthals." Catherine leaned back in her chair.

You're not the best spokesperson anyway. "Who then?"

"Deb Holt has been the president for years. The Humane Society's official position should come from her."

"Can I have her number?" I reached into my purse and grabbed my phone.

"She's coming over in a few minutes, so you can ask her when she gets here. A group of Girl Scouts held a food drive for us today at PetSmart, and we'll store the donations in my basement."

While we waited for Deb, I told Catherine about meeting Azmina's sister, and how she'd given me Manny.

"He's a great cat. I'm glad you're keeping him." Catherine snapped her fingers. "Hey, whatever happened with the nursing home? You said you were going to take him there as a therapy cat like Azmina used to do."

"Oh." I looked at my lap. I still hadn't told Barry about my botched attempt at being a therapy cat handler. I'd been trying to erase the whole fiasco from my memory, convince myself it never happened. "It didn't work out so well."

The doorbell rang, and Catherine rose to answer, sparing me from relating my tale.

At the door stood a tall, fortyish Black woman with oversized glasses and hair pulled into a tight bun like a librarian. Catherine didn't bother to introduce us. Perhaps Deb and Barry already knew each other. And Deb had met me once, although I doubted she remembered.

"Need help bringing in the donations?" Barry asked.

"That would be great," said Deb. "Thank you."

We all filed out to Deb's shiny black SUV and schlepped bags of pet food and cat litter into Catherine's house. As we descended the stairs to her basement, I wondered how Octomom and her kittens were doing. I knew better than to open the door to check on them; no way would I give the wily mother cat another chance to escape.

When we'd finished unloading and organizing the items in storage, we climbed back upstairs. Catherine showed Deb my document, which still lay on the dining-room table.

Deb skimmed over it. "Cat, this is exactly what you've wanted. If this revision passes, that cop won't be able to harass you anymore."

I basked in the warmth of her compliment. "Will you speak in favor of these changes when we present this proposal to the Board of Commissioners?"

Deb turned to me, vague recognition in her eyes as if she hadn't realized until now that I could speak. "Who are you again?"

"DeeLo's my helper," Catherine answered for me. "She's the one who wrote this. With the help of my lawyer." She tilted her head at Barry.

Deb studied me again. "Oh yeah. Community service." Not quite a sneer, but almost.

"You spoke at my volunteer orientation meeting," I reminded her. "Delores Myer. DeeLo."

"Thank you, DeeLo." Deb studied the document again. "This is good. But you know, working on this ordinance doesn't count toward your community service hours. The Pecan Point Humane Society's mission isn't to change legislation. Our focus is rescuing homeless animals and promoting spay/neuter. Trapping cats with Catherine and taking them to the clinic counts, but that's all we can authorize."

"I wouldn't dream of putting all those hours on my timesheet." I hadn't been tracking the time I'd spent working on the ordinance anyway. "But will you come to the Board of Commissioners meeting when we present this proposal and tell them the Humane Society is in favor of it? Assuming you are. I mean, it seems like you are."

Deb nodded. "I can do that." Her eyes swept my face with maybe a spark of respect. "And I'll spread the word among the volunteers that we'd like them there as well. Thank you for taking the initiative, DeeLo. Please keep us apprised of your progress with the commissioners and let us know when we can expect to see this proposal on the agenda."

After Deb left, I told Catherine about the unaltered cats I'd seen at Leonardo's. She said she'd contact the manager; she'd trapped cats for him before. "Are you going to help me? You haven't completed your hours yet."

Barry and I exchanged glances. He stifled a chuckle.

I told her about my trapping adventure with Lisa Ross and plans for a re-do Sunday night.

"No," said Catherine.

"No, what? I haven't asked you anything yet."

"I won't help. Lisa and I don't get along."

"What a surprise," murmured Barry.

"I didn't ask you to help," I said. "Lisa doesn't want you there."

"Oh." Catherine put her hand on her hip. "What then?"

"Can I borrow some of your traps? Unless you're going to use them at Leonardo's tomorrow night."

Catherine heaved a put-out sigh, but I could tell she was secretly pleased. She ended up being quite accommodating, helping Barry and me load traps and dividers into my car, and even offering a few tips I hadn't learned yet. "Do you have bait for the traps?" she asked.

"Believe it or not, Lisa's cats only eat Meow Mix." I waited for her to be amazed.

She shrugged, with maybe a hint of derision toward Lisa's choice of cat food. "Cats all have different preferences. Whatever works."

As Barry and I climbed into my car, Catherine wished me success. "You'll need it with that backstabber."

I didn't ask what she meant by "backstabber." I had to consider the source. "Look, if we catch those cats and Lisa becomes a believer in TNVR, she'll be a valuable ally when we go before the BOC."

"How so?"

"Not only is she married to a Pecan Point cop, but she works with Vince Connors, one of the county commissioners. If she likes our proposal, maybe she'll influence Vince."

"Vince Connors? No way he'll support a TNR ordinance."

"But he was one of the two commissioners who voted in favor of a spay and neuter policy at Animal Control." I'd been counting on Vince lining up with Roy Don to support our ordinance change.

"Different species," said Catherine. "When those guys claim they're in favor of laws to protect animals, they're thinking about pet dogs, not free-roaming cats."

I flashed back to our encounter at the memory care facility. Manny had gone berserk as soon as Victoria walked into the room; Vince had been afraid for his elderly father's safety. "All the more reason we need Lisa on our side."

Catherine shook her head. "DeeLo, you're something else!"

Barry patted my knee. "She certainly is."

I covered his hand with mine before starting my vehicle's engine. I couldn't help smiling. Catherine had called me "DeeLo" again.

Chapter Twenty-One

When I arrived at the Ross residence Sunday night, I had a good feeling about my second trapping exploit with Lisa. Catherine's traps were familiar to me, and the Meow Mix was easier to use as bait than the slippery, smelly mackerel that Lisa's cats didn't like anyway. I demonstrated the first set-up and then let Lisa know she'd be doing the rest. Playing the teacher, I hoped I didn't sound as bossy and condescending as Catherine.

Lisa's injured arm was bandaged but did not appear to restrict her motion. She was a good student this time, as I liked to think I was when Catherine taught me.

On her first try at set-up, Lisa set the food too close to the door.

I cleared my throat.

"No?" She sucked her lip in thought.

"You want the cat to go all the way inside to get the food, so when he steps on the trip plate, he won't get caught in the door."

"Oh." She moved the food to the correct spot.

"Good job," I complimented her. I handed her a ribbon to tie to the entrance door. "When we're waiting on the porch, this ribbon will help us see whether the door's down."

We set four traps as she only knew of four cats living on her property. I'd brought an extra in case one malfunctioned, and Catherine insisted I bring along transfer cages and dividers. I'd never tried to move a cat from a trap to a transfer cage, and I hoped not to have to do it for the first time in front of Lisa. We didn't need another injury.

"They're hungry, right?" I confirmed as we finished setting the last trap.

"I remembered not to feed them last night," she assured me. "It broke my heart, though. They kept eyeing us until we went inside, and I heard one of them howling later. I know they felt betrayed."

"No breakfast, either?"

She nodded. "I'm trying to do this right."

Like the last time, we settled on her patio to wait for the sound of metallic doors closing. The aroma of woodsmoke in the autumn air made me think it would soon be cool enough to build a fire in my fireplace. I imagined snuggling in front of it with Barry at my side and Manny on my lap.

Lisa brought out a pitcher of iced tea and two tall glasses. She poured. "You like sweet tea?"

I preferred my tea without sugar, and the "sweet tea" most Georgians served tasted more like tea-flavored syrup. I took a small swallow and nodded politely.

She sipped her tea and then ventured, "You were asking a lot of questions the other day about Azmina Patel. Did you know her well?"

"Not well. I've shopped in her store a few times to buy tea as well as books. She always offered good reading recommendations." I set down my glass. "I don't know if your husband told you this, but Catherine Foster and I found the body."

Lisa's head jerked.

"We were behind the bookstore last Sunday night, trapping some of the cats Azmina fed. It was such a shock to see her lying there like that..." I squeezed my eyes shut, as if I could ever block the image from my mind.

"How did you find her? I mean, why did you go into the bookstore?"

"Her cat was loose, and the door was open."

"Oh. Her cat." Lisa rubbed the condensation on her glass. "It must have been awful. Was she—?"

I turned the conversation back to her. "It must have been creepy for you to find out the next morning that Azmina had been killed. Especially after you'd just seen her, not long before she died."

Lisa gulped some tea.

"Did you see anyone else go in there?"

"No."

"What are the other tenants saying? Any idea who might have killed her?"

Lisa shook her head.

"Not even a guess? Everyone I talk to seems to have an opinion." Well, mainly Sandra. Catherine and Barry always changed the subject.

With a shrug, Lisa stared out at the darkening woods beyond the patio.

"You know José Garcia was arrested?" I ventured.

She nodded. "I heard it from Natalie Wojcik before my husband had a chance to tell me. Gossip travels fast in this town." She swirled the ice cubes around in her glass. "José hasn't been charged with Azmina's murder, though. He was arrested for beating up his wife. She'll cool off and drop the charges, and then they'll let him go, as usual."

"Do they fight often? To the point of violence?"

"It's happened several times," Lisa replied.

"Do you think José could have killed Azmina?"

She shrugged. "People can surprise you sometimes. He—"

A clatter of metal against metal interrupted our conversation, and I noticed one of the ribbons lay on the ground. By the time we raced to the traps with towels, a second cat had been caught.

"Oh… I'm sorry, kitty," Lisa whimpered as she tried to cover the trap containing a thrashing blur of ginger fur. The cat calmed down as soon as the towel blocked its view of escape.

I gazed at the other caged feline. "I thought you said all your cats were orange tabbies."

"They are."

"Where did this big tuxedo boy come from then?"

Lisa clasped a hand over her mouth and looked at me in alarm.

"Do your neighbors let their cat roam? If so, they shouldn't be surprised if he comes home with a tipped ear." I stole a glance at the tomcat. No ear tip, definitely intact.

"Can we do that?" she asked. "What if they object?"

I'd assumed I'd be doing the pet owners a favor by having their cat neutered. Neutering, and a rabies vaccination, would keep him healthier and safer, especially if they were going to let him wander outside. But some people had different ideas about what could be done with their "property." I remembered the comments Randall Sparks had made at the Board of Commissioners meeting. I turned to Lisa. "Why don't you ask around the neighborhood? See if this cat belongs to anyone."

She stared at the cat and then shook her head. "He doesn't look familiar. Doesn't belong to anyone around here. Someone probably dumped him, just like they did with Memaw cat."

"I'll have him checked for a microchip," I decided. "He doesn't have a collar, and you don't recognize him. If he doesn't have an owner, we're getting him neutered."

We lugged the traps to Lisa's garage, where I'd told her they'd need to remain overnight. "I gave you directions to the clinic, didn't I?"

Lisa nodded. "The LifeSaver. College Park."

"And the cats have to be there before eight."

"I'm an early riser."

I set down the trap containing the tuxedo cat, Lisa's unexpected guest. I looked around the two-car garage. "Do you and your husband have another vehicle?" I gestured toward the Smart Car parked on one side. The two-seater didn't even have a trunk.

"Paul has the pick-up truck he drives to work."

I made some quick measurements with my eyes. "These traps won't fit into your little car. Especially if we catch more cats tonight."

Lisa shrugged. "We'll manage."

I eyed the Smart Car. *No way.* The pick-up might work better, but would the cats be safe? Would Detective Ross even let his wife use his truck? She probably couldn't see over the dashboard.

I had a feeling I'd be making another trek to the LifeSaver in the morning. My Lexus still smelled like Big Mack.

By the time we walked back to the patio, another orange tabby thrashed in a surprise prison. I grabbed a towel, hurried to cover the trap, and then, together, we carried it to the garage and lined it up next to the others.

"How are you going to get to the clinic?" I asked Lisa.

She gulped, as if just now calculating the size of the traps.

"We have three so far. What if we catch another cat?"

She held out her hands, palms up in surrender.

I sighed. "What about your husband's truck?"

Her scrunched face told me the pick-up wasn't an option.

Lesson learned: Have a plan for transport.

While we pondered the dilemma of conveying the cats to the clinic, headlights appeared in the driveway. I shielded my eyes as the vehicle approached.

The engine shut down, but Detective Paul Ross remained in the driver's seat, his head bent.

Lisa rushed toward him. The driver's side door swung open.

"Honey, we caught three cats tonight—and one of them I've never seen before," she chattered as her husband slowly emerged from the vehicle. "Can you help us get them to the animal clinic tomorrow?"

He looked at her with bloodshot eyes and waved a limp hand. "Let DeeLo take them."

Lisa and I exchanged glances. I'd been expecting this.

Detective Ross started into the house. Lisa caught his sleeve and stopped him. "Paul, something's wrong. What is it?"

He sighed and answered as if I weren't standing there, listening to every word. "José Garcia committed suicide in his cell."

Chapter Twenty-Two

After Detective Ross delivered his shocking news about José's death, all thoughts of trapping vanished. No use arguing about transport arrangements, so I collected the traps—with and without cats—and showed myself out.

I rose early Monday morning for my trek to the LifeSaver clinic, with Lisa's two orange tabbies and the tuxedo tomcat Lisa had claimed was a stray.

On my drive to the clinic, questions ran through my head like scrolling headlines at the bottom of a television newscast. Was José's death truly suicide? How did it happen? I didn't know the man well, but he'd never struck me as depressed. However, many people hid their feelings of desperation, even from those closest to them.

I certainly hadn't imagined him as a wife batterer either. The family all worked together in the restaurant, appearing to get along as well as most families.

Being suspected of murder could add enough stress to send him over the edge. Was I complicit? After all, I'd confronted him in his restaurant the day after Azmina's murder and started the rumor mill. His daughter had called me out on that, making me question whether I was really a nice person.

Had José strangled Azmina and then decided he couldn't live with the guilt? That would be the obvious, convenient conclusion, which would enable the police to wrap up the murder investigation with a nice, neat bow and put the whole sordid chapter in Pecan Point's history behind us. But if José didn't do it, the real killer was still out there, with no one looking for him or her anymore.

If José's death wasn't suicide, then who would kill him? And how? He should have been safe in a jail cell. Perhaps his demise was an inside job. The duplicitous, evidence-tampering Officer Friendly? But what would be his motive? Did José know too much about Azmina's murder?

Detective Ross hadn't shared any details with us last night—or at least, not while I was around. His demeanor had signaled he wanted me gone, and I'd complied. Maybe Lisa would spill this evening when I returned the cats. Or maybe Jill knew something. I'd texted her last night, but she had not yet responded.

There wasn't much information on the radio. One brief statement about the death—an apparent suicide, but no specifics about the cause—and then the reporter moved on to the next story. I'd thought a murder investigation and the suspicious demise of one of the main suspects would have been bigger news, but a triple homicide and arson in Atlanta last night edged out the happenings in sleepy Pecan Point.

I arrived at the LifeSaver with plenty of time to spare. It helped that I knew where I was going this time.

The tiny lobby teemed with a line of pet owners checking in animals. The man with a long face holding the leash of a Collie mix reminded me how dogs and their owners sometimes resembled each other. There were people in business attire on the way to offices, people in casual clothes acting like they had nothing else to do today, and one woman in a robe and bedroom slippers. She hadn't bothered to put on make-up or even completely remove whatever cream she'd slathered on her face the night before.

The same vet tech who'd helped me last week worked at the counter, but she showed no sign of recognizing me. Just as well. I had no desire to stand out of the crowd, especially if labeled as a high-maintenance customer. "Next," she said when it was my turn.

"Reservation for Ross. Four ferals, but we only caught three."

"That's fine." She handed me the paperwork to fill out. Her long nails were painted fuchsia today. "How are you paying?"

I'd intended for Lisa to take the cats to the clinic, and then she'd have been the one to pay for their surgeries. I supposed she'd reimburse me, but the conversation might be awkward since I was doing the job as community service. "Do you accept Master Card?"

The receptionist nodded and held out her hand for my credit card. She ran it through her machine, and it churned out a slip, which she handed me to sign. I glanced at the total. Not a bad price for getting three cats sterilized and vaccinated against rabies and distemper. The last time I'd owned a pet, I'd spent more than that on one cat for an annual check-up at a regular veterinarian's office.

"Oh… can you check the tuxedo cat for a microchip?" I didn't think someone would microchip a cat and not get him neutered too, but one never knows.

"Certainly." She wrote something on the admission form. "Need help bringing in the traps?"

"Please."

A different intern followed me out to my car to help retrieve the cats. "Four o'clock," he reminded me, flashing a broad smile.

I supposed I'd be the one to pick them up since Lisa didn't have a suitable vehicle for transport. "Got it." It was good to have an understanding boss who thought he was in love with me.

* * *

I'd emailed my draft of the animal ordinance to Sandra Larson at Animal Control on Sunday but decided to call her when I reached my office to make sure she'd seen it.

"Reading it now." It sounded like she'd just flipped a page. "Looks good, but I have a few questions."

"Want to get together for lunch and talk about it?" I'd planned to give Sandra until the end of the day, but now I'd be spending my afternoon and early evening picking up cats from the clinic and delivering them to Lisa Ross, thanks to Lisa's conveniently tiny automobile.

"Can you come here?" Sandra asked. "I have a lot going on today."

"Sure. Want me to pick up some food? We can eat while we go over the document."

"How about Mexican?"

Was she in the mood for Mexican food, or did she not know about José? "I'm not sure José's will be open."

She paused. "Why not? Are they closed on Mondays?"

"Not usually… You didn't hear the news yet?"

"What?"

"José was arrested last Wednesday—domestic violence. And then yesterday, he killed himself in his jail cell."

Sandra gasped. "I told you he was Azmina's murderer. The guilt must have eaten him up."

"We still don't know—"

It sounded like Sandra put her hand over the phone, muffling a conversation with someone who'd entered her office. In a moment, she came back on the line. "Taco Bell is fine. Twelve-thirty?"

I agreed and hung up.

My inbox was empty, and I had caught up with all my digitizing. Guilt at being paid well for doing nothing nagged at my conscience. I rose and strolled over to Jane's desk.

She ignored me, although I could tell she knew I was standing there.

"Jane," I began sweetly, "Do you have any more files ready for me to scan into the database?"

She kept typing, eyes on the keyboard.

I pointed to one of the cardboard boxes next to her desk. "What about that one? Can I take those files yet?"

She looked up, her gray eyes cold. "I'll let you know when they're ready." With a grunt, she went back to typing, most likely still steamed because Barry had taken my side in our dispute over sharing files with Victoria.

* * *

The rest of the morning, I worked on enhancements to the firm's website and then did some modules for my online paralegal training course. At noon, I stuck my head into Barry's office to let him know about my lunch arrangements with Sandra.

"Good idea," he said. "It's important to get her buy-in for the ordinance changes you're proposing."

"That's the plan." I leaned against the doorjamb. "Can I bring you anything?"

"No thanks. I'll probably go out, too."

"Maybe you should invite Jane." I smiled.

He adjusted his glasses. "Why?"

"It might improve her mood."

Before he could ask me to elaborate, I was out the door. Though I'd wanted to plead with him to make Jane stop being so difficult, I didn't have time to outline the problem without sounding petty. And it was my fight anyway.

I swung by José's on my way to Animal Control. As I'd suspected, the restaurant was closed. Several would-be customers milled about on the sidewalk, peering in the windows, and shrugging at each other. I thought about stopping to tell them what was going on, but what would I say? Jill had not yet answered my text.

The line at Taco Bell's drive-thru moved quickly, and I arrived in Sandra's office, paper sacks of food in hand, at exactly twelve-thirty.

She pored over a printed copy of my document while I set our lunch on her desk.

"Want a water?" She looked up and pointed to a mini refrigerator in the corner.

I took out two bottles, handed her one, and made myself comfortable in the chair facing her. "What do you think?" I twisted the cap off my water bottle and drank.

We discussed the ordinance change as we ate. Sandra liked that I'd left in the leash law and that I hadn't tinkered with the maximum number of pets an owner was allowed to keep. Though she rarely had to enforce those sections, she explained that having the language in the ordinance gave her ammunition against negligent pet owners and hoarders.

"How's the part about TNVR?" I asked.

"Good. Very close to what we had in Wisconsin. I made a couple of changes regarding the role of Animal Control." She slid the pages across the desk so I could see her notes. "I'm glad you didn't add a Citizens' Advisory Committee. Roy Don Whitehead tried to pull that with my spay and neuter proposal."

"A Citizens' Advisory Committee?"

"Some meddlesome group, with one of the commissioners overseeing it. I said no way."

"Nothing like that in this proposal." I studied her changes. "I think we can live with this."

"Go ahead and keep that copy," she said.

"Once we get this proposal on the agenda, will you come to the Board of Commissioners meeting and voice your support?"

"Sure."

"I'd also like to invite you to a preliminary meeting with Roy Don Whitehead and whoever else he can persuade to sponsor this ordinance change."

"Commissioner Vince Connors is sympathetic to animal causes," she suggested. "He worked with me and Roy Don on the spay/neuter proposal for Animal Control. He's a smart man, very thorough. He'll make sure you have an answer for every question that could possibly come up."

"I remember. Theirs were the only two 'yes' votes. But would Commissioner Connors support a proposal that mainly benefits cats?" Vince Connors hadn't been happy when Manny went berserk around his father at the nursing home.

Sandra shrugged. "I don't see why not."

I wadded up the wrapper from my taco. "I still think we can pass your spay/neuter proposal eventually if we convince the budget guy—what's his name, Phillip Gates?—that it will save the county money."

"And how are we going to do that?"

"Accountants like numbers. Show the cost of staff hours spent on compliance. Let him know you'll use low-cost clinics like LifeSaver. They might even work out a volume discount with you." I showed her my receipt for Lisa's cats. "This was for three community cats—surgery, rabies vaccination, and distemper shot."

Sandra glanced at my receipt. "That's cheap."

"Look, I'm good at creating PowerPoints and spinning statistics. Help me get TNVR passed, and I'll help you pass Shelter Spay/Neuter."

Sandra chuckled. "What's in it for you?"

I rested my chin in my hand. "Watching Catherine Foster get arrested for releasing a cat she'd unintentionally trapped made me realize what a stupid law this county has on the books. Seemed like an easy thing to change."

"And now you realize it's not so easy after all."

"We'll get there." I took another sip of water. "With your help."

She held up her water bottle as if to toast. "You've got it."

"Good. The Humane Society is on board, too. My plan is to talk to all the stakeholders and address their concerns before we present our proposal. The meeting I'm most dreading is with Nick Norton, with the Pecan Creek Nature Reserve." I grimaced, thinking about Nick's letter to Catherine. "He's not a fan of feral cats."

"DeeLo, I have no doubt you'll be able to persuade him. Just say it's what Azmina would have wanted."

"Unless Nick killed her." I couldn't stop wondering about those text messages.

"What is it with you?" Sandra ran her fingers through her spiked red hair. "José's the murderer. His suicide was practically an admission of guilt."

"What if he didn't do it? What if the killer's still out there?" I leaned forward. "Maybe José's death wasn't even suicide."

She creased her brow. "He was in jail. Who would get to him? No, suicide fits."

"What do you mean?"

"He was on the anti-psychotic drug Clozapine, used to treat schizophrenia. It also helps prevent suicide." She tossed her wrappings into the trash can beside her desk. "He probably missed a few doses while he was locked up."

162

"If he was taking a critical drug like that, wouldn't he tell the police? Wouldn't they make sure he kept taking it while he was in custody?"

Sandra shrugged.

"How do you know what drugs he was taking?" I continued. Sandra had been determined to label José as Azmina's killer since we first started speculating about the case.

"Remember I told you how José tried to poison those cats Azmina was feeding?"

I nodded.

"He denied guilt when I came out to investigate the complaint. Claimed he didn't know how the poisoned meat got there. Said it must have been one of the other store owners in the strip mall, or maybe even a customer. Except I found a bottle of prescription tablets at the scene, with his name on it."

"Clozapine?"

"Bingo." She flashed a conspiratorial grin. "I agreed not to press charges if he'd give me his word to never harm those cats again."

"Did he admit he dropped his pills while trying to poison the cats?" I asked. "He could have said he dropped the bottle another time. Or that someone planted them to make him look guilty."

"He's not a good liar." She smiled. "And the prescription had been filled that day, so the window when he could have dropped them was narrow. I reminded him animal cruelty is a felony."

"But so is murder."

She frowned. "I sure didn't think he'd resort to that."

I still wasn't convinced he had.

Chapter Twenty-Three

When I returned to the office, Jane was gone, and Barry sat at his desk munching a pungent pastrami sandwich. So much for my suggestion that he take his receptionist to lunch.

I poked my head in his doorway. "No lunch date with Jane?"

He looked up. "She had plans." He set down his sandwich. "Do you want to tell me why you suggested I invite Jane to lunch?"

I sighed. "Can we have a team meeting in the morning? I don't think Jane understands the benefit of having our files stored electronically on a server where we can all access them easily. Not to mention the security."

"Have you tried explaining it to her?"

Explain it to her? He had to be kidding. "How have you been able to get by all these years with her filing system?" I gestured toward the stacks of cardboard boxes alongside Jane's desk. "Originals are only housed on her computer, not on the server. Copies of important documents are in unlabeled boxes in no logical order...what if there's a fire?" And one of our documents ended up at a crime scene. How did that happen?

He shrugged. I could tell it didn't matter to him how much of Jane's time and energy was wasted as long as she could retrieve what he needed. And it was easier for him to endure the chaos than to confront Jane and suggest she change her habits. His father had hired her before Barry became a partner, and until recently, she'd worked mostly with Victoria.

"I know she resents me, and I haven't made things easy for her." I pointed to myself. "But if this project is going to be successful, we have to function as a team. That's not happening now."

He nodded. "Okay."

I sensed resolving staff conflicts was not high on his to-do list. "By the way, I have to leave early to pick up Lisa's cats at the LifeSaver." I turned to retreat to my cubicle. "I'm all caught up, and Jane doesn't have anything more for me to archive today. I offered to help go through those boxes, but she said there's nothing I can do."

Barry picked up his sandwich again. "I'll talk to her."

* * *

The lobby of the LifeSaver bustled as much at four p.m. as it had that morning. Twice as many interns disappeared into the back room, emerged with pet carriers or leashed dogs, handed them over to customers, and then headed back for the next animal. Many of the same pet owners from the drop-off crowd waited for pick-up, chatting among themselves or checking their smartphones. I didn't see the woman who'd worn the bathrobe, but perhaps I wouldn't have recognized her without curlers.

When it was my turn, the desk clerk presented me with Lisa's cats' paperwork, which I perused while the intern fetched the animals. According to the surgical form, the two orange tabbies were both females. From the age estimates, they must be mother and daughter. Both had been in heat. That explained why the tuxedo tomcat—who did not have a microchip—had shown up on the property. Now they were all out of commission, and I congratulated myself on how many kitten births we had prevented.

I opened the hatchback of my Lexus for the two interns to load the traps. I peered into the cages to verify I was getting the right animals back. One of the orange tabbies could hardly hold up her head. "Is she okay?" I asked the intern who'd helped me that morning.

He eyed the limp cat. "She might have been one of the last surgeries. The anesthesia hasn't worn off yet." Before I could respond, he closed the hatch and headed back inside.

Prior to driving out of the parking lot, I phoned Catherine and described the condition of the kitten.

"He's probably right, but tell Lisa to keep those cats in her garage overnight," she instructed. "Give them time to heal a little and recover from the anesthesia before she puts them back outside. The females will need more time than the males, especially if they were pregnant or in heat. Sometimes, I mix pain medication into their food, if I can get them to eat."

"I didn't think to ask for any." As common as it was, spay was major surgery. "You don't need your traps back right away?"

"Not for a few days. Did you catch all the cats?"

I recounted our trapping experience—our surprise addition to the clan, our luck at capturing the two females in heat, and how the evening was cut short when Detective Ross came home and told us about José Garcia's death.

Catherine's breath caught. "What? José's dead?"

"They think it was suicide."

She whistled. "How did he do it?"

"I don't know. Had you already been released when they brought José in? Wednesday night, wasn't it?"

"I saw him as I was leaving. He didn't have anything good to say to me."

"How did he seem?"

"How does anyone seem when they get locked up?"

I closed my eyes, remembering my arrest. At least I didn't spend the night in jail, but it was bad enough hearing that heavy steel door slam shut behind me.

"Well," said Catherine. "The cats will be safer without him."

* * *

When I knocked, I expected Lisa to answer. Instead, Detective Paul Ross crossed in front of the picture window and walked toward the entryway. I considered turning around and leaving, but he'd already seen me.

He opened the door. "She usually gets home around six," he advised when I asked for his wife.

I consulted my watch. Five-thirty. Would he let me hang around that long? Did I want to? "I have the cats we caught last night." *Duh.* Stating the obvious. "I just came from the clinic."

He craned his neck to see past me. "Are they in your car?"

"They're still recovering from the anesthesia. Lisa needs to keep them in the garage overnight." I shuffled my feet on the wooden porch. "Can I go ahead and bring them in? Set up a place in your garage?"

"Let me help you." He stepped onto the veranda beside me.

Grateful for a task to occupy the time until Lisa returned, I stumbled into one of the rocking chairs before bolting down the porch steps en route to my SUV.

Raising the hatchback, I took a step back and almost bumped into him. A pleasant scent of fading aftershave mixed with masculine perspiration hung in the surrounding air. We both reached for the same trap simultaneously. Our fingers touched and instantly recoiled as if shocked by static electricity.

I smiled to mask my discomfort. "Grab that one, and I'll get this one over here."

He tried to pick up two but quickly assessed how bulky they were. One of us would have to make another trip for the third cat.

Straining to keep the traps level, we lugged them to the garage. "Careful," I admonished. "Let's not jostle the poor kitties after all they've been through today."

"They can spend the night in these contraptions?" the detective asked.

"They should be fine," I assured him, quoting Catherine. "It's better than letting them loose outside while they're recovering from the anesthesia. Confined in these cages, they won't be able to injure themselves." As I spoke, I thought about José, confined in a jail cell. And now dead.

Inside the garage, we selected a clear area where we could set down the traps. I peered at the cat who'd been listless at the clinic. She still appeared groggy, but less so. I adjusted the towels to cover the cages. "One more," I said unnecessarily.

"Lisa appreciates this," he said, as we headed back to my car.

"I'm happy to help." As if I had a choice. "There are still two more cats to go. Not sure when she wants to try to trap those."

He shrugged. Apparently, they hadn't discussed cat-trapping plans.

"I borrowed the equipment from Catherine Foster, so I don't want to keep it too long."

Detective Ross lifted the third cat from my trunk, and I closed the hatchback. The towel slipped to the ground on our way back to the garage. I picked it up and trotted after him, anxious to cover the trap before the cat got too freaked out.

With the cats settled, we both looked at our watches in a synchronized movement. It was only ten until six.

"She should be home soon," he said. "Want to come in the house while you wait?"

"Let me get the cats' paperwork before I forget."

He headed inside. I retrieved my folder of vet records and the LifeSaver receipt from the front seat of my car.

Stalling, I checked my phone. No urgent messages required my attention.

I composed a text to Lisa, "I'm at your house with the cats." I started to add, "Your husband helped me unload them," then backspaced to erase that line. Instead, I typed, "Please keep them in the garage overnight," and pressed Send.

"On my way," came her reply.

Knowing it would be rude to leave now, I headed back up the steps to the front porch.

Although the inner door stood open, I knocked on the screen door.

"It's unlocked," called Detective Ross. "Come on in."

The aroma of a spicy chicken dish simmering in a crockpot filled my nostrils. I almost tripped over a plastic toy truck as I navigated through the dimly lit living room toward the bright glow of the kitchen.

On a wooden end table beside a leather recliner sat a familiar-looking folder. Tiptoeing closer, I recognized Azmina's file from Barton and Barton. With a furtive glance around the room, I reached for it.

"DeeLo?" Detective Ross's voice interrupted the drumbeat of my heart. "In the kitchen."

I gave the file a lingering look, then changed course and continued toward the voice in the kitchen.

Detective Ross stood in front of the open refrigerator. "Something to drink?" His hand touched a bottle of beer.

Was this a trick? Offer me a beer and then sic Officer Friendly on me as soon as I got in my car to drive home? "How about some water?" I wondered if I was being paranoid as I seated myself on a stool at the breakfast bar that divided the kitchen from the family room.

Clutching a beer and a water he closed the refrigerator door and took the seat across from me, on the kitchen side. He handed me the water.

He held up his beer in a toast. "To getting those cats fixed." The fluorescent light overhead picked up the emerald green of his eyes.

He's married, I reminded myself. And I knew his wife—a real person with feelings, almost a friend. We touched bottles. "Two more cats to go."

"Thought you did three today," he said. "There should be only one left."

"The black-and-white cat is a newcomer," I explained. "Lisa thinks he's a stray."

He raised his eyebrows. "Our property is now a dumping ground for unwanted animals? Or is my wife attracting all the strays in the neighborhood?"

I shrugged. "Your two females were in heat."

"In heat?"

"Ready to get pregnant," I explained, realizing too late that maybe he wasn't asking for a definition. "The urge to breed is powerful in cats."

"I thought they only did that in the spring? Kitten season, I've always heard." He scratched his chin.

"Here in the South, since we have such mild winters, cats breed all year." I set my plastic bottle down on the Corian countertop.

He looked up at the ceiling. "Oh, great."

"Fortunately, we got them in time." I traced a line of condensation on the bottle. It felt awkward talking about sex with him, even if it only related to cats. "So, is your case wrapped up now?"

"Case?" He narrowed his eyes.

"Azmina Patel's murder." My voice broke. "By the way, did you ever locate that document she was holding when Catherine and I found her?"

"No one remembers seeing it."

"Except me." I wondered what yarn Officer Friendly had spun. Or if Detective Ross had even questioned him about the missing paper.

The detective's eyes met mine. "Why would you think the case is wrapped up?"

"Well, with José Garcia's suicide…"

"We're still investigating."

"You mean, maybe José's death wasn't suicide?"

The detective gazed at the countertop. "It was most likely suicide."

"How did he do it?" I'd blurted out the question before I had time to plan a more diplomatic approach.

Again, that look—right through me, as if I was the most obtrusive person he'd ever met.

"Is it confidential? Information you can't release to the public?"

"No, that's a fair question," he conceded. "José hung himself in his cell with the bedsheet."

"How awful!" I covered my mouth with my hand. "But how—?"

"Desperation finds a way."

"His wife…"

"She's devastated. Blames herself."

"How awful," I reiterated.

"José didn't have an alibi for Azmina Patel's murder," the detective continued. "You saw someone leaving around the time you found the body, which fits with what Mr. Garcia told us. But it doesn't prove José had been inside the restaurant all afternoon and evening, as he claimed. No one can verify that, since he was alone after closing."

"And he had motive?"

"It would be irresponsible to wrap up the investigation this soon." The detective took a deep drink of his beer. "There are other suspects with stronger motives than a disagreement over feral cats."

The screen door opened, and wood flooring creaked under soft footsteps. "Honey, I'm home," called Lisa.

Chapter Twenty-Four

I averted my eyes as Lisa and Paul exchanged a kiss and mumbled mushy words only the two of them could hear. Their towheaded son, trailing after Lisa, joined the powwow and hugged his daddy's thighs. I just wanted to hand over the vet records, give Lisa instructions about releasing the cats, and get out of there, leaving them to their cozy cocoon.

"I fixed your favorite chicken dish," she said, untangling herself from her husband's embrace to move toward the crockpot. "Smells like it's ready."

Licking his lips, he followed her. "I'm starved."

"Me too!" cried his Mini-Me.

I set down my water and stood. "Hi, Lisa." I picked up the folder containing vet records. "I have the cats' paperwork here. And the receipt for their surgeries."

"DeeLo." Her facial expression hinted she'd forgotten I'd be here, even though we'd just exchanged text messages.

"DeeLo brought the cats back," Paul chimed in.

"We put them in the garage already," I added. "As I said in my text, please don't release them until tomorrow. One of the orange females is groggy, so keep an eye on her. And you can give them food and water tonight. They'll be hungry."

Lisa took the folder and glanced at the receipt. Then she fumbled inside her purse, which still hung over her shoulder. "I must have left my checkbook at work. Paul?"

He threw up his hands.

She sighed. "I'm so sorry, DeeLo. Can you come by the office tomorrow?

I'd stop by yours, but I'm not sure I can get away."

"Not a problem; I'll pick it up from you." I'd been about to suggest she use Venmo or PayPal, but then realized the inconvenience might work to my advantage. She could formally introduce me to her boss, Commissioner Vince Connors, and I could pitch him my TNVR proposal. Hopefully, he wouldn't associate me with the scene involving Manny at the memory care center. And even if he did, an introduction from Lisa would give us a fresh start.

"Thanks. You've been a godsend." She lifted the lid to the crockpot and took a whiff.

I started toward the door. "When do you want to try to catch the other two cats? I have to return Catherine's equipment soon."

"How about tonight?"

"Tonight?" I stopped. "Your dinner is ready. I don't want to interrupt."

"Stay for dinner, then. We can trap when we're finished."

"I can't—"

"There's plenty." She stirred the contents of the crockpot. "You like chicken, don't you? You're not a vegan or anything?"

I stole a glance at Detective Ross, trying to read his reaction to his wife's invitation, but he was busy gathering utensils from a drawer. "Chicken's fine," I replied to Lisa. Maybe I'd learn more about the case by staying for a meal. But more importantly, the sooner we caught the rest of those cats, the sooner I'd be done with this project and thus, the Rosses. "Thanks. Can I help with anything?"

With a thin smile, she shook her head.

"Do you mind if I use your bathroom to wash up?" I started toward the living room, hoping for another opportunity to peruse Azmina's file.

Lisa pointed in the opposite direction. "That way."

If I'd thought waiting for Lisa with Detective Ross was awkward, sitting through family dinner with all of them proved excruciating. The food was fine, but the atmosphere crackled with tension. I made several false starts at cordial conversation—the house, the food, their experiences growing up in Pecan County—and each attempt was met with one-word, full-mouthed answers.

Their son sucked his thumb and stared at me as if I had three heads. He hadn't touched his meal.

I smiled and leaned toward him. "What's your name?"

He covered his face and burrowed his head into his shoulders like a turtle retreating into its shell. His parents had probably taught him not to talk to strangers.

"Eat your dinner, Paul." Lisa pointed to the untouched food on her son's plate.

I put on my most non-threatening smile. "Nice to meet you, Paul." Paul Jr.—I'd guessed correctly.

Detective Ross turned toward his son. "What do you say to the nice lady?" At least he described me as "nice."

The kid just stared at me.

"I'm DeeLo. How old are you, Paul?"

The boy looked down at his plate and slowly held up one hand, spreading all five fingers.

"Five years old. Wow. Do you go to school yet?" *A little old to be sucking your thumb.*

While Paul Jr. pondered the question, Lisa answered for him. "Kindergarten in the mornings. Then he spends the afternoon at daycare since we both work."

I nodded. I'd run out of conversation with the child like I had with the adults.

Lisa and Detective Ross barely looked at each other during the meal, in contrast to their lovey-dovey greetings earlier. I couldn't tell if their dinnertime demeanor was normal, or if they were holding back a sensitive discussion because of my presence. Perhaps Lisa felt betrayed to come home and find me drinking and chatting with her husband, although she should have expected me to be there. Did she suspect we were attracted to one another? Were we? However, she'd been the one to invite me to stay for dinner—not exactly the gesture of a jealous wife. Or maybe it was? Keep your enemies close...

Possibly, Detective Ross had wanted to talk with Lisa about something personal—or maybe even the murder investigation, à la Nick and Nora Charles in Dashiell Hammett's *The Thin Man*—and I was in the way. Yet, he'd started to open up to *me* about the case right before his wife arrived home.

I cleared my throat. The silence grated my nerves. I'd never been able to keep my mouth shut for long. "So… Lisa, how long have you worked at Connors Insurance?"

The chewing stopped. Detective Ross looked up from his plate and stared at his wife, his face as hard as a granite statue. Was her job a taboo subject? Another failed attempt at harmless chatter had stumbled over a land mine.

Lisa picked up her napkin and wiped her mouth. "Three years." She rose and began collecting plates.

I'd been about to ask what it was like to work for Commissioner Connors, gather some more information about my potential ally, but she'd signaled dinner was over. "Can I help you clean up?"

Detective Ross motioned for me to stay seated. "I'll take care of the dishes and get Paul ready for bed. You two can start your cat trapping."

* * *

Before setting up our equipment, we checked on the recuperating cats in the garage. Even though I'd only watched a few YouTube videos to reinforce what Catherine had taught me, I expertly showed Lisa how to stick a divider into the trap so she could corral the cat, open the door, place bowls of food and water into the cage, and close it up without getting bitten or allowing the cat to escape.

The female orange tabby, who'd been groggy earlier, had perked up. When we closed the door and removed the divider, she dove into the bowl of Meow Mix, which reassured me she was on the road to recovery.

We reached the tuxedo tomcat last. He seemed alert and anxious to chow down. My head swelled with pride that our feeding operation was going so smoothly, despite our lack of expertise. "Let's change the paper liner in his cage while we're at it; looks like it's wet."

From a stack of old newspapers, Lisa grabbed last week's *Pecan County News*. An article with Jill Hernandez's byline caught my eye. Little did Jill know a stray cat would be peeing all over her words.

I picked up the divider. "I hope your husband wasn't upset when I mentioned your job."

"Why would you say that?" Lisa set down the newspaper in front of the trap and lifted the door.

"Wait!" I hadn't inserted the divider yet.

Sensing a window of opportunity for freedom, the cat shot out of the trap in a blur of black-and-white fur. He scurried around the garage, searching for an exit, eyes a pair of black marbles.

Lisa's mouth dropped.

I shook my head. "We're not going to get him back in that trap."

"Well, I don't want him running loose in my garage! Paul will have a fit."

"Just open a door and let him go. You'd be doing this tomorrow anyway. He's been neutered and vaccinated."

"Will he be okay?" She watched the cat's frenzied scuttle.

"The males recover quicker than the females. He's moving well."

Lisa pressed the button to raise the garage door.

After an initial flinch at the noise, the cat stared at the opening and then dashed outside into the night.

"Maybe he'll find his way home," I suggested. If he had a home.

* * *

We set two traps in the same spots as the night before. Lisa didn't make any mistakes with hers this time. She told me she hadn't given the remaining cats breakfast that morning, so I figured they'd be plenty hungry. I hoped so; I wanted to be done and get home to Manny at a reasonable hour.

Settled in our spot on the patio to wait, I took a deep breath of the crisp fall air. "How did the other business owners at the shopping center take the news about José?"

"Shocked." Lisa pressed her lips together. "Totally unexpected."

"Were you aware he had problems with depression?" I asked. "I heard he was taking an anti-psychotic drug."

She raised her eyebrows. "I had no idea. He always seemed normal to me."

"I guess the drugs were working." I looked down. "If it's true..." Before she could ask me how I knew José took Clozapine and what business it was of mine, I shifted the topic. "Do you think the police will close the murder investigation now? Have they decided José was the killer?"

"People are certainly speculating. But, as usual, my husband hasn't told me anything more than what's been released to the public." She stared off into the woods. "Shh... One of the cats is sniffing around the trap."

The sliding glass door squeaked open, and Detective Ross tromped onto the patio. "How's it going, ladies?"

At the sound of his voice, the feline bolted back into the bushes.

Lisa whirled toward her husband. "You just scared the cat away."

Looking at the detective's crestfallen face, I said, "They'll be back. They're hungry."

"Did you put Paul to bed?" Lisa asked.

Detective Ross nodded. "But I'm sure he'll appreciate a goodnight kiss from you." He sat down at the table with us. "You seem to know quite a bit about cats, DeeLo."

Lisa rose. "I'll go tuck our son in."

When she'd disappeared inside, I turned to Detective Ross. "I'm new to this trapping business, but I've had pet cats off and on since I was a child. And I just adopted Azmina's bookstore cat, Manny."

The detective's brow furrowed. "The bookstore cat? I thought he ran off. You have him?"

"Remember, I told you Catherine Foster and I saw the cat roaming the parking lot behind the store? That's why we went inside, where we found Azmina's body."

"I remember you telling me that, but I didn't know you'd taken the cat. We thought he ran off."

"No, Catherine took him home that night, and now I have him." I searched his face. He was staring at me as if I'd withheld critical information from his investigation. "What? Is Manny wanted for questioning?" The sole witness to Azmina's murder?

"If only cats could talk." The hint of a smile crossed his face. "No, I'm just surprised you've had him all this time. People were worried about him. Glad the cat has a new home."

Lisa slid open the patio door. "What cat has a new home?"

"The bookstore cat," replied her husband. "DeeLo adopted him."

She stared at me. "You have Azmina's cat?"

Chapter Twenty-Five

The clatter of a metal door interrupted our conversation about Manny. Detective Ross followed Lisa and me to the edge of the woods to collect the cat. He and his wife grappled for the trap at the same time. In his attempt at chivalry, he accidentally knocked it out of her hands before we'd had a chance to secure the entrance door with a clip. The door popped open, and we scrambled to close and clip it before the cat saw a chance to escape.

As I covered our quarry with a towel, the second trap captured the last feline.

We put the cats in my SUV, since I'd already resigned myself to making another trip to the LifeSaver in the morning. That clinic was becoming my second workplace; my car could drive there on autopilot.

Once we'd loaded both animals into my vehicle, there was no reason for me to hang around, no hope of getting another look at that file in the detective's living room. I thanked them for dinner and announced I was heading out.

On my drive home, while I watched the rearview mirror for threatening headlights, I wondered why both Rosses were so surprised I'd adopted Manny.

* * *

When I arrived at the office the next day after dropping the cats at the clinic, Jane glanced at her watch but said nothing. I wasn't late.

"Good morning, Jane." I tried to make my voice sound cheery with no trace of my usual sarcasm.

She grunted and refused to look at me.

I stuck my head in Barry's doorway and said in a stage whisper, "Have you talked to Jane yet about a team meeting?"

He looked up from his pile of contracts. "I'm swamped. Maybe tomorrow?" He tapped a pen against a file folder. "But why don't you and Jane meet without me?"

I arched my eyebrows.

"Try it." With a hint of an amused smile, he returned to his paperwork. For a supposedly sensitive man, he was oblivious to tension among his employees.

Frustrated, I started to return to my cubicle, then did an about-face. "Barry?"

He raised his head and gave me his attention.

"Do you realize I don't have enough work to do? I appreciate your giving me this job, but I feel guilty taking a paycheck for doing nothing."

He smiled. "That's the nature of this work; it ebbs and flows. You'll be busy again before you know it."

"Jane is the roadblock. There's plenty of work I could be doing now, but she won't let me touch her precious files until she does who-knows-what to them."

He nodded. "We'll talk to her."

I wanted to bang my head against his doorjamb.

Change the subject. "I need to arrange a meeting with Nick Norton from the Pecan Creek Nature Foundation to go over the recommended ordinance changes. I want to be prepared to counter his objections before we present our proposal to the Board of Commissioners. Will you come with me?"

He set down his pen. "Are you sure you need me? You've been doing fine with the other stakeholders."

The other stakeholders weren't possible murderers. "I'd feel better if you were there. I'm expecting resistance, and it would help to have your legal muscle to support me."

Barry smiled. "As you wish. Let me know when you set up the meeting. Not today, though."

Adjusting his glasses, he plunged back into his work. I tiptoed away.

"Jane," I proposed as I passed her desk. "Can we meet this morning to talk about those files I'm trying to archive?"

She made a sour face. "I'm too busy."

"This afternoon, then?"

Her answer was a dismissive sniff.

"I can help if you let me. Once we have everything stored online, your work will be a lot easier."

"I don't need your help." She pointed at the nearest box of file folders. "Don't you touch anything!"

With another glance at her boxes, I wondered what she didn't want me to see in those files. I headed back to my cubicle and my empty inbox. At least I'd tried to tell Barry what was going on. Jane viewed me as expensive window decoration, the privileged girlfriend who'd prevented her from getting the raise she believed she deserved.

Sighing, I googled the Pecan Creek Nature Foundation. I read their mission statement and viewed photographs of the various tracts of land they had bought in the name of conservation. One of their goals was to preserve the native flora and fauna of the region, and they sponsored nature hikes and other educational events on their properties. A picture had been posted of Nick with the Boy Scouts who'd cleaned up the reserve, and there was another photo of the troop receiving their proclamation at the last Board of Commissioners meeting.

The foundation had an office in downtown Pecan Point. When I phoned, a secretary answered; she said Nick Norton could see me at two p.m. the following afternoon. Meeting Nick in a formal office setting with a secretary down the hall seemed safer than another encounter in the woods, like our first meeting, with only birds and feral cats around. And besides, Barry would be with me.

I sent Barry a text with the time and location of our meeting with Nick. "Will this work for you?"

He returned a thumbs-up.

My phone rang: Jill Hernandez. I answered, "It's about time. So much for getting me the scoop."

"You can catch my story in today's edition. José hung himself with a bedsheet."

"Yeah, I already know."

"But what you don't know—" Jill lowered her voice, "And I can't put it in the story, either—it wasn't a county-issue bedsheet."

"What do you mean?" Detective Ross had not revealed the origin of the bedsheet/suicide weapon.

"Scented pink satin," she whispered. "I can't confirm, but a source thinks his wife brought it."

Detective Ross definitely did not share that tidbit. "Is that allowed?"

"Someone let her give it to him."

I let out a puff of air. "His wife files charges against him, gets him locked up, but then she comes to the jail with special sheets from home? To make him more comfortable, or to tie a better noose?" Suicide was a serious topic, which was why Jill couldn't print all the details, but picturing a scented pink satin bedsheet in a holding cell brought out an inappropriate giggle.

"Hmm, that's the question," said Jill.

"When José's wife came to visit him, did she bring his meds?" I asked.

"His what?"

"I heard he was taking an anti-psychotic drug. Clozapine. I presume the staff would have to administer it."

From the way Jill's breath caught, I could tell she didn't know.

I backpedaled. "I'm probably not your best source, so please don't quote me."

"How did you get this information?" she pressed.

I related what I'd heard from Sandra about the medication she'd found at the scene of the attempted cat poisoning. "This is second-hand gossip from someone who thinks he's guilty of murder," I warned.

"It's a lead, though. I'll check it out."

"Jill… is there any chance it wasn't suicide?"

She covered the mouthpiece to speak with someone in the room with her, then returned a moment later. "I have to go."

* * *

I'd told Lisa I'd stop by her office at lunch so she could reimburse me for the clinic bill—including a new invoice from today. And hopefully, she'd introduce me to Vince Connors.

Barry had hinted I should make more of an effort to get along with Jane, so I vowed to offer to bring back lunch for her. Except she wasn't at her desk. Did that count as trying? Isn't it the thought that counts?

A twinge of sadness hit me as I pulled into the run-down shopping center that had been the scene of so much tragedy. Two of its business owners dead in less than two weeks. The Mexican restaurant was still closed, as was Black Cat Books. Apart from a few customers at the Dollar Tree and one car in the dry cleaner's drive-thru, the parking lot was almost empty.

The giant Whitehead Realtors poster in the window of one of the unoccupied storefronts had started to peel away from the plate glass. Victoria Barton's distorted smile mocked its stark surroundings.

Connors Insurance, set apart by a red-brick facade, shared a wall with Black Cat Books. I recognized Lisa's Smart Car parked in front near a black Cadillac Escalade. I thought of the three bears as I eased my mid-sized Lexus RX in between the huge Escalade and the tiny Smart Car.

A door chime announced my arrival. The reception desk facing the glass entry doors showed no sign of occupancy. I remembered Lisa telling me they'd had to furlough all their other employees. Two of the offices just beyond the reception desk had shuttered doors and blank nameplates. Light shone from a room farther down the hall.

"Hello?" I called.

Lisa emerged from the illuminated office. "DeeLo?"

"You asked me to come by today to get a check." I started toward her. "For the cats."

"Oh yes, of course." She beckoned me to follow. "Come on in."

Dark wood panels framed her office walls, and a large picture window overlooked the greenbelt. She retreated behind a glass-topped mahogany desk wider than she was tall. I sank into a leather side chair.

"I also have the bill for today's surgeries." I slid the receipt across the desk.

She reached into a drawer and produced a plaid checkbook. "What's the total?"

I tallied the two amounts in my head and gave her the number.

"Just make it out to you?"

I thought for a moment. "No. Make it out to the Pecan Point Humane Society."

She looked up. "I thought you paid for the surgeries yourself."

"I did. But let's pay it forward. The Humane Society can use the money to fix more cats. And it's tax-deductible if you itemize."

"Whatever you say." She wrote carefully in a looping script, then tore the document from the checkbook and handed it across the desk. "Here you go. I appreciate all your help with those cats. I don't know what we would have done with more litters of kittens living on our property."

"Thanks." I put the check in my purse. "I'm picking up the last two cats from the clinic at four, so I'll bring them by your house afterward if that's okay. Will you be home at the usual time?"

"I should be." She stood up.

I hesitated, not rising. "Lisa?"

"Yes?" She stopped.

"Do you know if Vince is busy?"

"I'm not sure. Why?"

I cleared my throat. How to begin? Lisa should be an ally after she'd seen the benefits of TNVR firsthand. "He's on the Board of Commissioners, isn't he?"

Lisa nodded.

"I have a proposal to present to the Board, and I need commissioners to sponsor it."

"What kind of proposal?"

"Pecan County's animal ordinance was written back in the mid-twentieth century, and some of its provisions are outdated."

She knitted her brow. "Why do you care?"

"If you follow the wording of the ordinance, TNVR—what you and I did with the cats on your property—is illegal."

She expelled a puff of air. "What? They're on my private property."

"The county has a leash law. And you've exceeded the number of pets a Pecan County resident is allowed to own."

"But they're not pets. They're strays. They just showed up on my property."

"You feed them, don't you?" I challenged.

"Well, yeah. I don't want them to starve."

"According to the ordinance, if you feed them, you're the owner. And by letting them loose after you've trapped them and provided care, you're abandoning them."

"But I'm not—"

"What about our tuxedo friend?"

Lisa shook her head. "That's just crazy. No one would ever enforce a law that stupid."

"Maybe your husband didn't tell you, but Catherine Foster was arrested last week under the abandonment clause of the Pecan County animal ordinance."

"What?"

"We were trapping strays behind Black Cat Books, and one of the ear-tipped cats went into the trap by mistake. The moment Catherine let it out, Officer Friendly slapped the cuffs on her."

"That's crazy! I heard Catherine Foster went to jail under suspicion of murder."

"Is that what your husband told you?"

"He doesn't tell me much of anything about his work. I heard it from Natalie at the dry cleaners."

"They held her as long as they did because she wouldn't answer their questions about the murder, but the initial arrest came from Pecan County's outdated animal ordinance," I said. "If we fix the wording, something like that can't happen again."

Open-mouthed, Lisa pressed her hand to her cheek.

I explained the passages in the ordinance defining ownership, the leash law, the abandonment clause, and how I'd proposed changing them to make exceptions for community cats and their caregivers. I didn't have my notes with me, but I'd talked about the proposed ordinance changes so much, I knew most of the wording by heart.

"My boyfriend is a lawyer, and he helped me put it together." I purposely referred to Barry as my boyfriend rather than my boss to subtly reassure Lisa that I didn't have designs on her husband. In case she'd picked up a weird vibe last night. "My plan is to meet with stakeholders and commissioners to seek support before it goes on the agenda."

She stood up. "I think Vince would support it. Let's go talk to him."

We headed down the hall to a larger office at the end. Broad-shouldered, silver-haired Vince Connors sat behind a mahogany desk almost twice the size of Lisa's. Framed certificates for degrees and awards decorated his paneled walls.

Vince looked up as we stood in the doorway. Not distracted by Demi this time, his eyes swept my body from head to toe, halting for a moment on my chest—the more typical male response I got when I wasn't with my niece. "Ladies, what can I do you for?"

"This is my friend, DeeLo," began Lisa. "She has, uh… I'll let her tell you about it." She pointed to me.

"Nice to meet you, Commissioner Connors." This was my moment. "I have a proposal I'd like to present to the Board about—"

The front door chimed, and spiked heels clicked on the tile floor. "Yoo-hoo? Vince?"

Preceded by her signature floral scent, Victoria Barton clattered down the hall.

"In here, Vicky," Vince called. He smiled at me. "I'm sorry, ladies, I have an appointment. Maybe we can talk about this another time?"

"You again," Victoria and I said in unison, glaring at each other.

She brushed past and closed the door, edging Lisa and me into the hallway.

Chapter Twenty-Six

L isa turned to me with an apologetic shrug. "I didn't know Vince had an appointment." She glanced at the closed office door separating us from the muffled voices inside. "That realtor woman has been coming here a lot lately, which is why I suspect we might be moving soon."

That realtor woman? Wouldn't Lisa know Vince and Victoria were siblings? If I'd heard correctly at the memory care center when Victoria referred to Vince's father as "Dad." Maybe Victoria was Vince's girlfriend, acting overly familiar with the elderly gentleman. But then, what about Roy Don? Victoria had been with him at Leonardo's the following day, so they must still be an item. Of course, cheating on her man was Victoria's style.

Lisa and I started down the hall. "Maybe I could—" I began.

The front door chimed again. In came a pale, forty-something woman whose elongated body and widespread, bulging eyes reminded me of a praying mantis. Her dishwater-blonde hair had been piled into a top knot. Dressed in a leotard and tennis shoes, she carried a gym bag over her shoulder. "Ready?"

"Just a minute, Natalie." Lisa ducked into her office. "I have to get my stuff."

"I'll be on my way," I said.

Lisa emerged from her office with a bulging gym bag. "I'll change there."

"Going to the gym?" I asked as we headed toward the exit.

"Natalie and I have been taking a self-defense class. A little judo, karate— mixed martial arts. Never can be too careful, you know." She pantomimed a few karate chops. "Especially with a murderer on the loose."

We'd reached the front door. "Natalie, this is my friend, DeeLo," said Lisa. "She's the one who's been helping me trap the cats on my property and get them fixed. DeeLo, Natalie Wojcik owns the dry cleaners across the way."

"Hello." As we walked outside, I gestured toward the shuttered bookstore next door. "So awful what's happened here lately. Did you know Azmina well?"

"She was our landlord. But we weren't friends." Natalie switched her gym bag to the other shoulder. "Still, it was a shock to find out José Garcia killed her."

"They don't know that for sure, do they?" Did Natalie believe José was the killer, or was he a convenient scapegoat? What about Lisa's "murderer on the loose" comment? José was no longer on the loose. "What does your husband say, Lisa?"

Lisa made a face, and both women laughed, perhaps at a joke I wasn't in on.

"Guess what, Natalie?" gushed Lisa, as we stood on the sidewalk outside the office. "DeeLo adopted the bookstore cat. He's not lost like we thought."

"You have him?" Natalie's bulging, steel-gray eyes focused on me. "We've been searching for that cat every day since the murder. I was sure something awful had happened to him."

I smiled. "No, he's doing fine."

"So glad," said Natalie. Although her words were kind, they lacked sincerity.

We'd reached the parking lot, and she folded herself into a red MINI Cooper. Lisa got in on the passenger side and waved as I unlocked my own vehicle.

Checking my phone, I lingered in the driver's seat for a few moments. I wondered how long the women had been taking martial arts classes; I had a feeling their enrollment wasn't just prompted by the recent murder. Because Lisa was so tiny, I'd assumed her incapable of strangling Azmina. But maybe she had some moves that would have given her the upper hand? And Natalie, with her gangly limbs, might have been able to overpower her smaller landlord, like a praying mantis biting off the head of its mate.

Natalie drove away, and within minutes, a fully loaded, silver F-150 blaring country music pulled into the vacated spot. The music stopped mid-song, the driver's side door slammed, and Roy Don Whitehead swaggered onto the sidewalk. Cowboy boots clunking against the pavement, he lumbered toward Connors Insurance. If Victoria really was two-timing him, I would have loved to stay for the fireworks.

I leaped out of my car and caught up with him. "Commissioner Whitehead."

He tossed a partially smoked cigarette onto the pavement and crushed it with a bootheel. The stench of his tobacco smoke lingered in the space he'd just vacated. His hazel eyes scanned my face and then focused on my chest. "Hey there, little lady."

I wasn't sure if his gaze conveyed recognition or just everyday lust for the female anatomy, so I reminded him. "Delores Myer. I talked with you last week about making changes to the animal ordinance."

The recognition I'd sought flickered onto his face. "Oh, yeah. How's that coming?"

"Very well, thank you. I'd like to set up a time to discuss my proposal, whenever it's convenient. And if you can talk any colleagues into joining us—"

He gestured toward the building housing Connors Insurance. "Vince here usually sees eye to eye with me on a lot of issues. I'm fixin' to meet up with him right now. Want to come do your spiel?"

I might have taken him up on the invitation if Victoria wasn't inside with Vince. She'd ruin everything. Her hatred of me might prevent the men from listening to a good idea, an idea that would help the community. No, my odds of a favorable reception would be better if I could present my case to Roy Don and Vince alone. Besides, I didn't have my documents with me and all my impressive pie charts. "I have to get back to work now," I told Roy Don. "But can we get together later in the week?"

"Sure, little lady. Just call Amanda and make an appointment." With a nod, he headed inside and activated the now-familiar door chime.

* * *

Jane was still absent when I returned to Barton and Barton. Buried in work, Barry had not left his desk. "Anything I can help with?" I asked, peering through his open door.

He sighed. "I hate to ask, but Jane will be out the rest of the afternoon. Can you make copies of these briefs?"

"No problem." I took a stack of papers from him and headed to the copy machine, grateful for something to do.

As I watched the machine spit out copies, I wondered where Jane had gone. None of my business, I reminded myself. Although Jane made it her business to keep up with *my* comings and goings.

"Anything else?" I asked Barry when I returned with his copies.

"Thanks, but no." He bent back over his work.

I hovered at the door. "I know it's bad timing with Jane gone, but I have to leave early again to pick up Lisa's cats at the clinic."

He raised his eyebrows.

"Last two, though. We're done with our trapping project."

"Good. Maybe you'll have some free evenings for a change. I miss spending time with you."

"Likewise. I'm almost done with my community service." While I still had his attention, I asked, "Does Victoria have a brother?"

He did a doubletake; I could tell my question came at him like a ball through a window. "Yes. Why?"

"Does he live around here?"

"He owns an insurance business here in Pecan Point, and he serves on the Board of Commissioners."

"Vince Connors is Victoria's brother?"

"Half-brother, yes, but they don't advertise it. They're not close."

They seemed pretty close to me. "I had no idea they could be related until I saw him with Victoria last week at the memory care facility where my mom stays. They were searching for a place for their father." I still couldn't bring myself to tell Barry about the altercation with Manny, my failed attempt at stepping into Azmina's role as a therapy cat handler. In front of Victoria, no less. She may have already told him.

He nodded. "I knew it was about time. The old man's health has been declining fast in the past few years."

"Do you get along with your brother-in-law?" I corrected myself, "Ex-brother-in-law?"

Barry shrugged. "We're good. Why?"

"Hello? He's on the Board of Commissioners. Is there any bad blood that would keep him from looking at our ordinance proposal objectively?"

"No." Barry looked at me. "When Victoria and I started having problems, Vince stayed out of it. Of course, he had his own issues. His wife was battling breast cancer."

"Oh, my God. Is she okay now?"

Barry shook his head. "She passed away right before Christmas. It took a lot out of Vince."

"I'm so sorry. Did you know her well?"

He nodded. "Sally Connors was a wonderful woman. Kind to everyone." He smiled. "You'd have liked her. She had a soft spot for animals."

"I'm sorry," I repeated. Poor Vince. And too bad I'd never meet his animal-loving wife, who might have been an ally. "What about Victoria?"

"Victoria?" Barry's face reddened. His blood pressure always elevated at the mention of his ex-wife.

"How much influence does she have on her brother?"

"Not a lot. Vince is his own man."

"You don't think she'd sabotage our proposal just because she hates me?"

Barry crinkled his brow. "Why would she do that? And why do you think she hates you?"

Men could be so dense, ignoring the catty, political machinations among women. Did he not see the way Victoria glared at me every time she waltzed into our office? Did he never hear the snide remarks she directed at me? I cleared my throat. "I'm planning to set up a meeting later this week with Roy Don Whitehead and maybe Vince Connors to present the proposal. Will you come?"

He pursed his lips. "Not with Roy Don. You want to meet with him, go ahead, but count me out."

I nodded. The pain of Victoria's betrayal still showed on Barry's face whenever Roy Don's name came up. "I respect that. You two have a history. But what about Vince?"

He stroked his chin. "Vince is okay. I can set up a meeting for us if you like. Just us, no Roy Don. Let me know when you're ready."

I'd thought getting Vince Connors's ear would be hard, and now I couldn't believe how easy it had become. "That will be great. The sooner, the better."

* * *

Even though I took my time getting to the Ross home after picking up the cats at the clinic, I still arrived before Lisa. Detective Ross came out of the house as my SUV pulled up the driveway. Somehow, I wasn't as rattled to see him as I'd been the day before.

He helped me unload the caged cats from my vehicle and carry them into the garage. The two females already housed there perked up at the scent of the new arrivals.

"They recognize their family members." I peered into the traps. Golden eyes blinked back at me. "These girls are looking livelier."

The detective gestured toward the captive felines. "Were these two in heat also?"

"They're males."

"Oh." We endured another awkward silence. Then he asked, "Should we keep them in here overnight as well?"

"It's probably best, although the neuter surgery for males is not as invasive as the spay for the females."

More silence.

"I better get their vet records." I started back to my car.

He followed. "Want me to sign your timesheet?"

"Sure." I fetched my log of community service hours and handed it to him, avoiding looking into his eyes. As he wrote, I said, "Please ask Lisa to call me when she's ready for me to pick up Catherine's equipment. I suspect Cat will need it before long."

"Aren't you going to stay and help Lisa release the cats from yesterday?"

"Does she need my help?" I dreaded the torture of another invitation to witness their domestic delight.

"I'm sure she'd appreciate it." He glanced at his watch. "She'll be home soon. Did Lisa ever pay you back for covering the vet bills?"

"I stopped by her office today, and she wrote me a check." I leaned against the car. "I was hoping to meet her boss, but it didn't work out."

"Just as well," he muttered.

"Why?" I recalled his prickly reaction last night at my mention of Lisa's job. "Don't you like him? I hear Vince has had a rough year."

The detective's face darkened. "I suppose. Why did you want to meet Vince Connors?"

"Because he's on the Board of Commissioners. I talked to Lisa today about a proposal I'm working on, to change the county's animal ordinance. I think both of you might be interested in supporting it. The provisions affect you personally."

Paul's brow furrowed. "How?"

I pushed on. "Remember when Catherine Foster was arrested?"

The furrows deepened. "We had questions about her role in Azmina Patel's death."

"But don't you remember why she was picked up in the first place?"

The light still had not come on. How much did he and Officer Friendly share? Pecan Point had a tiny police department.

"I was there when Officer Friendly arrested Catherine. The charge he cited was animal abandonment, all because she released a cat who had wandered into a trap by mistake." I explained how the antiquated Pecan County animal ordinance made TNVR illegal, and the few wording changes I was suggesting would bring it into the twenty-first century. "It would be wonderful if you and Lisa could provide a testimonial about the benefits of TNVR at the Board of Commissioners meeting when the topic comes up on the agenda."

I was still animatedly expounding on my plans for reforming the law when Lisa drove up. I'd missed my opportunity for a quick escape.

Chapter Twenty-Seven

L isa stepped out of her car and eyed us, her face stiff from a day that had not gone according to plan.

I waved her over. "We were talking about the ordinance changes I'm proposing to the Board of Commissioners. Remember what I told you at your office? It would be great if you'd give a testimonial about the benefits of TNVR when the issue comes up on the agenda." Her expression didn't change, and I kept talking. "We put the cats in the garage already. The ones who were fixed today."

"I asked DeeLo to stay in case you need help releasing the other cats." Detective Ross acted almost as nervous as I felt, which was irrational because we had nothing to hide. "The ones who've been here overnight."

Lisa's gaze shifted from me to her husband. "Sure," she said. "Thanks."

Did we remind her of two pets caught stealing table scraps?

"Are you ready now, Lisa, or do you need a moment?" I asked, anxious to be done with this task and leave them to their evening of marital bliss.

She turned and opened the car door to free her son from the back seat. Paul Jr. bounded out and ran to his father.

The detective tousled his son's hair and looked at his wife. "I'll help if you want."

"It will just take a minute," I said. "You saw how fast that tuxedo cat took off last night."

"Okay," said Lisa. "Let's go."

I still couldn't read her deadpan expression. Preoccupation with matters that had nothing to do with me? Not exactly jealousy, but perhaps annoyance at my encroaching on her territory? Mercifully for us all, the cat project was ending, and I'd soon be out of their lives.

The three of us headed for the garage. The detective's Mini-Me trotted after us. Seeing them together, I again marveled at how he was a perfect miniature version of his father, from the fair coloring to the quirky mannerisms. "Kitties," the boy cried, pointing at the caged orange tabbies.

Lisa knelt at eye-level with her son. "Wait here, Paul. Remember, we told you not to touch the kitties."

Detective Ross grabbed a tricycle and wheeled it over to Paul Jr. "Why don't you ride down the driveway and back? By that time, we'll be done letting the kitties out."

The child shifted his attention to the tricycle and hopped on. I picked up one of the traps, and the detective took the other. After ensuring her son was safely occupied, Lisa followed us.

As we headed toward the woods, I asked, "So, Detective Ross, are there any updates you can share about the murder investigation?"

Lisa eyed her husband. "Yes, Detective Ross. When can the business owners in the Patel Shopping Center feel safe again?"

A look I could not decipher passed between them.

"Have you ruled out José Garcia then?" I asked.

"He committed suicide." The detective's response did not answer my question.

"I'd say that's an indication of guilt," said Lisa.

I jerked my head toward her. The first time we'd discussed José's suicide, she hadn't thought he was guilty; now, she seemed as convinced as Sandra. Like Natalie Wojcik. Maybe she and Natalie had discussed the case during their martial arts class earlier. But if she believed José was the killer, why the question about safety?

Detective Ross stayed silent.

We'd almost reached the edge of the property when I asked, "Was José still taking his medications while he was in jail?"

"What medications?" A tad roughly, Detective Ross plunked down the trap he'd been carrying.

I cleared my throat. "I heard he'd been taking an anti-psychotic drug called Clozapine. For depression, I presume."

"He never mentioned it." The detective stared off into the woods. "I didn't know." He didn't ask how I knew, which surprised me. His jaw stiffened. "Neither did his wife when she came to see him."

"But she brought sheets?" Jill hadn't instructed me not to tell anyone about the suicide sheets, and the detective must already know.

"Sheets?" Lisa repeated. "Why would his wife bring him sheets? Aren't sheets provided in the jail? Are people even allowed to bring in stuff like that?"

"Not normally," replied Detective Ross. "But Mrs. Garcia told Stan Friendly that José would be more comfortable with sheets from home, and our officer gave them to him."

Stan Friendly? Why would that stickler choose this time to break the rules?

Lisa shook her head. "I guess new sheets didn't help José's state of mind." She glanced back at the driveway, where her son was still riding his tricycle, and then gazed down at the traps. "Are we going to let these cats out or what?"

"Go ahead," I said. "Remember how to open the cage?"

She nodded, then bent and raised the door of the first one. A whoosh of orange fur flew by, and the first feline dashed into the woods. Lisa grinned at me. "We did it!"

"Bravo." The detective mimed applause.

His wife moved to the next trap and opened the door. The cat didn't budge. Lisa leaned her face toward the opening.

"Don't!" I grabbed her shoulder and pulled her upright. "You don't want to get bitten or scratched." Lisa's arm was still bandaged from our first TNVR attempt. I nudged the contraption with my foot; maybe the animal was so used to being confined, she'd forgotten what freedom was like. The cat moved to the other side to avoid my foot, but she still wouldn't come out. "Maybe we can lure her out with some food?"

"I'll get it," said Detective Ross, already starting toward the house.

"And check on Paul, too," Lisa called after him.

Looking down at the uncooperative feline, I cajoled, "Don't you want to come out?" I couldn't remember if this was the one who'd been lethargic yesterday; the orange tabbies looked alike. They'd both seemed alert when we checked them earlier.

"What if she won't come out?" Lisa screwed her mouth into an expression no one would want to see frozen.

"She'll come out." With my foot, I gently rocked the wire enclosure from side to side. A flash of golden fur bounded out, and the cat disappeared into the woods. "See?" I smiled at Lisa. "There she goes."

We picked up the traps and headed back toward the house. I made a beeline for my car, but Lisa stopped me. "Why don't you leave them here for now? I'll wash everything and give you a call after I've released the other two cats so you can pick up all the equipment at once."

I hadn't expected Lisa to offer to clean anything, and I doubted she had the proper disinfectants. But if her wash job wasn't up to Catherine Foster's standards, Catherine would just do it over. "Thanks," I agreed. "I should get going now."

Detective Ross emerged from the house with the bag of Meow Mix. "You don't need this anymore?"

I looked at Lisa. "They're probably hungry. We didn't feed them before we let them go. And don't forget to feed the ones who are still in the garage."

She took the bag from her husband, and I opened my driver's side door. "Good night, and good luck with releasing the other cats tomorrow."

* * *

As soon as I opened the door that led from my garage to the laundry room, I sensed something was awry. The broom closet door stood open, and I knew I hadn't left it that way. Someone had been here.

Breath caught in my throat, I tiptoed into the kitchen. The doors to the cabinet under the sink and the pantry were ajar. A wave of nausea hit me. I felt violated.

Was the burglar still in the house? It might not be safe for me to stay here. Should I leave and call nine-one-one? I backed up.

"Manny!" I called. No response.

Cocking my head, I listened to the silence. My gut told me whoever had been here was gone. I continued forward, assessing the situation.

Someone had rummaged through the hall closet, scattering my belongings into the living room. If anything was missing, it wasn't of much value.

"Manny!" I called. The poor cat would have been terrified to confront an intruder. He must be hiding.

There was no answering meow.

"Manny!" Panic shook my voice as I searched room after room. No sign of my cat in the disarray.

What if the burglar let him out? I raced to the front door, flung it open, and called, "Manny! Kitty, kitty!" No response.

Visions played before my eyes, of the night Catherine and I found Manny wandering behind the bookstore after the brutal killing of his former owner. Manny, the sole witness to Azmina's murder. Was there some secret device or clue hidden on the cat's body? Was that why everyone seemed so interested that Manny had surfaced? What if the killer had come for me now?

I should call Detective Ross. I grabbed my cell phone and pulled up my contacts. What was I thinking? He was off-duty, and besides, he wasn't a beat cop.

Instead, I phoned Barry. My call went to voice mail. Tongue-tied, I mumbled, "Barry... Someone broke in. They've ransacked the place. Manny's gone. I don't know what to do." I looked around. Maybe "ransacked" was too strong a word for ferreting through a few closets. My expensive paintings and flat-screen TV still hung on the wall. My Baccarat crystal sat on the living room shelf in plain view. The intruder had not touched my jewelry box.

My eyes rested on the contents of the hall closet, now strewn around my living room. Winter coats, a vacuum cleaner, and an array of attachments. Missing was Manny's cat carrier.

I punched in nine-one-one. Regardless of the value of the items taken, I had to report the burglary.

"What's your emergency?" The operator's drawl made her sound like Scarlet O'Hara.

My voice quivered as I gave my name and address. "Someone broke in. My cat is gone."

"Ma'am, has anything been taken? Someone let the cat out?"

"My cat, Manny. They took my cat." I brushed the hair off my face, wet with beads of perspiration. "His carrier is gone too."

"What kind of cat is it?"

Oh dear, she thinks I've lost a valuable show cat. As if anyone could assign a price tag to a beloved pet. "Uh, Manny's just—" A witness to a murder.

A car door slammed. A second later, a key turned in the lock, and my front door opened. Manny's howls reached my ears before Demi tromped inside, slinging the cat carrier from side to side.

"Never mind," I murmured into the phone as I hung up. "Demi! What the—"

"Now, now, stop that yowling. You're home now." Demi set the carrier down and unlatched its gate.

Manny scooted out and rushed to me. Stroking his lush black coat, I eyed my niece. "You almost gave me a heart attack! I thought someone broke in and took Manny."

Unapologetic, Demi just laughed. "Who would steal a cat?"

"Where did you take him? How did you get in here?"

Demi held up my spare key. "I borrowed this the other day when you forced me to spend the night."

"You were too drunk to drive home. And that doesn't give you the right to come in and take my cat without my permission." I glared at her. "I was calling nine-one-one."

"You're such a drama queen, DeeLo." Demi put a defiant hand on her hip. "We went to see Grandma. She misses Manny."

"At the memory care facility? I thought they kicked us out."

"They let *me* take him to her room. Grandma shouldn't have to suffer just because *you* screwed up."

"Excuse me? You're one to talk about screwing up. Who took her out to lunch and lost her?"

"Okay," she amended. "But you couldn't control the cat."

Wincing, I remembered the awful scene during my last visit to my mother. Everything had been going so well... until Victoria walked in. Manny could probably sense what a witch she was.

Even though I was furious at my niece for taking Manny without my permission, scaring me half to death, I was glad my mother had a chance to see the cat again. For that, I was grateful to Demi. "You should have told me you were taking him. You left such a mess; I thought a burglar had trashed the place and let the cat outside."

"I couldn't find your carrier. And then Manny didn't want to get in it, so I had to chase him around the house."

"He doesn't like being caged." Still seething, I glared at my niece.

"Tell me about it." Demi started toward the front door. "I thought I'd surprise you and make Grandma's Fettuccine Alfredo. You didn't have all the ingredients, though. I stopped to buy heavy cream and fresh mushrooms. The groceries are in the car."

Demi thought she knew how to diffuse my anger, but I wouldn't forgive her so easily.

My phone rang while Demi was outside.

"Thank God, DeeLo." Barry exhaled. "Are you okay? I'm on my way over."

"False alarm," I assured him, regretting the panicked message I'd left. "The intruder was Demi."

He groaned. "Is she there now?"

Demi walked in with a bag of groceries and let the door slam behind her.

"She's making dinner. Would you like to join us?"

I imagined Barry's mind spinning through excuses like prizes on a wheel of fortune. "No thanks, I have some work to finish up. Call me later?"

So much for him coming right over to comfort me after my trauma.

Chapter Twenty-Eight

It had been a long time since Demi and I cooked together. Memories flooded back to simpler times when, as teenagers, we experimented with new recipes in my mother's sunny yellow kitchen in our Santa Monica bungalow. We'd made a good team when we weren't squabbling.

Since preparing Mom's Fettuccine Alfredo was Demi's idea, I let her be in charge. That meant no shrimp or jalapeño peppers—modifications I'd added in the last decade to make the recipe my own.

"Can you slice the mushrooms?" Demi handed me the package. "And don't cut the pieces so small this time."

I removed the cellophane wrapper en route to the sink. "How did Manny behave at the memory care facility today?"

"He was a little prince, as usual." Demi opened a pack of bacon. "Where do you keep your paper towels?"

"Under the sink. Didn't you see them when you ransacked the place?" Still annoyed at Demi for breaking in and taking my cat without telling me, I stepped aside from my mushroom washing so she could open the cabinet door. "Does that mean he's welcome back?"

Demi grabbed the roll, tore off several sheets, and spread them on a plate. "I didn't discuss it with anyone. Figured we'd keep a low profile for a while. Easier to get forgiveness than ask for permission."

I scrubbed specks of dirt from each mushroom before placing it on the cutting board. "Manny was doing great that time I took him—until Victoria walked in."

"Who?" Demi separated strips of bacon and laid them on the paper-towel-lined plate. She covered the plate with another towel and popped it into the microwave.

"Victoria Barton. Barry's ex-wife."

"Oh. Barry used to be married?" I'd confided my Victoria woes to Demi several times before, but they must not have made an impression. *Her* love life was usually the preferred topic of conversation. "Which one was she?"

"Remember that couple who came in with the old man in the wheelchair? Just before Manny freaked out?" I sliced through a mushroom with more force than I'd intended and banged my knife against the cutting board. "You were drooling over the guy before you noticed he was with someone."

"Yeah, I remember now. Rugged good looks. The best ones are always taken." She gazed at a spot on the stove, and I hoped we wouldn't have another cryfest tonight about her married ex-lover, Carl.

"His name is Vince Connors, and he might not be taken. He's a widower, and Victoria is his sister." I peered into the large saucepan, where a lump of butter had melted. If I'd been in charge, we'd have used olive oil. "Want me to sauté the garlic?"

"Yeah, but lower the heat before it scorches."

"I know how to sauté garlic."

Opening and closing cabinet doors, Demi found my bottle of vodka. "Douse it with this once it starts sizzling."

I took the vodka from her and set it beside the pan. "I think Manny freaked out because of Victoria. He's an excellent judge of character."

"Yeah, right," Demi scoffed. "He could sense you were freaking out." She opened the box of fettuccine. "Why does Victoria get to you so much? They're divorced, aren't they? Barry's crazy about you."

Demi always trivialized my emotions. I knew I wouldn't get any sympathy recounting all the nasty remarks Victoria had made about me. Demi wouldn't understand why the moniker, "Surfer Girl," was such an insult because I couldn't replicate the condescending tone Victoria used when she addressed me. My niece couldn't care less about the passive-aggressive work environment I endured because of Jane's loyalty to her old boss. Or the way Barry withdrew to lick his wounds after each new confrontation with his ex-wife. Was I the only one who saw that woman for the monster she was? She was the type who'd stop at nothing to get what she wanted. "I think Victoria may be a murderer," I blurted.

Instead of dropping into the boiling water, the dry fettuccine scattered on the granite countertop as Demi clasped her hand to her mouth. "What did you say?"

My remark surprised me as much as it had Demi. It was the first time I'd put those suspicions into words. "Manny's former owner was murdered. The cat might be the only witness."

"But why do you think Victoria did it? Wasn't the woman strangled? Is Victoria strong enough to kill someone?"

I helped Demi gather up the noodles and stick them into the boiling water. "Manny's afraid of her."

"Ha! I'd like to see someone try to prove that in court." Demi stirred the pot to ensure all the pasta was submerged and separated. "How do you know Manny's fear was directed at her? Why not the nursing home manager who was escorting them? The old man who tried to grab him? Or the brother? Does Victoria even have a motive?"

"She does." I checked on the garlic, doused it with vodka, then added mushrooms to the mixture. Fresh jalapeño peppers would have made a great addition, but Demi would balk; she said they burned her mouth. I tossed in red pepper flakes in keeping with Mom's recipe. "Barry says Victoria had been trying to coerce Azmina into selling her land to Oakwood Studios, and Azmina resisted."

"Oh, yeah, I heard Oakwood was shopping for land in Pecan County." Demi pulled oregano, paprika, and nutmeg from my spice cabinet. "How is Victoria involved?"

"She was Azmina's realtor, and the sale would have meant a big commission. Also, her boyfriend, the owner of Whitehead Realtors, is the buyer's agent for Oakwood. Their firm wouldn't have to split the money with another agent." I stirred the sizzling garlic and mushrooms. "Want me to grate some Romano?"

"Use the Parmesan I bought." Demi tossed me a brick of cheese. "Let me get this straight… Victoria was trying to motivate Azmina to sell her land to Oakwood Studios. Azmina didn't want to, so Victoria killed her? And Manny knows he's the witness she has to bump off now?"

Demi could twist my words to sound ridiculous. I opened a drawer and grabbed my grater. "Barry thinks there's something squirrelly about the deal."

"I thought the police had locked up a suspect already." Demi checked the bacon in the microwave and then reset the timer. "What about that restaurant owner Jill wrote the story about? And your cat-trapping girlfriend?"

"Catherine Foster was released; no charges were filed. She had an alibi." I checked the level of cheese in my bowl, then continued to grate. "And I guess you didn't hear, José Garcia hung himself in his jail cell."

Demi raised her finely arched eyebrows. "Seems like an admission of guilt to me. Did they close the case? Or has Detective DeeLo persuaded the cops to investigate Victoria?"

"They haven't closed the case." Giving my niece the side-eye, I turned off the flame under the boiling water. "I think the noodles are ready. They're still considering other suspects."

Another arched brow. Demi was proud of her eyebrows; she spent lots of money keeping them perfectly shaped. "And you're privy to the investigation?"

I drained the pasta and dumped it into the saucepan, stirring to coat it with butter, garlic, and mushrooms. "I've been helping Detective Ross's wife trap the feral cats who live on their property. In fact, I was over there earlier this evening. We discussed the case."

Demi giggled. "And, of course, the detective listens to you, the community service 'volunteer' and super-sleuth." She opened a pint of heavy cream and poured it into the pan, then added more vodka. "Why are you even involved?"

"I found the body, remember?" I dumped the grated cheese into the mixture and stirred vigorously. "My friend was wrongfully arrested." *Did I just call Catherine Foster my friend?* "And I owe it to Manny to get justice for his former owner."

"Like the cat is going to know it." Demi removed the crispy bacon from the microwave, crumbled it, and dumped the bits into the fettuccine.

"He might. Look how he recoiled when Victoria entered the room." I shook the spices into the concoction and continued to stir. "He's a very smart cat."

"Does he talk to you? Confide his theories?" Demi teased. "Manny, the crime-solving cat."

"Ha, ha." I scraped the bottom of the pan to keep the pasta from sticking.

"I guess you told Detective Ross to arrest anyone who's a cat hater." She grinned. "Based on Manny's reactions."

Demi made me sound like a cross between a crazy cat lady and a meddling Miss Marple. Even though I hadn't actually shared theories with Detective Ross, I'd asked questions, tried to point his investigation in the right direction. "Speaking of cat haters, there's another suspect who's still flying under the radar."

"Do tell!" Demi could have kept her voice a little less patronizing.

"Remember the last time you took my mother to Leonardo's? And lost her?"

With a wince, Demi looked away. She deserved to feel guilty.

"And remember how I found her wandering in the Pecan Creek Nature Reserve?"

"I just walked away for a minute. Grandma wasn't really lost."

"She was all the way down the hill, by the creek. She could have fallen in and drowned. And it would have all been on you!" For a moment, I relived the panic of learning my mother was missing, my anger at realizing Demi was responsible.

Demi bit her lip. "But she didn't fall in."

"I found her with the man who manages the reserve, Nick Norton."

"Oh, yeah. Nice-looking guy." Demi walked to the refrigerator. "Got anything we can make a salad with?"

"Spinach. And there are some mushrooms left." I continued to stir as the cheese melted and the cream thickened. "Nick Norton wanted to buy

Azmina's land and increase the size of the nature reserve."

Demi took a bag of spinach out of the chiller and carried it to the sink. "Let me guess. Azmina didn't want to sell it to him, so he killed her? How's he going to get the land now?"

I let out an exasperated puff of air. "In all the confusion that afternoon, Mom got away with Nick's phone. When I was trying to figure out who it belonged to, I found some incriminating text messages."

"Ooh...a confession?" Demi washed leaves of spinach, pulled off the stems, and threw them in the sink. The other side had a disposal, but she didn't use it.

"Wouldn't you like to know." I turned off the flame under the saucepan. "This is about done."

Demi picked up my leftover mushrooms and tossed them into the spinach salad. "You're not going to tell me?"

I selected a colorful Italian pottery serving bowl for our pasta dish. "Want to eat in here? Or shall we get out the good china and eat in the dining room?"

"Dining room." Demi picked up the salad bowl. "Do you have blue cheese?"

"You're not going to make Mom's vinaigrette?"

"Are you going to tell me what the text messages said?"

We carried our dishes into the dining room. Ignoring her question, I removed plates and salad bowls from the hutch and set the table.

Demi opened my silverware chest and took out utensils for our meal. "Why were the texts incriminating?"

I laid a linen napkin at each place setting. "I think that's everything. Want some ice water?"

"Do you have white wine?" Demi had already taken two wine glasses out of the cabinet. "Who were the text messages from?"

"There's an open bottle of Chardonnay in the fridge." I sat down while Demi returned to the kitchen for the wine. "You're not going to get drunk again, are you?"

Back in the dining room with the bottle, Demi poured us each a glass of Chardonnay. "Are you going to tell me about the text messages?"

I smiled and took a sip. "Are you going to laugh at my theories?"

"Cheers." Demi held up her glass in a toast. "You got me curious."

"I know." I helped myself to the Fettuccine Alfredo. "Smells great. We're pretty good cooks."

"DeeLo..." Demi poured blue cheese dressing on her salad.

"The text messages were between Nick and Azmina, on the night she died. She told him the sale was off. The last message he sent said he was coming right over." I folded my arms across my chest.

Demi's large hazel eyes widened. "Did you show the police?"

"I did. I pointed out the timestamps, and they let Catherine go." Well, not immediately. But eventually. And maybe I had something to do with it.

"Why haven't they arrested Nick?"

"I don't know. Maybe he explained his way out of it." I twirled some fettuccine around my fork. "I have a meeting with Nick tomorrow."

Demi set down her glass. "You *what?*"

"I'm trying to get the Pecan County animal ordinance changed, and Nick Norton is a stakeholder. I have to convince him that Trap-Neuter-Vaccinate-Return for the feral cats living in the reserve is a good idea."

"Animal ordinance? Trap-Neuter... whatever? I don't even want to know." Demi took a sip of wine. "Is that part of your community service?"

I continued to eat.

"Aren't you afraid?" Demi's brow wrinkled. "I mean, if you think he could be the killer."

"Barry's going with me."

"Thank goodness." Demi picked up her fork and waved it at me as if she were giving a lecture. "You've read enough mystery novels to know the amateur sleuth who meddles in the murder investigation always gets in trouble. You don't want to be that person."

"I won't. I'm careful." I looked down at my plate.

"In fiction, the heroine gets rescued in the nick of time, and the killer is stopped. But it might not happen that way in real life."

* * *

A steady stream of clients kept Barry in the conference room all morning. Jane was back in the office but unusually quiet and detached. I walked by her desk several times and she forgot to glower.

Barry and I had planned to go out for lunch and then head over to the Pecan Creek Nature Foundation office for our two o'clock appointment with Nick Norton. But at twelve-thirty, Barry apologized that his meeting was running late. He gave me a copy of a trust document to deliver to a client and assured me we'd meet up at Nick's office.

I finished my errand in plenty of time to grab a sandwich but couldn't think about eating. I'd easily won support from the other stakeholders because we were already on the same team. That early success had bolstered my confidence—perhaps too much. Nick would be a hard sell, and I needed time to study and hone my presentation to sharpen my reasoning. Luckily, Barry would be by my side to rein in my emotions and keep my arguments logical.

Ten minutes early, I arrived at the foundation. The office was clean and welcoming, but not plush, which I appreciated in a nonprofit. Framed poster-sized photos of local flora and fauna adorned the cream-colored walls. I checked in with the smiling, gray-haired receptionist, took a seat in the lobby, and pulled out my notes for a last-minute review.

Three minutes before two came the sound of a woodpecker, notifying me of an incoming text. With a knot in my gut, I glanced at my smartphone to confirm what I'd dreaded. "DeeLo, I'm so sorry, but something urgent came up. You'll do great without me!"

I had to face a possible murderer all on my own.

Chapter Twenty-Nine

Nick Norton looked different than I remembered. Instead of the signature safari outfit, he wore a tweed blazer that picked up the golden highlights in his hair. He'd slicked it back like a gangster's instead of letting it hang hippy loose. He rose from behind his plain wooden desk and came forward to shake my hand. "Delores Myer? What can I do for you?" His intense amber eyes squinted, deepening his crow's feet. "You look awfully familiar. Where have we met?"

I returned his firm handshake—not bone-crushing, but not wimpy. "You helped me with my mother last week when she was lost in the reserve."

He tapped his forehead. "Of course, the woman from the memory care home. How is she doing?"

"Fine, thank you." As I sat down, I was tempted to bring up the purloined phone and his text messages. Even though Barry couldn't accompany me, he knew exactly where I was. It felt relatively safe meeting in a downtown building across from government offices, with a charged cell phone in my purse and an attentive receptionist down the hall.

With a gentle knock, the receptionist stuck her gray head in the doorway. "I'm taking off now. Do you need anything else?"

"No thanks, Marlene," Nick replied. "This is my last appointment. Go ahead and lock up behind you."

I swallowed the lump rising in my throat. Recalling the words of Lady Macbeth, I screwed up my courage to its sticking place, determined not to fail.

Marlene's footsteps retreated down the hallway, and then a key turned in the glass outer door.

We were alone.

Nick turned to me. "Now, what is it you wanted to see me about?"

Inhaling faint odors of Lysol and furniture polish, I set my folder of papers on the edge of his desk. "Pecan County's animal ordinance." I took another deep breath to keep my voice even. "I plan to present a proposal to the Board of Commissioners to make some needed changes, and I wanted to notify all the stakeholders beforehand, so I can answer any questions they might have and ensure they can support it."

Nick stroked his chin. A tuft of blonde fuzz covered its cleft and the area above his lip, like he was trying to grow a beard but not having much success. "Okay. I'm not sure how an animal ordinance affects me, but I'm listening. I mean, there's plenty of wildlife in the reserve, but we don't manage it."

"The changes will legalize Trap-Neuter-Vaccinate-Return for feral and community cats. The way the law is written now—"

"For feral cats?" His facial features twisted as if he'd tasted something sour.

"The way the law is written," I continued. "Someone who traps a feral cat, gets it neutered and vaccinated, and then returns it to its outdoor home can be prosecuted."

Nick held out his hands in a broad shrug. "If they trap a feral cat, why put it back? Wild cats are nuisance animals. Someone who puts them back should be prosecuted."

"But they live in the reserve already. Just like the squirrels and the possums and the raccoons."

"I know, and cats don't belong there. I'm trying to have them all removed." He pressed his thin lips together. "Cats kill birds and other native wildlife. And they spread disease."

I'd anticipated this argument after seeing the threatening cease-and-desist letter he'd sent to Catherine. "Here, I think you should read this." Leaning across his desk, I handed him an article I'd printed about "the vacuum effect" and how studies showed that removing the cats from an area—i.e., trap-and-kill—didn't work because new arrivals replaced the ones who'd been eradicated. "As long as you have a favorable habitat, and as long as people abandon their pets, you'll have feral cats."

"They shouldn't be there." He jutted his bottom lip like a stubborn child.

"If you allow rescue groups onto your property to trap the cats who already live there, get them fixed, then put them back, the population will stabilize and eventually decline. Which means fewer bird deaths." I tapped my finger on the article I'd offered, which he had yet to read.

"They still spread disease."

"We get them vaccinated as well as neutered, so the animals will be healthier than before they were trapped."

Nick glanced at the paper, then waved a hand in the air. "Azmina tried to sell me on that stuff—TNR, or whatever they call it. But I've read plenty of stories to the contrary. There's no proof that those programs reduce the cat population."

I whipped out several more articles citing success rates in various communities. "If done right, they do."

He shook his head. "Ms. Myer, I'm sure you mean well. But you can't convince me that allowing cats to remain in the Pecan Creek Nature Reserve is a good idea."

"You can't keep them from living there. It's a huge area. People dump unwanted animals, unsterilized pets wander off, and they breed. Many will find their way to the nature reserve; cats don't respect property lines. We can't stop the problem, but we can mitigate the effects."

He crossed his arms. "People should be prosecuted if they dump their pets."

"And there are laws on the books against animal abandonment. But do you think a rescue volunteer or shelter employee performing TNVR should be in the same category as a pet owner who dumps a cat or dog he no longer wants?"

"Well, no."

"But the way Pecan County's ordinance is written, they're considered the same, punished the same. Which is why I want to make these changes."

Nick tapped his fingers on the desk. "What do you want me to do? I told you I don't support TNR."

"You don't have to support TNR. I just don't want you to oppose these ordinance changes." I thrust my copy of the ordinance toward him and pointed to the places where I'd added definitions and exemptions. "Let's make it so a rescuer doesn't get thrown in jail for trying to reduce cat overpopulation."

He chuckled. "So, you want me to stay home when this thing comes up on the agenda at the Board of Commissioners meeting?"

"Just don't speak out against it."

"Ordinance or no ordinance, I won't allow feral cats—or any kind of caretaking activity that encourages them to stay there—in the nature reserve." He leaned back in his chair.

"There's nothing in these ordinance changes that says you have to." I arranged my papers into a neat stack. "But think about what Azmina would have wanted."

He straightened. "Azmina?"

"You said she was your friend, right?" I swallowed. *Here we go.* "When we met by the stream that day…"

"Azmina." He closed his eyes. "I still can't believe she's gone."

"Shocking," I agreed.

Opening his eyes again, he stared at a spot on the wall. "Azmina and I didn't agree about her feeding those feral cats."

"But she loved them, didn't she?" I placed the papers back into my folder.

He nodded, still pensive.

"I remember you telling my mother about Azmina. How she fed the cats in the woods." I studied his face for traces of guilt, but the emotion he wore looked more like grief.

He pressed his hands against his forehead. "That was a horrible day."

"You seemed so distraught. Didn't you say you saw her the night she was killed?" Demi's admonition nagged at the back of my mind, the bleep of a stall warning on an airplane, but I ignored it.

His facial features twisted like he was trying to arrange pieces in a puzzle. Maybe the police hadn't told him who found his phone. And if so, he might not know I'd read those text messages, which could be a good thing. "I thought that's what you said when we were with my mother. Perhaps I was mistaken."

"My mind was a blur that day; I honestly don't remember what I said to anyone." He massaged his forehead. "But you're right; I tried to see Azmina the night before. We had a difference of opinion, and I thought it would be better to talk it out in person. I sent her a text saying I was coming over."

At least his story was consistent with what I'd seen on his phone. "Did you go over there?"

"I went to her house, but there was no answer when I rang the doorbell. Her car was gone, too." He let out a puff of air. "I talked to one of her neighbors who said he hadn't seen her all day. I decided to head to the bookstore."

I held my breath. "Did you?"

He nodded. "The place was dark inside, and she didn't respond when I knocked. But her car was in the parking lot."

"Did you try the back door?"

He shook his head. "I figured if she was in there, and she didn't answer my knock, she wasn't ready to talk to me. It never occurred to me that something had happened to her. If only..."

Unable to detect the usual signs of lying in his body language, I searched his face. Maybe Nick didn't kill Azmina. "So, then what did you do?"

He blinked. "I don't know why I'm telling you this."

"Sometimes talking about a traumatic event with a stranger can help," I encouraged, taking advantage of the opening he'd provided.

He rubbed his forehead. "I went home, and when I came back the next day... well, you know the rest."

So that was it? "Before you left the store that night, did you see anyone around?"

"Just as I arrived, I almost collided with a black SUV driving across the parking lot. The windows were tinted, but I could see the outline of two people in the front seat. When Azmina didn't come to the door of her shop, I presumed she was the passenger."

"But now we know she wasn't." Maybe Nick had seen the killer leaving. Not one person, but two? Or maybe he was fabricating a story to take the spotlight off himself. "Did you recognize the vehicle?"

He shook his head.

"Did you get the make and model?"

"That's what the police asked me, but no."

My lips curled into a half-smile. "Men usually notice stuff like that."

"Yeah, the detective grilled me, especially after I admitted going to the bookstore that night." He tapped his fingers on the desk. "Turns out, two of the business owners in that shopping center own black SUVs, so it wasn't unusual for one to be there. I guess their alibis checked out."

"How do you know this?" I wondered if Detective Ross had shared more information about the case with Nick than he had with me.

"No one has been arrested yet, so I just assumed." Nick pursed his lips. "I sure hope they hurry and find the killer."

"A lot of people think it was José Garcia, the owner of the Mexican restaurant." I pushed a strand of hair behind my ear. "José and Azmina had some run-ins about the cats she fed."

"I remember. They wouldn't stay out of his dumpster. Not a good look for business."

"You know he committed suicide in his jail cell?" I studied Nick's face for a reaction.

"It was all over the news. I don't think José did it, though."

"Why not?"

"José was a hothead, but he was more bark than bite. And who'd be foolish enough to kill a woman over some nuisance cats?"

"If not José, then who?" I didn't tell Nick *he*'d been one of my prime suspects.

"That's for the police to figure out." His phone vibrated on the desk. He looked down but did not attempt to answer.

"I shouldn't keep you." I stood. "Can I leave this file with you? Maybe if you read through the data, you'll find you can live with the ordinance changes I'm proposing."

"Go ahead." With a hint of a chuckle, he accepted the folder from me. "You remind me a little of Azmina."

I raised my eyebrows.

"I mean, you look nothing alike, obviously, but there's something about your subtle determination." He stared wistfully at the wall.

"I didn't know her very well, but I consider that a compliment."

He rose. "Let me walk you out. I'll have to unlock the front door."

We headed down the hall together, and then, with a twist of a key, he opened the door and freed me from my once-imagined prison.

Strolling along the sidewalk, I basked in the waning sunshine, no longer convinced that Nick Norton was Azmina's killer. But who was? And who were the two people leaving the area in a black SUV?

Chapter Thirty

Victoria's red Mercedes straddled two spaces in our tiny asphalt parking lot—her usual inconsiderate gesture. Her middle finger to the law firm that had provided her first job, and to the husband who had loved her faithfully.

Tempted to crowd in next to her, I played nice and parked on the far side of the lot next to Barry's dark green Subaru Forester. Such a dark green that it looked black in certain lighting...

I shook my head. There were a lot of black SUVs around town, and many more dark-colored vehicles that could pass for black at night under artificial light.

Still rehashing my conversation with Nick, I headed inside.

Victoria's former office remained unoccupied, and Barry's door was closed. My blood simmered as I wondered if his ex-wife had been the reason he'd stood me up for our meeting at the foundation.

Jane stared at her computer, fixed like a mannequin in the same position she'd been in when I left. Glimpsing my empty "in" tray, I pointed to one of the cardboard boxes at her feet. "Are you done with those files yet?"

I took her limp shrug for acquiescence, picked up the box, and hauled it to my cubicle. She did not react. Something must be wrong with Jane, but I didn't care enough to ask what it was. She wouldn't tell me anyway.

Before tackling my new pile of work, I called the Board of Commissioners. Amanda, the office assistant, answered promptly, remembering immediately who I was. She scheduled a meeting with Roy Don Whitehead at ten the next morning and asked me to email the documents for his review. She'd try to invite another commissioner to our meeting but couldn't promise anyone's availability.

I thanked her, hung up, and then cast a defiant look in the direction of Barry's closed office door as I emailed Amanda the requested documents.

The first folder I tackled contained bankruptcy papers for a client named Eric Graham. Commissioner Eric Graham? Skimming the filing, I learned he'd owned a men's clothing store in the Patel Shopping Center, and his business had failed last year. All that remained now was another empty storefront contributing to the neighborhood blight.

One of Graham's major creditors was Azmina Patel, for unpaid rent. My heartbeat quickened. A motive for murder? Unlikely. She'd be the one after him, not the reverse. But what if they'd argued about it, and he became violent?

Another creditor listed in the filing was Connors Insurance, for overdue premiums. Such a small town; I was beginning to learn all the players.

Since the file contained no photo, I googled his name. Old ads for Graham's Menswear popped onto the screen. Also, articles from the local news about the bankruptcy, several written by my friend Jill.

My cell phone buzzed. Catherine Foster's name appeared on the screen.

"Do you still have community service hours?" Catherine asked before I could say hello.

"Why?"

"I'm trapping at Leonardo's Sunday night, and I could use your help. And are you finished with the equipment you lent to Lisa Ross?"

I spun away from my computer screen, resisting the urge to keep reading about Eric Graham. "We caught the last two cats and got them neutered yesterday. Most likely, she'll turn them loose tonight. And Lisa offered to clean all the traps."

Catherine made a noise between a snort and a scoff.

"If you need the traps earlier, I can ask her if it's okay to pick them up tonight, but she might not have time to clean them."

"You really got all those cats?"

Maybe it was my imagination, but Catherine sounded impressed.

"And one extra," I replied proudly. "Two of her females were in heat, and a new male showed up."

With a hint of a chuckle, Catherine asked, "Did Lisa drive you crazy?"

I thought about Lisa's antics the first night. But maybe I wasn't the best teacher, and Catherine would be sure to point that out. "She was okay. She tries."

The chuckle moved deeper into Catherine's throat to become a chortle.

"Did Lisa help feed the cats behind Black Cat Books?" I asked.

The chortle became a huff. "Mainly when I was coming to trap, and I'd asked Azmina to withhold food."

Now I could see how Catherine would find that behavior annoying. "Since Azmina's gone, Lisa said she and Natalie, the dry cleaner, plan to take over the feeding."

"Ha! The cats will move on. Maybe to Leonardo's. Better cuisine."

I didn't ask Catherine why she thought the feral cats would refuse food from Lisa and Natalie. And with no more harassment from José, they would be safe staying put. "Did Azmina and Lisa get along?"

Catherine sighed. "How should I know? I couldn't be bothered with their drama."

"Do you think—"

"Look, D.D., get those traps from Lisa and meet me at Leonardo's Sunday night at nine-thirty."

I'd wanted to ask Catherine to speculate about murder suspects, but I should have known better. She was strictly TNVR business. "Yes, ma'am. See you then."

I hung up and went back to reading about Eric Graham.

His race for the Board of Commissioners had been contentious. His opponents had capitalized on the bankruptcy, pointing out that it demonstrated a lack of fiscal responsibility, which would carry over to his handling of taxpayer dollars. "You don't hire a fox to guard the henhouse," quoted an editorial.

Competing for the position was none other than my nemesis, Victoria Barton. I had to laugh. I'd had no idea she had political aspirations, but it totally fit what I knew of her character.

The Graham team fought back with charges of nepotism; they'd uncovered that Vince Connors, already on the Board of Commissioners, was Victoria's half-brother. They suggested the pair might form an unfair voting coalition. Her affair with Roy Don Whitehead, hot news then, had also surfaced, but more as innuendo than established fact. Barry's name was dragged through the mud; it saddened me to see him portrayed as a wimpy victim who continued to campaign for his cheating wife.

Another argument the Graham team made was the conflict of interest presented by Victoria's real estate ties. Motions involving real estate issues routinely appeared on the agenda, and Victoria, as an aggressive, up-and-coming realtor, had a hand in many of the deals.

Downplayed was the fact that Roy Don Whitehead, one of the senior commissioners, owned the real estate firm for which Victoria worked. Apparently, conflict of interest hadn't been so much of an issue when he was elected.

Victoria had fought back with allegations of sexism. Barry had remained by her side, her biggest supporter.

I leaned back in my chair. I felt no feminine allegiance to Victoria. Eric Graham hadn't impressed me either, but I was glad he'd beaten Victoria. What if she were sitting on the Board of Commissioners now, when I was trying to effect an ordinance change?

"DeeLo?"

I hadn't heard Barry approach my cubicle. So engrossed in my Google research, I'd only archived a few of the documents from the first file I'd handled—Eric Graham's.

I spun around in my chair. Like the ball in a roulette wheel, my emotions bounced from guilt at being caught surfing the web, to annoyance at being stood up, to curiosity. The ball stopped on curiosity. I peered past the walls of my cubicle. "Did Victoria leave already?"

Barry nodded. "Let's get out of here."

* * *

Barry offered to take me out to dinner, but I suggested eating in. I had plenty of leftover Fettuccine Alfredo, and since adopting Manny, I preferred staying home.

While I heated the pasta and washed spinach for a salad, Barry whipped up my favorite vinaigrette. I liked the way he knew how to find everything he needed in my kitchen without asking.

"So..." I fingered the dark green leaves in my hand. "Was Victoria the emergency? The reason you couldn't make it this afternoon?"

"There was a problem with the Power of Attorney for her father." Barry sprinkled thyme into the aromatic mixture of sesame oil, pressed garlic, and rice vinegar.

"And it couldn't wait?"

"They're getting ready to admit him to the memory facility, and she has to sell his condo to pay for his care."

"I guess you got it all straightened out?" I tried to make my tone light and understanding, rather than accusatory and nagging, which more closely reflected my feelings.

"All done." With a final whisk of the dressing, he brought it over to pour on the salad. "I'm sorry I missed your appointment at the foundation. But I knew you'd do fine without me."

Your appointment? I bit my lip, trying to stifle my annoyance. Barry was with me now, not Victoria. He wouldn't have chosen her situation over mine if he'd thought I needed him. Part of me felt pride for the confidence he had in my abilities. But why did his ex-wife always turn up at the wrong time? "You don't know the half of it."

"I want to hear all about it."

When we sat down to eat, I told him about my discussion with Nick, leaving out my initial terror that Barry had left me alone with Azmina's murderer, since now I was fairly certain Nick didn't do it.

"Do you think he'll support the ordinance?" Barry twirled some fettuccine around his fork.

"He's not a fan of TNVR, but I hope I convinced him there's nothing in the revised language that requires him to allow trapping in the nature reserve."

Manny rubbed against my legs. I bent down to pet his head. "I bet if Azmina were alive, she'd persuade Nick to support it."

"You talked about Azmina?"

I nodded. "We both hope the police find her killer soon. I don't know about you, but it creeps me out that there's a murderer loose in this town, and we don't even know why Azmina was targeted."

"The police arrested the owner of the Mexican restaurant next door, José Garcia. The one who committed suicide in his cell." Barry set down his fork. "News about the case has been quiet lately, so I figured they were about to close it."

"Detective Ross told me the case is still open." I watched Barry's face for a reaction, but he'd returned his attention to his food.

* * *

After dinner, we adjourned to the living room. As soon as we sat down on the couch, Manny hopped onto my lap. I turned to Barry. "If José didn't kill Azmina, who do you suspect?"

"Me?" His face turned a shade lighter. "I haven't thought much about it. Like I said, José—"

"But don't you wonder?"

He patted my knee, which normally wouldn't bother me, but now I found it condescending. "I know you like to read murder mysteries. And this one hit close to home since you found the body."

"No theories at all? Azmina was your client. Half the people in Pecan County are your clients. You know things about them that others don't."

"I can't imagine any of my clients committing murder." Barry threw his arm around me and pulled me close. Manny held his position on my lap. "I suppose you have a suspect in mind?"

"Victoria had something to do with it."

Barry's eyes widened, and he retracted his arm. "Victoria?"

"You told me she had a strong motive."

"What motive? Now that Azmina's dead, so is the land sale, and Victoria won't earn her commission. At least, not until the estate is settled, and the beneficiary decides what to do."

"But look how she's trying to falsify documents to say the sale was already final. Look how she's trying to find a loophole in Catherine's foundation—"

"DeeLo."

"Well, isn't she?"

Barry adjusted his glasses. "Victoria may be involved in some questionable business dealings, but she isn't a killer. I've known her since high school."

"You said she's changed since she left you for Roy Don. But you still have blinders on when it comes to your ex-wife."

He reached out and pulled me toward him. "Why are you jealous of Victoria? Our marriage is over. Don't you know you're the only woman I want to be with?"

I leaned into his embrace, which displaced Manny from my lap. The cat eyed us for a moment and then settled into another corner of the couch.

As we kissed, I should have felt comforted and reassured, but for some reason, I didn't.

Chapter Thirty-One

I chose my outfit carefully as I prepared for my meeting with Commissioner Roy Don Whitehead. I didn't want to wear anything too risqué, but subtly playing up my best attributes should help keep his attention without distracting him from my presentation.

Remembering the lascivious way he'd ogled my legs during my last visit—when I'd been wearing a skirt—I opted for a navy gabardine pantsuit. The fit was perfect, flattering the trim lines of my figure; the color both complemented my blond hair and brought out the dark blue flecks in my eyes. The neckline of my beige silk shell dipped just enough to frame my mother's pearl necklace without revealing cleavage. Matching pearl earrings completed the ensemble. After a twirl before my full-length mirror, I decided I'd struck the right balance between professional and demurely attractive.

My entrance generated the desired response.

Roy Don rose from behind his desk, and his hazel eyes sparkled like fool's gold. "Hey there, little lady. Nice to see you again."

I flashed a polite smile and seated myself in the side chair, crossing my ankles. "Nice to see you as well, and thanks so much for meeting with me. Did you have a chance to read the document I emailed over?"

He tapped his computer monitor and gave me one of those the-dog-ate-my-homework looks.

"It's okay," I replied. I hadn't expected him to study my proposal before our meeting. "I brought you a hard copy." I passed the packet of papers across the desk and opened my folder to my own copy of the revised ordinance. "I've highlighted the parts that have changed. Please look at the Definitions section. We've added the terms 'community cat' and 'community cat caretaker.' We've also modified the meanings of 'owner' and 'animal abandonment.'"

He skimmed my changes, lips moving slightly, and I watched his face for reactions. A nod, a wrinkled brow, but nothing negative.

When he flipped over the last page, I asked, "Do you have any questions?"

He stroked his silver mustache. "This is a good start."

"Start?"

"Yeah, if we're going to rewrite the animal ordinance, there are a lot of changes I've been itching to make, and you've opened up a golden opportunity."

"What other changes?"

"Tethering. We need to add an anti-tethering clause." He shook his head. "No one should be tying up their dog all day. It's inhumane. As a volunteer for the Humane Society, don't you agree?"

My shoulders sagged. "I don't disagree, Commissioner. But tethering has nothing to do with TNVR." Not being a dog owner, I didn't know much about the tethering issue, but I'd heard it was controversial in Pecan County. Not something I was ready to tackle. Certainly not before implementing TNVR, which had become my passion.

"Gotta strike while the iron's hot." He winked. "Get as much as we can."

I opened my folder again and pulled out the copy of the PowerPoint presentation I'd prepared. "Banning tethering doesn't save the county money, so it's going to be a harder sell. But supporting TNVR will result in significant cost reductions for Animal Control, especially if they partner with nonprofit rescue groups like the Pecan Point Humane Society that can do most of the trapping and transporting with volunteer labor and private donations." I showed him the cat intake and euthanasia statistics Sandra had provided, contrasted with the before-and-after stats of other communities running successful TNVR programs, including the Wisconsin county where Sandra last worked. Using those figures, I'd projected potential cost savings for Pecan County's animal shelter.

Roy Don barely glanced at my impressive numbers. "Another thing we need, what I've been pushing for since I've been in county government, is a Citizens' Advisory Committee. You know, a group from the community, appointed by the Board of Commissioners, to oversee the operation of the animal shelter. And, of course, we'll invite a representative from the Humane Society to sit on the committee." A dimple formed in his cheek. "You interested?"

No! I pressed my hand to my forehead. If I went along with the Citizens' Advisory Committee, I'd lose Sandra's support, which was crucial to the success of a TNVR program. "The Director of Animal Control is not in favor of a Citizens' Advisory Committee."

He let out a throaty guffaw. "She'll come around."

"But why don't we start with something less contentious? I have Animal Control and the Humane Society on board with the TNVR reforms. And Nick Norton with the Pecan Creek Nature Reserve has agreed not to oppose it." When Roy Don's expression didn't change, I added, "We can work on those other issues later, if you like."

"Well, little lady, you sure did your homework." He leaned back in his chair.

"When can we get this proposal on the agenda?"

There was a knock on the door. I turned to see Chairman Graham poke his bald head in. Eric Graham, the bankrupt clothier who beat out Victoria Barton for a seat on the Board of Commissioners. After my earlier research, I couldn't help viewing him as the businessman whose shuttered storefront remained an eyesore in the Patel Shopping Center. "Sorry I'm late," he said as he entered the room and took a seat across from me.

"We were just having a nice little chat about the animal ordinance," Roy Don explained.

I jumped into action, handing Eric a packet of papers. "I'm proposing changes to the wording that will make it easier and more cost-effective for Pecan County to control the overpopulation of free-roaming cats." Leaning over him, I pointed to the key passages as I explained the benefits of TNVR.

"Ain't she something?" said Roy Don, grinning, when I took a breath.

"Chairman Graham," I said, ignoring Roy Don's leer as I returned to my chair. "Do you have any questions about my proposal?"

The chairman stacked the papers neatly on his lap. "You've done an excellent job presenting your case, Ms. Myer."

I smiled. "How soon can we get it on the agenda for a vote? As you can see, we're ready to implement this program once we get approval from the Board of Commissioners. The sooner this happens, the sooner we can start saving feline lives and, most importantly, saving the county money."

He rose. "Our docket is full for the next few months, and this isn't a priority. Let's talk about it again after the first of the year."

My face fell as the chairman left the room, dropping his copy of my presentation into the wastebasket.

Roy Don stood, signaling our meeting was over. "Thanks for coming in, little lady. Always nice to see you."

Furious, I rounded the corner, stepped into the lobby, and froze. Officer Stan Friendly and Victoria Barton circled each other like boxers in a ring, their faces red with rage.

"You heard me. What's it worth to you?" Officer Friendly's smile looked more like a snarl, emphasizing the misnomer of his surname.

"Pitiful man! Not a penny." Victoria tossed her head of auburn hair, which barely moved, as if it had been shellacked in place. "Why do you think you can hurt me?"

"Just you wait. Evidence has a way of reappearing." He spun toward the front door.

"You're playing with fire, Officer," she called after him. "There will be more questions about where that paper has been all this time. No one will care what's written on it."

Her cold blue eyes met mine as she shifted her gaze toward the hallway leading to Roy Don's office.

"Hello again, Victoria." I put on a smile fake enough to rival one of hers. "We have to stop meeting like this."

As I strode toward the exit, I felt her icy glare and smiled even more. What could Officer Friendly and Victoria Barton be arguing about?

Chapter Thirty-Two

Deflated after my meeting with the commissioners, I trudged back to the law office to salve my wounds. Jane wasn't at her desk, which was a blessing, as I couldn't have handled another of her barbs.

I retreated to my cubicle, slumped in my chair, and stared at my computer screen. I'd been so sure Roy Don was going to love my proposal and promise to put it on the agenda for the next Board of Commissioners' meeting. My PowerPoint projecting cost savings for the county was going to wow everyone in attendance. My allies would speak in favor of TNVR, and, after the formality of a unanimous vote by the commissioners, the revised ordinance would become law. Rescue volunteers like Catherine would never have to face harassment from the likes of Officer Friendly again.

Instead, I was almost back to the drawing board. "Let's talk about it again after the first of the year." What did that mean? Chairman Graham hadn't even bothered to take the pages with him. And Roy Don wanted to derail the whole proposal by adding hot-button issues that had nothing to do with TNVR. Partnering with him would lead to months of debate and eventual defeat.

I wanted to break something.

To top it off, I'd run into two of my least favorite people. What was going on between Officer Friendly and Victoria? Could one or both have something to do with Azmina's death? "Evidence has a way of reappearing," the cop had threatened. What evidence? It had to be the paper I'd seen in Azmina's hand, the one with the Barton, Barton & Barton logo. Officially first on the scene, the patrol officer had the opportunity to tamper with it. How was Victoria connected?

"DeeLo?"

Like a sunflower toward the light, I turned to the sound of Barry's voice. "Yes?"

"I have some bad news."

"Bad news?" What could be worse than my latest failure?

His voice was somber. "Jane has been diagnosed with stage three colon cancer. She'll be taking an extended medical leave while she undergoes treatment."

My breath caught; this was the last news I'd expected. "I had no idea she was sick. I'm so sorry. Is there anything I can do?" Had my last words to Jane been kind? Probably not.

"Nice of you to be concerned, but I don't think there's anything we can do right now. I'll keep you posted."

I felt ashamed that I hadn't been more cordial to Jane. Perhaps her shortness with me had come from her illness. Cancer was a horrible curse I'd never wish on anyone.

Barry was still speaking. "And unfortunately, I won't be able to take you with me to Savannah next week for the estate lawyers' conference like we'd planned. I'd been looking forward to it, but I need you here to manage the office."

I'd forgotten the conference started next Monday. Barry invited me weeks ago, and it had seemed like a fun, romantic getaway. We'd made those arrangements long before my orderly life had been upended by a D.U.I., community service, and the world of TNVR. Not to mention, finding a dead person. The trip would have represented a pleasant return to normalcy. Or an escape from my new reality. Trying to keep the disappointment out of my voice, I replied, "I understand. And I know you'll only be a phone call away."

He smiled sadly. "I'll make it up to you."

I put on my most mature, magnanimous face. "It's okay."

"We'll get a temp to help out while Jane's gone, but I can't expect someone new to run the office alone."

"We'll be fine," I assured him. "I promise to pull my weight—better than I've been doing lately."

"You've had a lot going on," he rationalized for me. Again, I felt grateful for Barry's understanding nature. I'd never meant to take advantage of his feelings about me to garner special treatment in our working relationship, but I knew I had. "By the way, I also have some better news," he added.

"Let's hear it."

"I spoke to Vince Connors this morning, and he's agreed to come by tonight after dinner to look at your ordinance revision." Barry folded his arms and gave me a self-satisfied smile.

I almost fell out of my chair. "For real? Oh my gosh! Thank you!" I didn't tell him how I'd struck out earlier with two of the other commissioners since Barry had not been thrilled about my working with Roy Don. Perhaps if Vince was impressed with my proposal, he could persuade the others.

"I thought you'd be pleased." Barry was still beaming.

Casting a cursory look to ensure there was no one else in the office, I rose and threw myself into his arms to thank him properly. He held me tight, as if he didn't want our embrace to end.

* * *

After an early dinner of Chinese take-out, I set about tidying the living room for our guest. "Should I make coffee? Decaf?" I asked. "Does Vince drink it?"

"It couldn't hurt," Barry replied. "I'll have some even if he doesn't."

Reminding me it was time for his evening treat, Manny wove himself between my ankles as I bustled around the kitchen preparing the coffee.

The doorbell rang. I had cat treats in one hand and coffee mugs in the other. "Can you get that?" I called to Barry, who was already in the living room.

Footsteps crossed the floor. The door opened, and bro-backslapping ensued. "Vince, great to see you," said Barry.

"Nice place your friend has," came the deep baritone of Commissioner Vince Connors as he entered my living room.

"Hey, Barry," Demi's shrill voice pierced the air.

"Demi," came Barry's lukewarm greeting over my niece's clomping footsteps.

Manny's ears flattened with a hackle-raising growl. He dropped the treat he'd just been begging for and beelined into my bedroom.

"Manny? What's got into you?" I asked my cat. "Are you afraid Demi's going to kidnap you again?"

After picking up the dropped cat treat and putting away the bag, I headed into the living room to join the others.

I eyed my niece, who was standing too close to Commissioner Connors for this to be a chance encounter. "What are you doing here, Demi?" Was she going to ruin my presentation by taking over the spotlight?

Demi grinned, enjoying my baffled look. "We were out for dinner, and Vince said he was coming over here. I hope you don't mind."

Vince? We?

Commissioner Connors was taller than I remembered, and his broad shoulders made me again picture him as a football player whose best memories were of high school triumphs. His hair was more silver than black, and he looked too old for Demi. But then again, she'd dated a lot of older men. I wondered how the two of them had met.

"Commissioner, thank you so much for coming," I said as we shook hands. "Can I get you some coffee? Something else to drink?"

"No thanks." He flashed me one of those charming, politician smiles, and his blue eyes twinkled. "I'm fine." And then... did he squeeze Demi's arm? In an intimate way... He gestured around the room. "You have a lovely home, Ms. Myer."

"Thank you." I tipped my shoulder toward the couch. "Please have a seat." I turned to Demi. "Barry and I invited Commissioner Connors over to discuss some county business. Are you sure you want to hang around?"

"Why not?" Demi shrugged and plopped down next to Vince, their thighs touching.

When everyone was settled, I launched into my explanation of Trap-Neuter-Vaccinate-Return and touted its benefits. My speech became more fine-tuned with every performance.

Vince watched me with rapt attention, and Barry radiated with pride. Demi examined her freshly manicured nails.

"Here are the ordinance changes Pecan County needs to make TNVR legal." I handed Vince a copy of the document I'd given Roy Don and Eric earlier, with the proposed additions and changes highlighted.

Demi peered over Vince's shoulder. Yawning, she got up and left the room. I hoped she wasn't going to help herself to my wine and get soused again.

The commissioner read through the text while Barry and I waited, watching his face for a reaction. Like Roy Don, he did a lot of nodding and brow creasing. When he finished, he looked up and smiled. "Looks good. I don't see any problem with these changes."

Barry and I exchanged triumphant grins.

"I have the support of Animal Control and the Humane Society. The sooner we can get this revision approved, the sooner we can start saving feline lives and, most importantly, saving the county money."

"Do you have any supporting data that says the county will save money?"

"As a matter of fact, I do." I picked up a copy of my PowerPoint, with its persuasive graphs and statistics, and held it toward him.

His cell phone vibrated. With a glance at the phone's screen, he raised his hand. "Excuse me."

Still holding the papers, I watched impatiently as he listened to the caller. His face paled. "Vicky, slow down. Vicky—"

Vicky? His sister Victoria? My nemesis had interrupted our critical meeting; somehow, I was not surprised. Could she see through walls?

I stared at Barry in alarm; his expression remained unreadable.

Vince hung up and threw us an apologetic look. "I'm so sorry, but something has come up." He grasped the copy of my PowerPoint. "Can I take this with me, and we'll talk about it next week?"

Barry cleared his throat. "I'll be in Savannah all next week."

"Week after, then?" Vince headed for the door, papers in hand.

"I'm staying in town," I said. "Let me know when you want to finish our discussion. Next week is fine."

He studied my face as if seeing me for the first time. "Okay. I'll be in touch."

The door closed behind him. He hadn't even said goodbye to Demi, who had not returned from the kitchen or the bathroom, or wherever she'd gone.

I peered out the bay window, relieved to spot Demi's turquoise MINI Cooper parked on the street. They must have come in separate vehicles, so at least my niece wasn't stranded.

"What do you think?" I turned back to Barry.

Barry smiled. "Vince was impressed. Too bad he got called away before you could dazzle him with your numbers, but it sounds like he's interested in hearing more."

I moved across the room to give Barry a hug. "Thanks again for setting up this meeting. You don't know how much I needed some positive feedback. I was beginning to feel like all our work had been in vain."

We kissed, then Barry looked up. "Where did Demi go?"

I groaned. "I better check on her. The cat freaked out when she arrived. He must remember how she kidnapped him the other day while I was gone."

Barry shook his head in commiseration.

* * *

I found Demi in my bedroom with Manny on her lap, an open bag of cat treats by her side.

"Looks like he's forgiven you." I sank onto the bed next to her and gave Manny's head a pat, earning an appreciative purr.

"Of course," she said. "Manny likes me."

"He likes anyone who bribes him." I pointed to the treats.

My niece just smiled.

"So," I eyed her, "what's the deal with you and Commissioner Connors?"

"We met at the memory care home. Vince's father just moved there, and I was visiting Grandma." She glanced at me sideways, gauging my reaction. "I haven't seen you there lately." Her exultant look told me she'd been keeping score, which she only did when she was winning.

"I'm going there tomorrow," I retorted.

She rolled her eyes as if she didn't believe me. "Anyway, Vince asked me a lot of questions about the facility. We talked for a while, and the next thing I knew, he'd invited me to dinner." She stroked Manny's silky, black fur, and his body rubbed against her hand as he reveled in the attention.

"I guess you're over Carl." Only a few days ago, Demi had sat here, getting drunk and bawling her eyes out over her lost love.

"Carl Who?" She winked.

"I'm glad you have a new man in your life." I tapped my knees and made a kissing sound to my cat. To my delight, Manny abandoned her and hopped onto my lap. I rewarded him with more petting. "But why did you come here tonight?"

"I thought you might have an update on the Pecan Point murder mystery." Demi flashed a conspiratorial smile. "You left me hanging."

Had she blabbed to Vince my suspicions about his sister? "You didn't mention—"

"Did you confront that scary Nick guy? I was worried about you going to meet with him." Demi touched her cheek. "Or do you still think Victoria did it?"

Before I could answer, Barry appeared in my bedroom doorway. "What are you two talking about?"

Chapter Thirty-Three

D emi's eyes shifted from Barry to me as she adjusted her position on the bed. "Guess I interrupted your evening."

Neither of us rushed to disagree.

"Barry will be out of town all next week," I explained. "I was supposed to go to the conference in Savannah with him, but now it's not possible."

"Got it." Demi rose. "You need to stock up on some alone time." She stroked Manny's head again.

"Thank you," said Barry. I knew he was exercising restraint by not adding a snarky comment about Demi's lack of perception.

I rose, too, so I could escort my niece to the front door, keep her from lingering. "Let's get together next week and catch up."

When Demi had gone, I found Barry reclined on my bed, the lights dimmed. Batting my eyelashes seductively, I unbuttoned my blouse.

* * *

The next morning, it felt weird walking past Jane's empty desk. She'd been out of the office a lot lately, but this time was different; her stuff had been cleared out, like she was never coming back.

The phone rang, and it took me a second to remember Jane wasn't going to answer. I picked it up. "Barton and Barton." No third Barton. *Take that, Jane and Victoria.*

"Good morning," came the voice of Kyra Chowdhury, Azmina's sister. "Is that you, DeeLo?"

"Yes, good morning, Kyra," I replied. "How have you been?"

"Fine, thank you. How's Manny?"

My heart fluttered as if there were a hummingbird trapped in my chest, struggling to escape. Had Kyra changed her mind? Was she going to take my cat away after all? "He's doing great. So happy." *With me. Where he belongs.*

"That's wonderful."

When she paused, I sensed, with relief, that Manny wasn't the reason for her call. "How can we help you?"

"Is Barry available?"

"He's in a meeting, but I can have him call back." I twisted a strand of hair around a finger. "Or, if you run your question by me, maybe it's something I can handle." Despite my lack of legal training, there were tasks I could take off his plate. I'd have to, now that we were short-staffed. "Or at least, I can brief him."

"Okay, maybe you can clear something up," she began. "I was going through the list of Azmina's assets, and it looks like she was the beneficiary of a life insurance policy her husband purchased."

I wasn't surprised; the Patels owned lots of property. I'd have been more surprised if the couple didn't have life insurance. But why was Kyra bringing it up now?

"For five million dollars."

"Wow." I hadn't reviewed the list of Azmina's assets, but five million dollars should have helped her maintain the shopping center better than she had done after her husband's death.

I flashed back to the night of the murder when Catherine mentioned Azmina had been waiting for an insurance check.

"But I can't see where the proceeds were ever paid."

"What?" Azmina's husband had been dead for over six months. I'd never filed a claim for life insurance, but it seemed like the bureaucratic wheels should turn faster than that. When my stepfather, Al, died, my mother received his death benefit in about two months.

"Unless the funds went into an account that I'm missing," Kyra said.

I picked up a pad of paper. "Can you give me the policy number and the name of the insurance company? I'll call and see if I can find out what's going on."

After Kyra hung up, I located Azmina's file in Barry's office. Fortunately, the police had returned it; with Jane's haphazard filing system, I wasn't sure if we'd kept copies of every critical document.

We had no record of the life insurance policy in our office file. But since Rajindra Patel was already dead when Barry prepared Azmina's latest will, his life insurance policy wouldn't have been among the assets listed in her estate. Nevertheless, she would have told Barry she was expecting a payout. She'd apparently kept the paperwork because Kyra had it now.

I called the company, American Life, and explained I was from the law firm representing Azmina Patel's estate and that Azmina was a beneficiary of one of their life insurance policies. I gave them the account number Kyra had provided.

The representative put me on hold. In a moment, she returned to the line. "I'm sorry, Ma'am. We can't give out information about our policies over the phone."

Letting out a puff of air, I repeated my status as a legal representative of the beneficiary. "Perhaps I can speak to your supervisor?"

"One moment, please."

After a few minutes of hold music, a different voice came on the line. "I'm sorry, but we can't give out information about our policies to a third party."

"Okay," I said in my most authoritative tone. "What is your name, please? We'll need to subpoena those files." I had no idea if we could really subpoena their files, but my bully tactics seemed to scare her.

"Just a moment."

I listened to three smooth jazz songs before switching to speakerphone.

Someone came on the line to verify the policy number and name of the deceased.

"Rajindra Patel." I repeated the policy number and his date of death. "The beneficiary was his wife, Azmina Patel."

"Thank you." I heard a click and then more hold music.

Two more songs played, and then a commercial for life insurance.

236

"Ms. Myer?"

I was across the room watering a plant and had to rush back to Jane's desk. My desk now. "Yes?"

"I'm sorry, but that policy was canceled two years ago."

"Excuse me..."

"The policy is no longer valid."

"Why?"

"The client stopped paying the premiums."

"But... you're sure?" Five million dollars! Gone because of missed payments. How was I going to break the news to Kyra?

"We already explained that to Mrs. Patel two weeks ago. I'm very sorry."

Stunned, I thanked the representative and hung up.

I called Kyra back. "Bad news." I cleared my throat. "The insurance company said Mr. Patel stopped paying the premiums, so the policy was canceled."

"No!" Kyra's voice rose an octave. "That's impossible."

"I'm sorry. All I know is what they told me."

"Raj paid the premiums every month. Direct debits. I have the bank statements to prove it."

I slumped in my chair. "You're sure that's what the payments were for? And that the company was American Life?"

"Yes! I have the policy, and the agreement with the insurance company to have the payments debited each month from their checking account." Over the sound of shuffling papers, she read, "Connors Insurance, Ltd. Lisa Ross was her agent."

"Lisa Ross?" I relaxed. "I know her. Connors Insurance is in Azmina's shopping center. We'll get this matter straightened out." I thumbed through our file. "Can you email me that last statement, showing the debit for the premium?"

"Will do." Kyra's voice had returned to normal. "Thank you, DeeLo."

"Don't worry. We're on it."

* * *

When Barry came out of his meeting, I briefed him on the situation with the unpaid life insurance benefit. "Did Azmina ever mention it to you?" I asked.

He adjusted his glasses. "She did. But when I prepared her will, her husband had only been dead for a couple of weeks. At that time, no one had any reason to believe she wouldn't receive the funds."

"It must be a clerical error. I've asked Kyra to send me verification of the payments, and we can follow up from there."

"Thanks, DeeLo. I appreciate your initiative."

Before I could bask in the glow of Barry's compliment, the front door opened to admit his next client. The two of them headed into the conference room.

As promised, Kyra emailed me multiple bank statements and the purchase agreement between Rajindra Patel and Connors Insurance. The policy with American Life carried a death benefit of five million dollars, naming Azmina Patel as the beneficiary. The last debit from their joint checking account, in the amount of the agreed premium, had been posted the week of Mr. Patel's death. His life insurance policy should have been current.

American Life must have made a horrific mistake, and I needed to correct it.

I called the company back, got put on hold again. The original representative I'd spoken with was unavailable, so I had to start over with someone else, go through the whole stonewalling process again.

"I'm sorry, Ms. Myer," the supervisor said after listening to my story. "But we haven't received any payments from Connors Insurance in over two years. They no longer hold any current policies with us."

"You're sure?" I tugged at my hair. "They collected the money for the premiums, but never forwarded it to you?" Why wouldn't the payments go directly to the insurance company?

"That's something you'll have to take up with the agent," she replied. "Perhaps they switched the policy to a different company. We were making some changes to our rate and commission structure around that time. A lot of insurance brokers aren't exclusive; they shop around to find the best rates for their clients."

I thanked her and hung up.

My next call, to Lisa, went to voicemail.

I started to leave a message about Rajindra Patel's policy with American Life, then decided the situation was too complicated to explain in a voicemail. It might sound like I was accusing her or Vince of wrongdoing, which could set a negative tone for our conversation. Surely, there would be a logical explanation, and the Pecan Point police detective's wife wasn't scamming her clients.

When asking Lisa to call me back, I reminded her of my intention to stop by that evening to pick up Catherine's traps.

* * *

Working late not only helped me get organized in my new role at the office, but it also ensured Lisa would beat me to her house. I didn't relish another awkward dialogue alone with Detective Ross, even though I was dying to quiz him again about the missing document from the crime scene. After mulling over the exchange I'd witnessed between Officer Friendly and Victoria Barton, I was growing more certain the patrol cop had taken it. Why did he think a letter with the Barton, Barton & Barton logo would interest Barry's ex-wife? Could it implicate her in the murder?

Lisa was feeding the cats on the edge of the patio when I pulled into her driveway. The clowder had grown to five felines; the tuxedo male we'd caught and fixed had stayed.

She waved, and I walked toward her.

"I guess Tux didn't find his way home." I gestured toward the new addition, vying for position at the feeding station with an orange tabby.

"He likes it here," she said, filling another bowl with Meow Mix. "Your traps are all clean and sitting on the porch. I'll get Paul to help you with them."

"Thanks, but I can manage. And I'm sure Catherine will appreciate your cleaning them. We're trapping at Leonardo's on Sunday night."

"Thank you again for all your assistance with these cats."

"You're welcome." I shuffled, not quite ready to head back to the porch to pick up Catherine's traps. "By the way... something came up today at work that you might be able to help with."

"Oh?"

"Do you remember selling a life insurance policy a few years ago to Azmina's husband, Rajindra Patel?"

She closed the bag of cat food.

"With American Life," I added. "The death benefit was for five million dollars. Azmina was the beneficiary."

Lisa watched the felines gobble their food.

"Apparently, the death benefit was never paid," I continued.

"Really?" Lisa's face had paled. "Are you sure she filed a claim?"

"It was denied. American Life said the policy had been canceled for nonpayment of premiums."

She shrugged, still not meeting my gaze. "Well, if Mr. Patel didn't keep up with the payments, there's not much we can do."

"Except he was current on the premiums when he died. The Patels' checking account had been set up for automatic debits, and the monthly statements show those payments were made." I tried to keep my voice even and not accusatory.

"Maybe something went wrong," she suggested. "Bad account number?"

I shook my head. "The payments went to Connors Insurance, Ltd. Why would they go to your office instead of directly to the life insurance company?"

"For many of our clients, we act as intermediaries."

"But for some reason, the money was never remitted to American Life."

Lisa flinched.

I'd expected her to be more surprised, indignant even.

"You're sure the company was American Life?" she asked. "We haven't used them in over a year."

"That's what the policy says. Would you have switched Mr. Patel to another company?" I wondered why she still refused to look at me.

"Maybe." Lisa's voice shook. "I'll have to check our records on Monday."

Detective Ross came out the sliding door and strolled across the patio.

"Please do," I said to Lisa. "We're working with Azmina's sister to settle her estate, and I'm sure she'd be grateful if you can help us get this matter straightened out."

"Hello, DeeLo. I guess you came for the traps?" The detective eyed his wife. "What 'matter' are you talking about?" His emphasis on the word "matter" struck me as more lawyerly than cop-like.

"Oh, just an insurance thing." Lisa picked up the bag of cat food and started for the house. "Can you help DeeLo take the stuff to her car?"

I followed Detective Ross around to the front of the house. Now was my chance. "Detective," I began. "Did you ever ask Officer Friendly about the paper Azmina Patel was holding when she died?"

He stopped. "Why do you think a police officer did something with this supposed document?"

"Did you ask him?"

The detective sighed. "Officer Friendly denies finding a document. He suggested if there was one, maybe you or Catherine Foster removed it. He said Catherine was concerned about the will; Azmina had implied she might make her a beneficiary."

My mouth flew open. *The audacity!* "Officer Friendly was the one taunting Catherine about the will. Catherine didn't even know she was a beneficiary. I wouldn't put it past him if he snooped in Azmina's papers while he was alone in the bookstore, and that's how he found out."

Detective Ross began walking again, and I trotted after him. "I told you," he said. "And I showed you photos. We didn't find anything in Azmina's hand at the crime scene."

We'd reached the porch, and he picked up one of the traps. I grabbed another.

"Yesterday, I overheard Officer Friendly arguing with Victoria Barton," I said as we headed to my car. "You might not know this, but she used to work at our firm. She designed our logo—the logo on that document."

I opened the hatch, and we loaded Catherine's equipment.

"It sounded like Officer Friendly was trying to blackmail Victoria," I continued. "He said, 'Evidence has a way of reappearing.'"

Detective Ross harrumphed and headed back to the porch for the last of the traps. I followed.

"Why don't you ask the officer what he meant by that?"

The detective grunted as he picked up the trap. "DeeLo, I appreciate how you want to help with this case. But you have a very active imagination. This isn't one of those cozy mystery novels like Azmina sold in her store. You're not starring in *Murder She Wrote*."

Stung, I stared at him. "I thought the police would be interested in following all the evidence, not pretending some of it doesn't exist. If you don't want to challenge your fellow officer, why don't you bring Victoria Barton in for questioning? Ask her what was on that paper Azmina was holding." I slammed the hatch. "What does the chief say about it all?"

As I spoke, Lisa emerged from the front door and stepped onto the porch, her face frozen like a rabbit in a spotlight.

Chapter Thirty-Four

Leonardo's closed at nine p.m. on Sunday, so Catherine and I had agreed to meet there at nine-thirty. The elegant, Italian villa-style restaurant looked different in the dark—spooky, if I allowed my imagination to run free. Trees in the adjacent nature reserve cast menacing shadows across the patio, and hoots from an owl pierced the eerie silence.

Catherine watched as I set and baited the traps. "You're getting pretty good at this, DeeLo. I shouldn't tell you, but I might actually miss you when you've finished your community service hours."

I touched my heart in mock awe. "Such an honor!"

"Don't get a swelled head," she laughed. "TNVR isn't rocket science."

We settled at a table on the patio not far from the one Barry and I had shared when I first spotted the cats we were now trying to catch. An orchestra of insects in the greenbelt was tuning up for their evening concert, and wild honeysuckle displaced the fading aromas of garlic and tomato sauce. I checked my phone to ensure it was muted but kept it close. Barry was en route to Savannah and would probably text me when he arrived.

Catherine drummed her fingers on the table. "How's it going with those ordinance changes?"

I sighed. "My meeting with Roy Don Whitehead was a disappointment. I thought he was on board with TNVR, but then he wanted to make a lot of other changes to the animal ordinance that had nothing to do with community cats."

"Like what?"

"Adding anti-tethering laws for dog owners, creating an advisory board to oversee Animal Control…"

"That will never pass," Catherine scoffed.

"I know. We'd lose Sandra's support." I gazed out at the reserve. "Chairman Graham joined us later. He seemed interested in my proposal, but then he suggested we table the issue until next year."

Catherine shook her head. "I told you it wouldn't be easy."

I held up my hand. "But Thursday night, Barry introduced me to Commissioner Connors. Vince is his former brother-in-law."

"I know. Small town, remember?"

"Vince got called away before I finished showing him my presentation, but he seemed impressed. We're getting together tomorrow night to resume our discussion. If I can convince Commissioner Connors to move forward with this proposal, I believe he'll persuade the others."

"Always the optimist," Catherine snickered.

"Also, he's dating my niece. Secret weapon, right? She's a scatterbrain, but maybe I can get her to put in a good word for us."

"Your niece?" Catherine eyed me. "How do you have a niece old enough to date a middle-aged man? That guy must be pushing fifty."

"My sister is sixteen years older than I am. She'd already had Demi when I was born."

"Oh… so you're one of those 'accident' babies. Oops!" Catherine's mocking laugh resembled good-natured joking, except she didn't do good-natured joking.

Regardless of intent, her words stung. I'd heard them often while I was growing up, even though my mother had always assured me I was a blessing. Mom had repeated that platitude yesterday when I visited her at the memory care center. Mercifully, she'd forgotten all about the disruption I'd caused on my last visit.

The clunk of a trap door kept me from firing off a defensive zinger.

"I'll get this." Catherine picked up a towel, rushed to secure and cover the trap, and then hauled the bulky, bouncing cage to her van.

When she returned, she asked, "Did you ever meet with Nick Norton to tell him about the proposed ordinance changes? I can't imagine he was receptive."

"He doesn't like the cats living in the reserve," I conceded. "I tried to persuade him that allowing TNVR there would help control the feline population and thus reduce the bird deaths he's so concerned about."

"Ha!" jeered Catherine. "Do you think he bought it?"

"No. But I think I convinced him not to oppose our proposal."

"We'll see."

"I told him it was what Azmina would want."

Catherine tilted her head and gave me a cryptic half-smile, half-frown.

"For a long time, I suspected Nick might be Azmina's killer," I said.

"Nick? No way. I thought José Garcia did it. After all their fights over the cats, he must have snapped."

"Detective Ross—Lisa's husband—said they're still considering other suspects."

Catherine straightened in her chair. "What other suspects?"

"I don't know."

"Why did you think Nick killed Azmina?"

"Remember when I told you I met him in the reserve, the day I was searching for my mother?"

Her brow furrowed.

I told Catherine how my mother had taken Nick's phone, and I'd found those seemingly incriminating text messages between him and Azmina the night of her death. "Those text messages might be the reason the cops had to let *you* go," I said. "You and I were loading traps at your house at the time they were sent."

Catherine's eyes widened, but she didn't thank me for my efforts to prove her innocence. "What made you change your mind about Nick?"

"He had a reasonable explanation."

"You confronted him about the text messages?"

"It came up in conversation."

"What if he'd been guilty?" Catherine shook her head. "DeeLo!"

"He saw someone leaving the bookstore that night. In a black SUV."

"Lots of people have black SUVs. Deb Holt, president of the Humane

Society, has one. Your guy, Barry, has one too."

"It's dark green."

"Green can look black at night under dim lighting."

I gazed up at the heavens. Despite the full moon, the sky was clear enough to make out the stars of the Big Dipper. An owl hooted again, and then, like a stealth bomber, a dark shape swooped toward the ground.

Catherine shuddered. "We need to get all these cats fixed as soon as possible. I'd hate to see them bring kittens into this world just to become meals for birds of prey."

As if a cat had heard her, another wire gate clattered closed.

After we'd secured and retrieved the trap and settled on the patio again, I ventured, "When we found Azmina, do you remember her holding a piece of paper?"

Catherine bit her lip. "All I could think about was getting out of there as quickly as possible."

"I noticed the paper because it had a Barton, Barton & Barton logo. But when I made my statement to Detective Ross, he showed me pictures of the crime scene, and the paper was gone."

"We weren't in the bookstore very long, but I don't remember seeing it."

"I know what I saw," I insisted.

"Officer Fiendly probably took it." She sniffed. "The jerk."

"Why?"

Catherine snorted. "Why does he do half the things he does? That man likes to create chaos. Remember, he ordered us to scram, and then later, he accused me of leaving the scene of a crime I committed. He hates me."

"He hates you because of the accident? The lawsuit?"

She nodded. She didn't have to ask me how I knew; I worked for Barry, and the information was in his files. "Officer Fiendly must want everyone to think I took that paper, whatever it was. It probably had nothing important on it, but people will assume it contained something to incriminate me."

I mulled over her words, trying to make her theory fit. If no one believed the paper existed, why would they think it might incriminate Catherine? Under the moonlight, it was hard to read her facial expression.

"When I was in jail, he taunted me about being a beneficiary in Azmina's will. Which was news to me, but I guess he figured it made me a suspect." She wrung her gloved hands. "How did he know about her will? Did he snoop through her files? Do you think the paper you saw had something to do with her estate?"

"Maybe, but it didn't look like a page from our Last Will & Testament package," I flashed back to the image of Azmina clutching that paper. "It looked more like a letter. In fact, the stationery we use now just says 'Barton & Barton' since Barry's ex-wife left the firm. This logo had the three Bs." I leaned forward. "The other day, I overheard Officer Friendly arguing with Victoria; it sounded like he was trying to blackmail her. He said, and I quote, 'Evidence has a way of reappearing.' I think he was talking about that document Azmina was holding when she died."

Catherine touched her chin. "You think Victoria wrote Azmina a letter on old Barton, Barton & Barton stationery?"

CRACK!

A brick in the wall separating the patio from the greenbelt exploded, sending bits of shrapnel flying, pelting the metal furniture.

"The cats!" Catherine bolted out of her chair and dashed toward the traps. She threw herself across the entrance of one, right in the line of fire.

Another shot ricocheted off a nearby tree trunk. The tabby who had been hovering nearby scampered into the brush.

I froze as another bullet whizzed past. "What the—?" As I ducked under the table, my fingers found my phone and shakily punched in nine-one-one.

Catherine hadn't moved since her heroic dive to save the cat. Moonlight shone on a darkening wet spot on her shoulder.

"Cat—"

"What's your emergency?" the operator answered in a slow Southern drawl.

"Someone's shooting at us!" I gasped. "Leonardo's restaurant... on Pine Boulevard... by the nature reserve."

"Is anyone injured?"

"My friend has been hit. Please send an ambulance." I gazed anxiously at

Catherine, still not moving.

"What's your name, ma'am?"

"DeeLo Myer. My friend who's been shot is Catherine Foster."

"Did you see the shooter?"

At the vroom of an engine, I gazed toward the road. Illuminated by the streetlight, a Pecan Point police car pulled away from the curb. Frantically, I tried to snap a photo, but my hands shook so much, the image came out too blurry to decipher.

"The police—" I began.

"The police and paramedics are on their way."

A sick feeling overtook me as the taillights of the police car moved farther down the street. "The police... he was here. I think a police officer was the shooter."

The operator obviously didn't believe me. "Ma'am, the police and paramedics will be there shortly." As if to confirm the veracity of her words, a siren wailed in the distance.

No more shots had been fired since the patrol car drove away, the rumble of its engine now barely audible, which supported my theory about the shooter's identity. Who else but Officer Friendly? To be fair, I hadn't seen him. But he was the only one crazy enough and hateful enough to shoot at us.

Was he really trying to hit us? If so, he was a lousy shot. Maybe he just wanted to scare us.

Warily, I crept from my hiding place and made my way to Catherine's side. With a towel, I put pressure on her shoulder wound. "Catherine," I murmured. "Can you hear me?"

She emitted a faint groan. "The cat... Did she get away? Is she okay?"

I continued to exert pressure on her wound, which had not stopped bleeding. The sound of sirens grew louder. "The cat's okay. Not sure about you, though."

"What happened?" She blinked.

"You've been shot!"

The sirens stopped as emergency vehicles pulled into Leonardo's parking lot. Two paramedics jumped out of an ambulance and ran past a police car to my fallen friend.

In a moment, they had pushed me aside to assess Catherine's condition. Someone brought over a stretcher, and I watched them lift her onto it.

"Will she be okay?" I trailed behind the EMTs as they loaded the stretcher into the ambulance.

"We need to get her to the hospital," one of them replied. They closed the rear doors, climbed back into the vehicle, and drove away, siren blaring.

A uniformed Pecan Point police officer strolled up to me. "Ma'am, can you tell me what happened?"

He was as skeptical as the operator when I told him I suspected the shooter was a patrol officer. "How do you know it was a police car? Did you get the license plate number?"

"Not the license number, but I saw the car. Blue and white, with a cherry on top. Just like yours." I showed him my photo, but his prune-like squint told me he wasn't convinced. "Can't you check to see who was patrolling the area around that time?"

The officer gestured toward the darkened building. "What were you ladies doing out here anyway? The restaurant is closed." He narrowed his eyes. "Were you trying to break in?"

Of course. Protect your own. "Sir, we're volunteers for the Pecan Point Humane Society, and we have permission from the owner of Leonardo's to trap the feral cats on their property." I started to explain the benefits of Trap-Neuter-Vaccinate-Return, but his eyes glazed over.

"Got it." He held up his hand and gave me an eye roll.

They wouldn't let me remove Catherine's traps until the crime scene investigators had a chance to examine the site. Nevertheless, I persuaded the patrol officer to disable the mechanisms so we wouldn't catch another cat while the traps were unattended.

While I waited for permission to leave, I tried to reach Barry several times, but my calls went straight to voicemail. He didn't answer my hysterical texts either.

Once the police were finished with me, I transferred the trapped cats from

Catherine's van to my SUV. I'd be making another trek to the LifeSaver spay/neuter clinic in the morning.

As I pulled away, I wondered if Officer Friendly knew where I lived. It would be easy for him to find out.

Chapter Thirty-Five

My phone rang when I was about to leave the LifeSaver parking lot. I glanced at the screen showing the name Jill Hernandez and shut off my engine.

"DeeLo, are you okay?" she began. "You gotta give me a statement about last night."

"Are you talking about the shooting?" *News travels fast. Oh wait, Jill reports the news.*

Muffled voices deliberated in the background, and Jill momentarily covered the mouthpiece before returning. "Yes, please tell me about your role in the shooting last night. Did you see what happened?"

"My role? I'm lucky I wasn't hit. Catherine Foster and I were trapping cats behind Leonardo's, and someone shot at us. Catherine was wounded." I glanced in my rearview mirror to ensure I wasn't blocking traffic. Two cars hovered like buzzards, searching for a parking spot.

"Catherine's awake," Jill replied. "The bullet only grazed her shoulder, and she should make a full recovery. I interviewed her at the hospital this morning."

"Good. I'm going to try to see her."

Jill paused as if listening for a drumroll. "They arrested the shooter."

I almost dropped the phone. Last night, no one had been interested in my statement about seeing a police car drive away right after the shots stopped. "Who was it?"

"Your old buddy, Officer Stan Friendly. He confessed."

"Confessed? Already?" That news surprised me. The sleazy officer must have been caught red-handed. Had someone listened to me? Checked the patrol schedule for the area? "What's going to happen to him? He should be facing multiple charges."

"He claimed he wasn't trying to hurt anyone; he only wanted to scare you two. But he's been suspended," said Jill. "And he agreed to a mental evaluation. You remember all that stuff we dug up about the traffic accident, and the lawsuit that bankrupted his sister, and his grudge against Catherine Foster?"

"This would make a great follow-up to the story you never ran, about Catherine's arrest last week for violating an obscure, ridiculous animal ordinance that needs to be changed."

"I'll definitely work that in," promised Jill. "I haven't forgotten. Just waiting for a good time to run it. And trying to convince my editor it's newsworthy." She again covered her mouthpiece to address someone in the room. Then, "It's sad. Stan Friendly had a complete breakdown. His life is ruined."

"He's the one who ruined it. And he almost ended Catherine's life." Someone honked, anxious for me to vacate my spot. The LifeSaver parking lot was too small during peak times of the day. I started my engine. "Did Officer Friendly confess to any other crimes?"

"Other crimes? Like what?"

"Maybe a murder?" I suggested.

"Whose murder?"

"Azmina Patel. Remember, he officially found the body, and I happen to know he removed a piece of evidence from the crime scene."

Jill made a sucking sound through her teeth. "DeeLo, what have you been holding back from me?"

Glancing at the swarm of impatient motorists jockeying for parking spots, I murmured, "Gotta go."

"DeeLo, you can't leave me hanging."

"We'll talk more later."

"Holding you to it." She sighed. "I'm trying to interview Stan Friendly as soon as he can have visitors. But in answer to your question? As far as I know, he has not confessed to killing Azmina Patel."

* * *

Barry and I had been playing telephone tag since last night. He'd texted that he arrived safely in Savannah and was going straight to bed in order to wake up refreshed for his conference. I'd phoned several times after the shooting incident, but the calls went to voicemail. The message I left shared few details; I merely said I had a lot to tell him. This morning, he'd sent a text letting me know his break schedule. He said he missed me and signed off with a heart emoji.

I replied with a text stating I'd have to open the office late because I was stopping at the Pecan Point hospital to visit Catherine. That should get his attention.

As Jill had indicated, Catherine lay awake when I arrived in her hospital room. According to the doctor who was just leaving, the patient had already snapped at two nurses and demanded repeatedly to be released. I rapped tentatively on her door jamb.

"Who is it now?" she grumbled.

"DeeLo." I sauntered to her bedside. A medicinal smell tinged with Lysol tickled my nostrils. "How are you feeling?"

She eyed me. "Did you take care of those cats we caught?"

"Just dropped them at the LifeSaver." I touched her bed rail. "However, the police wouldn't let me pick up the empty traps yet. Not until the crime scene investigators are finished with them."

Catherine grimaced, and I suspected her shoulder hurt more than she wanted anyone to know. "Yeah, I think a bullet hit one of the trip plates. I hope the trap wasn't damaged beyond repair."

"They arrested the shooter," I announced.

Her eyes popped. "Who?"

"Your hate-buddy, Officer Stan Friendly."

Catherine squeezed her eyes shut. "Why am I not surprised?"

"He can't hurt you anymore. He's been suspended from the force and is undergoing psychiatric evaluation."

Catherine's mouth opened in an "O" but no sound came out.

"I imagine the police will be in to talk to you if they haven't already," I continued. "You'll want to press charges."

She shook her head vigorously. "No. I've done enough to that man. I just want it to be over."

"*You've* done enough? He had you thrown in jail! He shot you!"

"I never meant to hurt him or his family. My fight wasn't with them."

"You mean, after the accident?"

She nodded. "I wanted the truck driver to pay. And the company that allowed him to get behind the wheel intoxicated. I lost everything that night."

"No one could blame you."

A tear seeped down Catherine's cheek. "I never realized my actions would affect innocent people. I didn't think about collateral damage."

"It was a chain reaction. It started with the drunk driver."

"Of course." She massaged her forehead. "But I made it a lot worse. And I never meant to. I just wanted justice for my husband and daughter."

A knock on the door jamb interrupted our conversation. "Ms. Foster?" Detective Ross poked his head inside. "May I have a word?"

My eyes met his as I retreated from Catherine's bedside to make room for him. "I need to get to the office. Want me to feed your cats later, Catherine, or will you be released today?"

With a glance at the detective, she replied, "I hope to be released, but I'll call you if there are any surprises."

As I started out the door, Detective Ross held up his hand. "Ms. Myer?"

I stopped. "Detective?"

"Can we speak later?" The fluorescent light made his eyes sparkle like emeralds.

"Sure. I'll be at my office."

He nodded. "I'll stop by in about an hour."

"See you then." With this new development about Officer Friendly's erratic behavior, would Detective Ross be more willing to accept that his colleague was capable of evidence-tampering in the murder investigation?

***

The darkened office felt empty without Barry and Jane. I checked voicemail; there were only two calls to return, and neither was urgent. Most of Barry's clients knew he'd be gone all week.

After returning the messages, I called Lisa Ross at Connors Insurance. Voicemail. I stared at the phone. Was she avoiding me? I tried not to read too much into it.

While I was still staring at it, the office phone jingled, and I answered on the first ring. "Barton and Barton."

"DeeLo, thank God." Barry's friendly voice purred in my ears. "I left three messages on your cell and sent you two texts. Are you okay? What happened to Catherine?"

I hadn't checked my cell phone since I left the hospital; Barry must have really been worried. Blow by blow, I related the shooting incident from the night before. His gasps punctuated my tale at the appropriate points.

"DeeLo," he murmured once I took a breath. "Are you sure you want to keep doing this Trap-Neuter-Return stuff? You must be almost finished with your community service hours by now."

"I am." My completed timesheet lay on my desk, waiting to be signed by Catherine and sent to the court. "But I don't think Stan Friendly will bother us anymore. And once we get the ordinance changed—"

"Still," said Barry. "Don't you think it's dangerous for you to be alone in deserted areas late at night?"

"Thanks for your concern, but we can talk more about it later." Glad to hear he cared about my safety, I moved on to office business. "Remember, I told you about Kyra Chowdhury calling on Friday?"

"Something about Azmina's estate?"

"The death benefit from American Life hasn't been paid yet. On Azmina's husband."

Barry covered the mouthpiece to speak to someone in the room with him, then returned to our call. "Sorry, DeeLo. What did you find out?"

I told him about my calls to the insurance company and how Kyra had sent me copies of the Patels' bank statements showing monthly debits to Connors Insurance.

"Very strange," he remarked. "There has to be a simple explanation."

"Lisa Ross and I have become quite well acquainted since I've been trapping for her," I said. "I asked her to look into it, but so far, she seems to be avoiding the issue."

"I'll talk to Vince when I get back." Barry projected his voice away from the phone. "I'll be right there, Chris."

I tried to phrase my suspicions as delicately as possible. "You don't think they might be doing something underhanded? Like collecting premiums on a fake policy?"

Barry's indignant gasp was expected. "No way. I've known Vince for years. I don't know Lisa well, but Vince would never hire someone that dishonest."

His confidence in his former brother-in-law reassured me. "Vince is coming over tonight to discuss the ordinance. I'll—"

More voices in the background claimed Barry's attention. When he returned to our call, he said, "My session is about to start. I'm sure Kyra appreciates you following up."

* * *

I finally reached Lisa Ross after lunch. The conversation began cordially, with me asking about the cats and her telling me how well Tux had integrated with her orange tabby clan. Then, I brought up Rajindra Patel's life insurance policy.

She grew quiet.

"Lisa?" I prompted, afraid we'd lost the connection. "What did you find out? Did you switch Mr. Patel to a company other than American Life?"

"Not that I can find."

"What do your files show?"

"My files?"

"You must have a record of selling the policy. If not, I can send you a copy of the agreement."

"I have it."

"What about the payments?"

"The file says the policy was canceled for nonpayment of premiums."

"Lisa, I told you, the payments were current. I have the Patels' bank statements to prove it." I read her the account number where the debits had been sent. "That belongs to Connors Insurance, correct?"

"Yes." Her voice was barely audible. Papers shuffled. A phone rang, and it sounded like Lisa was answering the other call. *What's going on?*

"Sorry," she said after a moment. "I'm the only one here, and I had to take that."

"Same here," I commiserated. "My boss is out of town this week." I fingered the copies of the Patels' bank statements. "Did Azmina ask for help in filing a claim for the death benefit after her husband passed away?"

Lisa cleared her throat. "Listen, DeeLo, I need to talk to Vince about this situation. I'll get back to you."

Before she could hang up, I suggested, "Vince is coming to my house tonight to discuss the county animal ordinance changes, Lisa. Maybe I'll just ask *him* about the life insurance policy."

I thought I heard a gasp before the line went dead.

Unlike Connors Insurance, we didn't have a bell on the door to announce arrivals. I looked up to see Detective Ross walk in. The "hour" he had estimated when we were at the hospital had stretched into at least four.

"Was that my wife you were talking to?" he asked.

Chapter Thirty-Six

The detective pulled up a chair. "Was Lisa able to help you with that 'insurance thing' you mentioned the other day?"

Not wanting to burden him with irrelevant matters, I replied, "We're still working on it."

He nodded. "Is this a good time for you to give me a statement about what happened at Leonardo's last night? I thought you'd rather do it here than at the station."

"Sure. What else do you want to know? I told the whole story to the patrol officer at the scene."

"Mind if I record this?" He'd already pressed the record button on his cell phone, but it was nice of him to ask.

With a nod at the blinking red light, I replied, "Fine with me, since you're going to anyway."

Speaking into the phone, he stated the date, time, and participants in the interview. "Ms. Myer, please walk me through last evening, starting with when you arrived at Leonardo's. Don't leave anything out."

I told Detective Ross about setting traps and chatting with Catherine on the patio while we waited for the cats to take the bait. Careful to include the fact that Catherine had secured permission from the owner of Leonardo's to be on the property, I provided a brief explanation of TNVR. My tale comprised much more detail than I figured he wanted, but he'd asked me to be thorough.

The detective yawned after I described the second feline capture. "I get the idea. Did anything unusual happen?"

"I was about to tell you. You said not to leave anything out." I smiled sweetly. "At approximately ten p.m., someone started shooting at us." I described how the first shot ricocheted off the brick wall, and Catherine threw herself over a trap to save the cat lurking nearby.

"You saw the shooter?"

"Not the shooter. But I saw a police car drive away as soon as the shots stopped."

"Why did you think the shooter was Officer Stan Friendly?"

"He hates Catherine Foster, and he's always harassing her." I stared into the detective's eyes. "I didn't accuse Officer Friendly, but I heard he confessed."

"He did," Detective Ross acknowledged. "Thank you, Ms. Myer." He stopped the recording.

"What did Officer Friendly confess to? Attempted murder? Discharging a firearm in public? Assault with a deadly weapon? Did he say why he did it?"

Detective Ross swallowed. "He admitted to being the shooter. He claimed he was just trying to scare you two, not to hurt anyone. The chief is still reviewing the specific charges."

"Now that you've seen what Officer Friendly is capable of," I motioned toward his phone, "you'll want to record this too."

The detective pressed the record button again.

"Ask Officer Stan Friendly why he removed a piece of evidence from the scene of Azmina Patel's murder." I leaned toward the microphone. "And why he thought Victoria Barton would like it back."

The detective's hand hovered over the stop button. "What does this have to do with Victoria Barton?" His face no longer showed the skepticism I'd grown used to seeing whenever I brought up Officer Friendly's questionable actions.

I recounted the exchange I'd witnessed outside the commissioner's office the other day.

As he listened, the kaleidoscope of his facial expressions shifted from disbelief to horror, to apprehension. "Is that all, Ms. Myer?"

I nodded. "Just trying to help solve the murder."

* * *

Jill called shortly after Detective Ross left. "I snared an interview with Stan Friendly this afternoon."

"They'll let you talk to him?" I'd expected his colleagues to circle the wagons and protect their own. Or that he'd lawyer up.

"I think he wants to get things off his chest, and I can be very persuasive," said Jill. "What did you want to tell me about him?"

In dramatic detail, I described the encounter I'd witnessed between Officer Friendly and Victoria Barton earlier in the week. How he was trying to blackmail her by threatening to make evidence reappear.

"Ask him what he knows about Azmina Patel's murder," I suggested.

"You think he had something to do with it?"

"Ask him what that letter said, and why he took it from the crime scene. It might contain a clue to the killer's identity or motive."

Jill was quiet. Was she taking notes, or mulling over my revelations? Then she said, "You're not setting me up because you hate Victoria?"

My breath caught. Was I?

"DeeLo? Are you?"

"To be fair," I conceded. "Victoria didn't take the bait from Officer Friendly. If she was Azmina's killer, I think she'd have reacted differently." I drummed my fingers on my keyboard. "Besides, I can't imagine Victoria strangling someone. She'd mess up her nails."

Jill joined me in a nervous giggle. "What could be on that paper?"

"I don't know. But it must be something Victoria wrote. It was typed on our old Barton, Barton & Barton stationery." I stared at my computer and my untouched paralegal training modules, regretting how little work I'd accomplished today. So much for my promise to Barry. "Victoria was Azmina's realtor, so there were many reasons she might be writing Azmina a letter. It's just odd she used that stationery. Unless the letter was written back when she was still Barry's partner. But why would Stan Friendly think he could blackmail her over it?"

"I'll ask him when we do our interview," said Jill. "I'm on the case."

Chapter Thirty-Seven

My hands shook with anticipation as I tidied the living room and made space on the coffee table for the Pecan County animal ordinance paperwork. Manny watched from his favorite perch on my bookshelf.

Should I bring up Rajindra Patel's insurance policy tonight? Would it be appropriate to burden Vince with a matter better discussed during office hours? I'd given Lisa plenty of opportunity to explain, and she was obviously avoiding the issue. I hated to involve her boss, but he deserved to know if his employee was hiding something that would reflect poorly on his business. If Lisa had embezzled the Patels' premiums, she might be doing it with other clients.

I gazed at my cat, crouched like a panther stalking prey. "What am I going to tell Kyra if I don't bring up the problem with the life insurance policy?"

Manny didn't offer any advice.

The doorbell rang.

Vince Connors stood on my stoop, shower-fresh and wearing his politician smile. A whiff of after-shave followed as I stepped aside to admit him. "Thank you for coming, Commissioner." Focused on the purpose of our meeting, I extended my hand, and we shook. "Barry's away at a conference this week, but I just talked to him, and he's available by phone if we have questions."

"I doubt that will be necessary," said Vince, as we headed into the living room. "Your document looks solid. We'll have the county attorney review it before we put it on the agenda, but I don't anticipate any snags. Let's see what else you've got."

We sat down on the couch. I picked up paper copies of my PowerPoint slides. "Here are projections for how much money the county can save by practicing TNVR instead of impounding, sheltering for the mandatory stray-hold, and ultimately killing free-roaming cats."

He studied my paperwork. Nodded, raised his eyebrows, smiled—all the desired reactions.

"My plan is to present this slideshow at the meeting when the ordinance changes are on the agenda," I explained. "We'll have hard copies too. I think my data will convince any skeptics."

Stacking the papers neatly on the coffee table, he agreed, "You've done a thorough job, DeeLo. It was smart to research all those numbers instead of emphasizing the emotional appeal for animal lovers. Commissioners can hardly turn down a plan that will save the county money." The politician beamed. "You have my full support, and I believe this proposal will pass."

"Thank you, Commissioner." His praise warmed my spirits. But the insurance matter gnawed at me. "So, how long will the review process take? When do you think we can get this item on the agenda?"

He scratched his chin. "A few weeks. Depends on how busy the county attorney is."

"Let me know when it's scheduled. I'll invite supporters to the meeting in case the other commissioners have concerns about how this law will affect the community. Representatives from Animal Control and the Pecan Point Humane Society plan to speak in favor."

"Good to know," said Vince. "You've turned my assistant, Lisa Ross, into a believer."

I smiled. "Yes, I helped her trap and fix some stray cats on her property. Now they can live their outdoor lives without reproducing and burdening Animal Control."

"Great testimonial for your program." He flashed the politician smile again. This was almost too easy.

But his mention of Lisa created an opening. I hated to dampen our pleasant conversation, but I couldn't help myself; what would I tell Kyra?

"Speaking of Lisa, I've been trying to get information from her about a life insurance policy she sold a couple of years ago to Rajindra Patel, Azmina Patel's deceased husband. Our law firm is handling Azmina's estate, and her beneficiary noticed Rajindra's death benefit was never received."

Vince's face darkened and the smile faded. I should have heeded the warning, dropped the subject, and let Barry deal with Vince when he returned, bro to bro. But our earlier rapport had given me a sense of bravado.

My hand trembled as I fiddled with my papers. "Apparently, Azmina filed a claim after her husband passed away. It was denied. The company told her the policy had lapsed due to nonpayment of premiums."

"Nonpayment of premiums is a valid reason for denial."

"But Mr. Patel was current on his payments. Azmina's sister sent me copies of the Patels' bank statements showing the debits."

Vince pressed his lips together. "How do you know the debits were for life insurance?"

"The amounts match, and the entry says, 'Connors Insurance, Ltd.' Lisa verified the account number. In fact, I have them—" I reached for my American Life folder.

He held up a hand to stop me. "That doesn't prove anything."

"But I think it does. Let me show you." I made another move for the folder.

"DeeLo, you know how easy it is to fake a document these days."

Why was he having so much trouble believing there could be an irregularity at his company? Possibly involving a trusted employee. "I've talked to American Life."

His face paled. "It was a misunderstanding."

"You knew?" My jaw dropped.

Silence.

"But you can correct it." I fixed my eyes on his face.

He ran his fingers through his thick head of hair. "I can't."

"What do you mean, you can't?"

Vince expelled a long sigh. "American Life reorganized. They raised their rates and changed most of their product lines. We had a deadline to notify our clients and rewrite the policies under the new terms." He pressed his forehead into his hands. "DeeLo, my wife was in the late stages of cancer, and I barely left her side. I didn't know what day it was, much less what was happening at the office. Sally lasted for two weeks in hospice and then passed away."

I extended my hand toward his shoulder, then pulled back. "I'm sorry about your wife. Barry said she was a wonderful person."

The rims of his eyes had reddened. "Thank you."

"So, you never renewed Rajindra Patel's policy under the new terms, and they canceled him."

Vince nodded.

"Without notice?"

He buried his face in his hands. "They sent notice to our office. I thought it was being handled. I couldn't focus on anything except Sally."

"But why did you keep collecting premiums?" And not tell Rajindra Patel about the policy changes?

"I assumed... I suppose it's my fault."

I studied his face for signs of regret.

Vince wrung his hands. "We took a second mortgage on the house to pay for Sally's care. My business almost went under. I had to let most of my staff go."

"Except Lisa."

"Someone had to help run the office."

Why Lisa? "What did Lisa know?"

"Not much, until recently." He wiped his forehead. "She had a heavy workload of her own."

"How recently?" Lisa should have told her client what was going on with his policy. She wasn't the one with a dying spouse.

Vince straightened and took a breath to compose himself. "Look, I'm sorry that happened, but there's nothing we can do about it now. The company won't pay the death benefit."

"But—"

"Azmina Patel is dead; she no longer needs the cash."

I stared at him, hesitant to digest what I'd just heard. "But the beneficiaries? Her sister Kyra! Those funds should be part of Azmina's estate."

"It's just a windfall for the sister." His nostrils flared.

This was one of our county's lawmakers? Barry's friend? "Whether she needs the money is not up to us."

My cell phone vibrated with a text.

I glanced down. The message was from Jill. She'd attached a photo of the missing letter on Barton, Barton & Barton stationery, signed by Victoria. I slid my fingers across the screen to enlarge it.

"Something wrong?" Vince peered over my shoulder as I read the text. "I hope it's nothing—"

"You—" I tried to hide the horror on my face, but from the way he scrutinized me, I could tell I hadn't.

"Look," he said. Like a swell in an angry ocean, his blue eyes had turned a steely gray. "We made a mistake. I'm sorry it happened, but I can't fix it. The beneficiary is dead. Nobody profited. You need to let this go."

"Let it go? How?"

He pointed to the ordinance papers on the table. "That is, if you still want my support for your proposal."

My eyes strayed to the ordinance changes and supporting documentation I'd worked so hard to research and fine-tune. We were on the verge of making TNVR legal in Pecan County. But how could a county commissioner tie his support of my proposal to a promise to keep silent about insurance fraud?

Vince was still watching me. "What will it be, DeeLo?"

I shook my head and met his gaze. "I can't do that, even if I wanted to. Azmina's sister is Barry's client, and she's not going to drop it."

"She will if you tell her to."

"I can't. We're talking about insurance fraud!" The words slipped out before I could think of a less pejorative euphemism.

He clenched his teeth, and his features distorted like a Zoom caller with a bad internet connection. "Insurance fraud!"

Yes, "fraud" was too strong a word. Even if true, the word was incendiary.

But I couldn't stop. How did he think he could get away with such an unethical business practice? "What do *you* call it? Negligence? You took money for a product you didn't deliver, and Azmina Patel got cheated out of five million dollars!"

"But I didn't steal five million dollars. I tried to explain that to her." He picked up my papers and ripped them in half. "You obviously don't care about my support for your silly ordinance change if you dare to accuse me of fraud."

I felt my cheeks grow hot. "It would be one thing to acknowledge your mistake and make amends. But you tried to deny responsibility and cover up your negligence. You had your sister send Azmina a cease-and-desist letter ordering her to drop her claim!"

He stared at my phone, still displaying the text from Jill. His eyes narrowed in a predatory manner.

I tightened my grip on the device, wishing I could erase the last ten minutes and start over. Rewind our conversation to his comment about the ordinance having a good chance of passing. Before I accused him of insurance fraud.

"Why are we still talking about Azmina Patel?" His eyes glinted. "The injured party is dead."

"How convenient for you." I appraised the lines in his face, wondering how I could have misjudged him, how I could have viewed him as an upstanding businessman and lawmaker focused on doing the right thing. I stood, ready to show him the door. "I think we're done here."

"No." He moved closer to me, invading my space, making me aware of our size difference.

Our eyes locked, and a chill crept over me as if someone had opened the door to a deep freeze.

Was this how Azmina had felt confronting him about his attempt to deny culpability? And his nerve to enlist Victoria, her realtor, in the deception. Azmina had probably accused him of insurance fraud as well.

Shivering, I remembered that night at the bookstore: Azmina's twisted body lying on the floor, her neck bruised, the letter on Barton, Barton &

Barton stationery clutched in her hand. A burst of nausea hit me. My finger hit the dial pad.

Before I could press the nine, Vince batted the phone from my grasp and seized my neck with both his large hands.

I tried to protest, but my words came out in gurgles. His thumbs pressed into my jugular, and objects in the room grew fuzzy.

Trying to writhe away from his vise-like grip, I fought to remain conscious. *Why?* Others knew he was coming over tonight—Barry, Lisa, Catherine, Demi—so he'd become the prime suspect.

Unfortunately, none of them would figure it out in time to save my life.

My vision faded, and dizziness swallowed me; I struggled for a last breath of air.

A low growl rose in pitch until it became an eardrum-piercing yowl. In a blur of black fur, a panther flew from the bookshelf onto Vince's shoulders.

The grip on my throat loosened, and a blood-curdling bellow rang in my ears.

"Get that animal off me!" Vince's arms flailed, swatting at the angry feline who clung to his back, sinking sharp fangs into his neck.

Catching my breath, I took advantage of the diversion to scoot out of his reach. My phone had landed across the room, but I was close to the fireplace, and I grabbed the nearest object that could be used as a weapon: the brass poker.

With a burst of adrenalin, I raised it over my shoulder like a baseball bat, waiting for his renewed onslaught like a batter at home plate.

Vince tugged Manny's bum leg and yanked at the cat on his back.

Manny bit down hard on Vince's hand.

"You devil cat!" He flung my pet across the room.

Manny landed with a thud and a howl.

"Leave us alone," I shouted, swinging the poker as Vince lunged for me.

The metal object cracked against his knee, and he grasped it with a yelp.

The front door opened.

We both looked up as Demi let herself inside. I'd never been so happy to see my niece.

Her eyes swept the room. She was too far away to notice any marks on my neck, and I must have looked ridiculous standing over her new boyfriend with a fireplace poker in my hand. "Aunt DeeLo, what have you done?"

"Demi, call nine-one-one!"

"Help me, Demi," cried Vince, still rubbing his knee. "Your aunt's gone crazy!"

"Just call," I begged her. "Let the police figure out who's crazy."

Demi pulled her phone out of her bag, her head swiveling from side to side, taking in the bizarre setting. I refused to put down the poker.

Wincing in pain, Vince took a step toward her. "Demi, hold on a minute. Let's talk."

"Don't listen to him," I said. "Magic carpet!"

Demi blinked. *Magic carpet* was a code word from our childhood that our family members used to signal each other when we were in trouble, but we hadn't used it in years.

Her finger must have pressed the right button because I heard a voice say, "What's your emergency?"

Still eyeing us suspiciously, Demi rattled off my address. "There's a domestic disturbance."

"Come arrest Azmina Patel's murderer," I shouted, hoping the operator could hear me from across the room. "Vince Connors! He just tried to kill me!"

With a glare at me, Vince appealed to Demi. "Your aunt has gone off her rocker."

Demi's face twisted with uncertainty as she replied to the voice on the phone, "I don't know, I just got here. A weapon?" She eyed me, still wielding the fireplace poker. "Maybe."

A siren sounded, growing closer. Even for a small town, the response seemed unusually fast.

The three of us were still in a stand-off when someone pounded on my front door. "Police! Open up!"

Detective Ross? What was he doing here?

"It's unlocked," called Demi, stepping aside to watch the show.

Into my living room tramped Detective Ross, followed by a uniformed officer.

"Drop the weapon!" The officer pointed his gun at me.

I let the fireplace poker fall to my side and rubbed my neck.

"DeeLo, are you okay?" The detective's eyes focused on my throat, which must be purpling like Azmina's. "Lisa had a bad feeling about your meeting tonight, and then I heard the nine-one-one call on the radio while I was on my way over."

I pointed to Vince, slumped against my couch, his hands massaging his injured knee—those hands that strangled Manny's former owner and almost killed me. "Ask Commissioner Connors why he murdered Azmina Patel. It has to do with 'an insurance thing.'"

"Her accusations are absurd." With a scowl, Vince pointed at his knee. "She attacked me."

Ignoring her new boyfriend, Demi stooped to check on Manny, who whimpered and cowered in the corner.

Detective Ross and his colleague moved toward Vince, still glowering but defused. "Commissioner, we'll need to take you down to the station."

Chapter Thirty-Eight

On the floor of Octomom's room in the basement, Catherine and I sat cross-legged, each of our laps covered in squirming kittens. The little ones wobbled across the floor exploring their surroundings—which included our legs—and now that their ears were poking out, they looked more like miniature cats than mice. Their feral mother lurked in a corner, surveying us suspiciously, but did not intervene.

"So, Lisa came through for you in the end?" mused Catherine. "Who'd have thought?"

"She suspected Vince killed Azmina but didn't want to believe it." I picked up a wandering tabby and kissed it, inhaling its milky, furry kitten smell before corralling it on my lap with its mewing siblings. "He was her boss, the source of her livelihood. And she was afraid of how he might react if she brought it up. He already blamed her for the policy fiasco."

"I never thought she was very bright."

Discounting Catherine's commentary, I continued, "Detective Ross thought Lisa was hiding something, which caused tension in their marriage. I'm glad he put it all together when he did."

Catherine shivered. "I can't fathom what Azmina must have felt when she confronted Vince about that insurance money. Such a waste." She scooped up a tuxedo kitten, rubbed noses with it, and set it back down. "And you, DeeLo. I almost lost my best trapper."

I touched my neck, trying to remember if I'd seen my life pass before me when that monster had his hands around my throat.

"Barry must have freaked out. His former brother-in-law tried to kill his girlfriend."

I nodded. "He was in shock. And feels guilty, too. Which has been good for some fancy restaurant dinners this week."

Catherine gave my shoulder a playful nudge, which was very un-Catherine-like. "And what about your niece? She was dating that killer."

"Demi took it in stride." I sighed. "She'd picked another loser."

One of the kittens on Catherine's lap had rolled onto its back, and she tickled its belly. "Was Lisa the one in the car Nick saw driving away that night?"

"Yes. She didn't realize Vince had just committed murder. She thought he'd had another futile conversation with Azmina about lowering the rent."

Catherine started to open her mouth.

Before she could bad-mouth Lisa again, I continued, "I noticed Vince's black Escalade when I visited the insurance office, but there was a good reason for that SUV to be in the parking lot when Nick saw it. Lisa told me they'd worked late on Sunday." I stroked a tiny black kitten who'd fallen asleep in mid-play. "And I still half-suspected Nick."

"I told you he didn't do it. Most people thought José was the culprit." Catherine looked down. "And then he killed himself, which made him look even more suspicious. It was suicide, wasn't it?"

"No one has proved otherwise. His wife claims he was depressed. So sad, especially if being falsely accused of murder pushed him over the edge."

"I wouldn't be surprised if Officer Fiendly goaded him into it." Catherine flared her nostrils. "At least that sick cop is out of our lives now."

"You know," I eyed Catherine, "if you'd let me call nine-one-one when we found Azmina's body... if you'd let me look at that paper she was holding... the police would have solved this murder weeks ago."

Catherine let out a puff of air. "I was afraid. You know Officer Friendly had it in for me."

"He still tried to pin the murder on you. And we didn't have the proof." I picked up another wandering kitten. "If we'd called nine-one-one right away, Officer Friendly would never have stolen that evidence and tried to blackmail Victoria Barton."

"Someone you wish had been the murderer." Catherine's eyes lit with amusement—a rare sight. "Then Barry's ex-wife would have been out of your way."

I'd let my personal bias affect my judgment, and it had almost cost me my life. "I should have paid closer attention to Manny's signals."

"Manny, the hero cat." Catherine smiled. "Is he going to be okay?"

"His limp is more pronounced now. The vet said he bruised his bad leg, but nothing was broken."

"I'm so relieved."

"Vince was around every time Manny went berserk, but I always assumed it was for another reason—not that my cat was reacting to the presence of Azmina's killer. I didn't want Vince to be the murderer. He was helping us get the animal ordinance changed."

"You thought he was one of the good guys." Catherine exhaled. "What does this mean for TNVR?"

"Back to the drawing board. After the special election, I'll approach the new commissioner. But realistically, we're looking at next year."

"You still want to be involved?" probed Catherine. "After all, you've completed your community service hours, and then some."

With a laugh, I shifted my weight, careful not to disturb the sleeping kittens warming my lap. "Deb Holt didn't let me count the time I spent on the ordinance anyway. Lots of work remains to be done." I stroked a kitten's head. "These cats need us."

Acknowledgments

I would like to thank Marcia Hendershot, TNVR guru of the Fayette Humane Society, for taking me out trapping as part of my research for this book. She also served as a beta reader, correcting my many errors about the workings of TNVR. Her trapping expertise and love of cats are the only traits she has in common with Catherine Foster.

Cindy Lauer, Linda White, and Susan Griffith also provided answers to my questions and TNVR stories. Stacy LeBaron, with Community Cats Podcast, was kind enough to grant me an interview on her platform to help get the word out to cat lovers about this book.

I also thank my many critique partners: the Peachtree City Writers Circle, the Renegades from the Atlanta Writers Club, and especially my morning Sisters in Crime Zoom write-in buddies: Angela Costa, Linda Sands, and Liz Tully.

And I can't forget my many beta readers who provided valuable feedback as this story was being shaped: Paul Lentz, Julie Johns, Donna Pacho, and Donna Black.

Many thanks to the team at Level Best Books for believing in this story and bringing it to market. And of course, my loving husband, Michael, who does most of the yardwork and housework while I sit at my computer all day.

About the Author

Sharon Marchisello is a long-time volunteer and cat foster for the Fayette Humane Society (FHS). Because she earned a Master's in Professional Writing from the University of Southern California, her fellow volunteers tasked her with writing grants for FHS, including procuring funds to support Trap, Neuter, Vaccinate, Return. She's the author of two mysteries published by Sunbury Press—*Going Home* (2014) and *Secrets of the Galapagos* (2019). Sharon has written short stories, a nonfiction book about personal finance, training manuals, screenplays, a blog, and book reviews. She is an active member of Sisters in Crime, the Atlanta Writers Club, and the Hometown Novel Writers Association. Retired from a 27-year career with Delta Air Lines, she now lives in Peachtree City, Georgia, and serves on the board of directors for the Friends of the Peachtree City Library.

AUTHOR WEBSITE:
  sharonmarchisello.com

SOCIAL MEDIA HANDLES:
  https://www.facebook.com/SLMarchisello

https://twitter.com/slmarchisello

https://www.goodreads.com/author/show/4297807.Sharon_Marchisello

https://www.linkedin.com/in/sharonmarchisello

https://www.instagram.com/slmarchisello/

https://www.bookbub.com/profile/sharon-marchisello

Also by Sharon Marchisello

Going Home (Sunbury Press, 2014)

Secrets of the Galapagos (Milford House, fiction imprint of Sunbury Press, 2019)

Live Well, Grow Wealth (2018-nonfiction)

www.ingramcontent.com/pod-product-compliance
Lightning Source LLC
Chambersburg PA
CBHW020606110726
47899CB00002B/393